W9-BEF-217

MINUTE ZERO

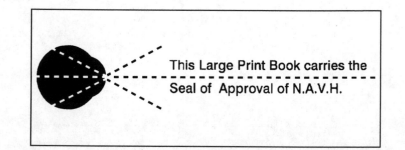

This Large Print Book carries the
Seal of Approval of N.A.V.H.

MINUTE ZERO

TODD MOSS

THORNDIKE PRESS
A part of Gale, Cengage Learning

GALE
CENGAGE Learning·

Farmington Hills, Mich • San Francisco • New York • Waterville, Maine
Meriden, Conn • Mason, Ohio • Chicago

GALE
CENGAGE Learning·

LIBRARY OF CONGRESS CATALOGING-IN-PUBLICATION DATA

Moss, Todd.
    Minute zero / Todd Moss. — Large print edition.
      pages cm. — (Thorndike Press large print thriller)
      ISBN 978-1-4104-8599-1 (hardback) — ISBN 1-4104-8599-4 (hardcover)
      1. Large type books. 2. Political fiction. I. Title.
    PS3613.O785M56 2016
    813'.6—dc23
                             2015035716

Published in 2016 by arrangement with G. P. Putnam's Sons, an imprint of Penguin Publishing Group, a division of Penguin Random House LLC

Printed in Mexico
1 2 3 4 5 6 7 20 19 18 17 16

AUTHOR'S NOTE

Minute Zero is entirely a work of fiction, yet it was inspired by the author's real-life experiences inside the U.S. government and the story draws on true historical episodes. In the early 1980s, thousands of civilians in Zimbabwe died during a military operation known as *Gukurahundi* (or "Early Rain That Washes Away the Chaff" in the local Shona language), an atrocity for which no one has ever been held to account. Zimbabwe's president Robert Mugabe, in power since 1980, lost the 2008 election but refused to step down and instead deployed the army to attack the opposition and ensure he won a second-round vote. In the 1970s, up to half a million Ethiopians perished from the Red Terror campaign of dictator Mengistu Haile Mariam. Mengistu was overthrown in 1991 and has lived ever since in exile in Zimbabwe's capital, Harare.

A Note on Time Zones

Washington, D.C., is Eastern Standard Time; Great Britain is + 5 hours; Zimbabwe and South Africa are + 6 hours; Ethiopia is + 7 hours; Thailand is + 11 hours.

Our policy is directed not against any country or doctrine, but against hunger, poverty, desperation and chaos.
— **GEORGE MARSHALL,**
U.S. Secretary of State, 1947

Chaos often breeds life, when order breeds habit.
— **HENRY BROOKS ADAMS,**
historian, 1907

PROLOGUE

Victoria Falls, Zimbabwe
Wednesday, 5:52 p.m. Central Africa Time

Before he saw the smoke, he heard the thunder. His ears hummed with white noise, the infinite, deafening rumble of the Zambezi River. It would also be the very last sound he heard.

The man, in his late twenties, was obviously American. His thick designer glasses, white socks, and neon-yellow running shoes gave him away to the German and Chinese tourists. He was also easily spotted by others watching him across the hotel lobby.

The American felt a twinge of adrenaline as he departed the colonial-era hotel to meet his contact. He had just gotten off the phone with his girlfriend back in Michigan, who had playfully peppered him with too many questions about his latest trip to Africa.

"Isn't it dangerous?" she had asked with a

9

giggle. The American exposed nothing classified, of course. But he told her just enough to hint that what he was doing was secret. And critical to national security.

Satisfied that he had projected a hint of intrigue without compromising the mission, his face flushed as he imagined his triumphant return to Detroit and another passionate reunion. After his last overseas trip, his girlfriend had greeted him wearing only a raincoat and a mischievous grin. "Hello, Mr. Bond," she had purred.

A loud "Good evening, saah!" snapped his mind back to Zimbabwe. The doorman was wearing a nineteenth-century British military uniform, an oversized ostrich feather on his hat. Both men averted their eyes, the Zimbabwean out of deferential habit, the American out of awkward embarrassment.

The American hurriedly descended the grand steps, dodged a pack of aggressive taxi drivers, and veered through a garden of jacaranda trees and a finely clipped lawn. As he crossed the line at the end of the hotel's private property, the ground turned abruptly from lush green to parched brown. Among the unkempt scrub grass, he noticed burn marks where someone must have been setting fires.

The man's stride quickened and his heartbeat accelerated as his body prepared itself for the encounter. The rumbling of the falls grew louder, and eventually the noise blocked out all other sounds. A light mist cooled his skin, reminding him of his summers spent at the lake. He suddenly found himself amid an oasis, a tiny rain forest living off the permanent cloud of the great roaring waterfall.

The American regained his bearings as he arrived at a stone patio marking the scenic overlook. A plaque shared key details of what stood before him. Victoria Falls, one of the Seven Natural Wonders of the World, was a sheet of water over a mile wide and 354 feet high formed by the Zambezi River plunging over an escarpment. The vapor rose more than a thousand feet in the air. The locals called it Mosi-oa-Tunya in the Tonga language, or "the Smoke That Thunders," and in 1855, Dr. David Livingstone had named it in honor of his queen.

No time for ancient history, he thought. The American placed both hands on the railing along the cliff's edge and peered into the haze. His glasses immediately fogged. Just then, sharply on time, an older dark-skinned man with a gray beard and a black business suit gripped the railing beside him. Without

11

making eye contact, the African spoke.

"My brother, all this smoke. I need to quit smoking."

"What is your brand of cigarette?" asked the American.

"Marlboro."

The American nodded. "Where's my dossier?"

"First, the gift."

The American glanced over both shoulders, then eyed his contact. After a hesitation, he reached into his jacket and withdrew an envelope. It quickly disappeared into the old man's pocket. "We walk."

"That's not the deal," said the American, grabbing the other man's forearm. "Give me the dossier or I am leaving. With my money."

"No. Too many eyes here," he said. "Not safe." He pulled away from the American's grip and dialed a number on a cheap flip phone. In short bursts he whispered, "The Marlboro man is here. We are on our way." He snapped the phone closed and grabbed the American's hand. "This way, my brother."

Silently the two men walked down another path toward the bridge spanning the 650-foot gorge between Zimbabwe and neighboring Zambia. The bridge had been built to signal friendship between the two allies, but instead it provided a constant reminder of the stark trajectories of the two countries.

Two nations, two anchors of the British Empire in Africa. Zambia had been granted independence in 1964 and Zimbabwe, then called Rhodesia, was supposed to have been next, but white settlers preempted London and declared Rhodesia independent. As Zimbabwe descended into a long and nasty civil war, Zambia basked in the confidence of a new nation, even allowing guerrillas to use its territory to fight the Rhodesians and the South African apartheid juggernaut. In 1980 the Rhodesian war ended and Zimbabwe gained its own independence, but by this time Zambia had slumped into a morass of corruption and debt. Zimbabwe was the new hope.

Two decades later, the tide had turned again. Zambia was back on the rise, while Zimbabwe was rotting. As the young American stepped onto the Victoria Falls Bridge, Zimbabwe was poisoning itself with a toxic cocktail of greed, dictatorship, and fear.

At that moment, however, the American wasn't thinking about that. After a few steps, he stopped. "I . . . I . . . I don't like this. I'm going back." He peered over the railing, scanning for crocodiles 420 feet below.

"My brother, it is up to you." The African hid his impatience. "You have come all this way. The choice is yours."

Shit, the old man is right. The American had spent most of the past eight months working toward this moment. All the hours spent digging into files, all the late nights tracking bank records, the long, hot days taking testimony in a sweaty thatched hut. He was now so close. Success depended on the final piece: the dossier. Success and a big promotion.

"Let's do it," he said, pointing at his contact's chest. "But if you fuck me, you and your boss are dead."

The old man laughed — not the reaction the American had expected. "There is no need for that, my brother."

"Dead meat," the American muttered under his breath.

The two strode across the bridge, passing a Swedish couple holding hands and a young Zimbabwean family. Most of the other tourists had retreated to their hotels for a sundowner — gin and tonics were still popular among certain crowds in this part of the world — and an early dinner of plate-sized steaks.

Two middle-aged African men, also in suits, approached from the opposite side of the bridge. One was holding a legal-sized manila envelope. The four men met at the very center, the border, the highest point.

The American accepted the envelope in silence, turning his back to the others to open it and claim his prize. The cover page was a fuzzy black-and-white photocopy of an Ethiopian passport. So far, so good. The next page was blank, and the next, and the next. He scrunched his forehead as anger rose within him.

"What the fuck . . ." He twisted his body to turn back, but strong hands grabbed his arms and his ankles and lifted him high up over the railing. "No, no, nooooo . . ."

As he fell, his mind raced with thoughts of his mother, his little brown dachshund, Alfredo, his messy loft apartment, his girlfriend's laugh, his unfinished, incomplete life.

The white noise of Victoria Falls filled his ears and, 5.2 seconds later, was replaced by total silence and a bright white light as the American's skull cracked on the rocks of the mighty Zambezi River.

The old man peered over the bridge railing and watched the body hit.

"Dead meat, my brother."

■ ■ ■ ■

Four hundred miles to the east, in a high-brow suburb of Zimbabwe's capital city, Solomon Zagwe sat alone in the garden courtyard of his villa. A light breeze was keeping him cool, and the light of the setting sun turned the jacaranda trees a bright purple. But Ethiopia's former president and supreme general didn't notice any of his surroundings.

"Now. I need the money now," he said, squeezing the phone tightly and clenching his jaw. Zagwe was concentrating on controlling his temper. He knew that he had to convey the necessity of an accelerated timetable without revealing any vulnerability. If the man on the other end of the line knew his true predicament, it would cost him more money. "Let us agree today, Max," he said. The line went dead.

"Ah, *dedabe,*" he swore to himself in Amharic, slamming down the cell phone. A few seconds later his phone buzzed and he quickly answered. "My apologies. No names. I won't use names on the phone again."

A servant boy in an all-white uniform entered the garden carrying a polished silver

16

tray holding a pot of coffee, a plate of small triangular sandwiches, and a single orchid in a glass vase. Zagwe scowled and shooed him away with a dismissive wave of the hand.

"I understand time is short," Zagwe whispered once the boy was gone. "If it was up to me, I would say very well. But my partners, they are difficult. They need the shipment now. This is not like it used to be with our Saudi friends. These people are impatient. It has to be now, even if it is a smaller package than usual. . . . Good. . . . Good."

Zagwe's shoulders relaxed. "No, there are no troubles," he said. "Victoria Falls went well." He laughed. "The mosquito buzzing in our ears has been taken care of. No more buzz. It has been crushed."

PART ONE:
THURSDAY

1.

Judd Ryker, half-asleep with his eyes still closed, could hear the gentle tap, tap, tap of the laptop. One eye opened.

"Uh, Jess?" he groaned.

Sitting up in bed next to him, Jessica smiled. "Hi, sweets. Good, you're awake."

"Not yet. What are you doing?"

"I'm up early for my video call with Papa. I told you already."

"No, you didn't."

"Well, that's what I'm doing. I didn't think I'd wake you. But now that you're up, be a sweetie and get me some coffee."

Jessica gave him that puppy-dog look she knew always worked. With one eye still closed and his face creased from sleep, Judd swung his legs heavily off the bed and stumbled out of the bedroom, scratching his stomach. He checked his BlackBerry —

21

no urgent messages — and slipped the phone into the pocket of his robe as he walked toward the kitchen.

The smell of the brewing coffee helped him clear the cobwebs in his head. Had Jessica mentioned she was having an early morning call with Papa Toure? Things at work had been so crazy lately, he couldn't keep anything straight.

Judd Ryker's experimental office at the State Department, the Crisis Reaction Unit, was struggling. His baby was in trouble. Three months earlier, a crisis in the West African nation of Mali had gone well, more or less. Judd had saved an important American ally from a coup d'état and rescued the daughter of a powerful senator who had been kidnapped by a previously unknown terrorist cell. But rather than celebrate his triumph, the corridors of the State Department had seen Judd as an irritant — or a direct threat.

Assistant Secretary of State for African Affairs William Alfred Rogerson was the U.S. government's top diplomat for relations with the forty-nine countries south of the Sahara Desert — and now he was viewed by his peers as uncharacteristically weak. Rogerson had taken a beating over the Mali affair from the other senior officials. He had allowed an interloper, a rookie outsider — a college professor no less — to tread on his turf.

"Never would've allowed that sort of thing in NEA," the Assistant Secretary of the Bureau of Near Eastern Affairs had declared openly at a senior staff meeting.

Rogerson was determined not to let it happen again. The other offices around State were similarly immunizing themselves from Judd Ryker and his ivory tower ideas. Not only had Judd been excluded from meetings since — hurricane response in Haiti, riots in Ankara, and a bombing in Rome — but he'd been increasingly shunned. The State Department treated him like a virus no one else wanted to catch.

This was why his first meeting today was so crucial. And why he needed to be thinking clearly this morning.

Judd reached the kitchen and filled two mugs, each displaying the White House seal, souvenirs from a recent meeting with the National Security Council staff. He topped off his mug with a splash of milk, but his wife always preferred her coffee strong and black.

Jessica was his rock. Through all the struggles at work, she had been his support.

She'd told him to ignore the passive-aggressive backbiting and just do his job. Beat them by being better than anyone else. Let success be his revenge. That was her philosophy. That, and what she actually said after one particularly frustrating day: "Fuck those guys."

Yeah, fuck 'em, he thought. Jessica always knew what to do, always knew the right next move. And how to play it.

Judd pushed open the bedroom door with his foot, carefully delivering the two coffees. His wife, her hair pulled back into a tight ponytail, looking fresh and clean despite wearing sweatpants and his faded Amherst College T-shirt, was talking into a headset and nodding into her laptop.

Jessica had been an agronomist, one of America's leading experts in drought-resistant crops, before she took time off to stay home with their two young children. She was an authority on growing plants where there was no water, a specialist at finding ways of making something from nothing. Jessica had encouraged Judd's choice to leave his professorship at Amherst to try his hand at real-world problem solving. She'd gracefully agreed to move from the comforts of central Massachusetts to Washington, D.C. She'd accepted the financial risk to their family, the impact on her own career. But now Jessica was dipping her toe back in the water, working part-time, and Judd wanted to be supportive.

Judd set down the coffee on the nightstand.

"Say hi to Papa!" she said, beckoning him onto the bed.

Judd leaned in and saw on screen the face of his old friend from Mali, Papa Toure. Papa had been on the Haverford Foundation water research team that Professor BJ van Hollen had assembled in northern Mali twelve years earlier. That was when Judd had first met Jessica. When BJ van Hollen had put them all together.

"*Bonjour,* Papa. How is everyone?" Judd asked, straining to show some early morning enthusiasm.

"Ahh, Judd! Good to see you. So strange to see you on the computer!"

"Not as strange as seeing you talk to Jessica while she's still in bed."

"Oh, Judd," Papa laughed. "You are a lucky man, yes?"

"How are things in Mali, Papa?"

"Everything is calm now. *Inshallah.* I am hopeful we are back on the right road. I wouldn't have left Bamako and come to Ethiopia if I was worried."

"You're in Ethiopia?" Judd asked.

"I told you that he was," Jessica said, shaking her head.

"Oh, yes, of course," replied Judd quickly. "Papa, how is Addis Ababa?"

"I'm not in Addis. I'm in Lalibela," Papa replied.

"There's no water problem in Addis," Jessica interrupted. "Papa and I are working together on the clean water and irrigation project in Lalibela. For the Haverford Foundation. Don't you remember?"

"Haverford? In Ethiopia?"

"I told you all of this, Judd. You never listen," she said, suddenly looking serious.

"Oh, Judd, I am sorry. I have gotten you in trouble already, yes?" asked Papa, looking overly pleased with himself.

"Lalibela has those old churches," Judd said, trying to change the subject.

"Ahhh, yes, the eleven churches of Saint George are here. Twelfth-century. Carved out of the rock. Judd, you should come see them. You and Jessica together. Bring the boys."

"I will, Papa. I've never been," Judd said. Jessica nodded in agreement. "*We've* never been. Is this your first time?"

"I was here many years ago," said Papa. "It's been a long time. Things have

26

changed."

"Well, enjoy it while you can," said Judd, moving out of the screenshot. "*Au revoir,* Papa."

"*Au revoir,* my friend."

Jessica blew Judd a kiss and then turned her attention back to the computer screen.

As he left the bedroom, Judd stole one last glance at Jessica, her high cheekbones, perfect coffee-colored skin, and bright, dark eyes. Papa was right, in fact. Judd had heard it often: He was a very lucky man. *Jessica's way out of my league.*

Judd closed the door and walked down the hall to check on Toby, who had just turned six, and Noah, their mischievous three-year-old. Thankfully, both were still sound asleep.

Judd took his coffee downstairs to a stool in the kitchen by the window looking out on the back garden. He checked his Black-Berry again, scrolling through the dozens of messages about overnight events around the world. A Greek bank collapsed. North Korea tested a missile in the Sea of Japan. A British journalist was imprisoned in Moscow. An American tourist committed suicide in Zimbabwe by jumping off a bridge at Victoria Falls. Nothing out of the ordinary.

Time to prepare for his meeting at eight a.m. — and hope it worked.

2.

Eastern Highlands, Zimbabwe
Thursday, 1:12 p.m. Central Africa Time
(7:12 a.m. Eastern Standard Time)

"Wang ba!" the operations director shouted, a Chinese insult the old man didn't understand. *"Wang ba!* Don't make me call the army boss man again!"

The old man, wearing a tattered shirt made of burlap, bowed his head and mumbled a weak apology: *"Ndine urombo."*

"English! Speak English, *Wang ba!"*

"Sorry, sorry. I work now," said the old man, shuffling away.

The manager stood on the edge of a giant hole, scanning the workers below. They functioned in small teams of six, each working a designated area, the same hierarchical model the company used at its mines in Burma. The youngest member of each team swung a pickax, breaking up the soil and rocks. The second youngest worked the

29

shovel, loading wheelbarrows, while the next three pushed their cargos up the circular paths out of the great hole and to the adjacent sifting camp. The last and always most senior member served as captain, ensuring the team stuck to its designated zone and met its load quota. These captains all reported to the operations director.

Despite the clear design, the director was not happy. The teams were working too slowly, and his bonus was based on volume. "Lazy," he scoffed. These workers reminded him of the carpenter ants he had watched as a little boy in his village in northeastern China. The ants he liked to stomp.

The operations director was also bitter because he knew the real money, the *big* money, from this mine was being made by his joint partners, the men who watched over him. In well-pressed Zimbabwe National Army uniforms, they hovered over everything, watching from an observation deck outfitted with fans and refrigerated sodas. Like the pit bosses in the casinos of Macao, they scrutinized every detail as teams picked amid the gravel and mud for small specks of light, tiny fragments of compressed carbon. The army made the big money because they controlled the diamonds.

The military men also, naturally, handled mine security. The ZNA bosses deployed regular units around the perimeter of the mine and along the main road toward town, all the way up to the large roadside sign warning: **PROPERTY OF THE EASTERN HIGHLANDS MINING COMPANY: ACCESS RESTRICTED, TRESPASSERS WILL BE PUNISHED.** More troops patrolled the border with Mozambique, just a few kilometers away. The boundary was porous and bandits might try to take advantage of the sudden sprouting of extreme wealth. The show of military force was also a deterrent to any domestic troublemakers.

The best-paid army troops were assigned to protect the airstrip. The sand path cut into the hills of Zimbabwe's Eastern Highlands was the company's lifeline into the buying markets of Belgium, Dubai, and Thailand. And because security and exports were essential to their business model, the army held the balance of power.

The operations director seethed with resentment. Making it worse, his bosses back in Chengdu didn't seem to care, either, as long as the production and sales targets were met. The director's phone rang. He recognized the number and cursed in Mandarin before answering.

"It is your partner," said the deep voice of General Simba Chimurenga on the other end. "How is business?"

"Slow. I told you already. These boys too slow."

Chimurenga laughed. "Zimbabwe is not China, my friend. It is not even Mongolia."

"Too slow," he repeated.

"I don't want to hear about your problems. We have more important matters. I need you to double production."

"Impossible."

"I don't care how you do it, but I am telling you: You will double production."

The director turned to face the giant hole below him and saw one of his excavation teams smoking cigarettes rather than digging. *"Wang ba,"* he cursed under his breath.

"What did you say?"

"Yes, I do it. I need more men."

"Not a problem. We can round up more workers. I will have my men sweep the village. I knew I could count on you. I also need you to do something else."

"Yes?"

"This is urgent."

"Yes?"

"Are you listening carefully?" asked Chimurenga.

"Yes."

32

"We must change the delivery. What is the order for this month?"

"Same, same. Ten. Five Bangkok, five Dubai."

"How many packages are ready today?"

"Three."

"Only three?" snapped Chimurenga. "I told you, these men too slow."

"Very well, three. Go to the stockpile in the vault and send them now. Send three packages to Bangkok tonight. All three. This can't wait. Do you understand?"

"I check with Chengdu first."

"No. This is *my* operation," said Chimurenga. "You and your partners are here as my guests. You are under my protection. I am telling you three packages will be on the Falcon to Bangkok tonight."

The operations director weighed his options for a moment. "I tell the pilot, General. Three to Bangkok."

"Yes, you tell the pilot, my friend."

3.

U.S. Department of State, Washington, D.C.
Thursday, 7:41 a.m. Eastern Standard Time
Nestled in the heart of Foggy Bottom, on
the far western edge of the nation's capital,
sat the Harry S. Truman Federal Building,
the headquarters of the U.S. Department of
State. Judd approached the limestone edifice
and its grid of sixty-six windows across and
seven stories high. He scanned the rows to
try to find the window for his office, but he
quickly lost his bearings. The Crisis Reaction Unit — S/CRU in State Department
parlance — was up there somewhere.

A stream of employees was arriving, just
like at any other factory, heads hung low,
eyes bleary, carrying coffee in brown paper
cups. Except these workers weren't writing
software code or assembling automobiles.
They were cogs in the massive diplomatic
presence of the United States government
around the world. Their task was to advance

the interests of the American people, and, as the Secretary of State said on television the night before, "Our job is to promote freedom and build a more democratic, secure, and prosperous world of well-governed states that respond to the needs of their people, reduce poverty, and act responsibly."

Judd edged past a group of visiting Korean diplomats in business suits to open the heavy glass doors at the front entrance. At the rear of the lobby stood the backdrop for the nightly television news, a wall of 189 foreign flags, one for each country with diplomatic relations with the United States of America.

He flashed his identification to the armed security guard, swiped his card, and punched his six-digit PIN. The glass security barriers swung open with a vhuuump. He strode down a long hallway to the cafeteria.

"Morning, Brenda," he said, forcing a smile. "Two large coffees with double espresso shots."

"G'morning, Dr. Ryker. That's two red-eyes!" she replied, a bit too loudly for this time of day. "I know: one with milk, the other black," she said with a wink.

Judd smiled and dropped a dollar in the tip jar.

He trekked carefully, balancing his coffees, to the elevators, up to the sixth floor, and then down another long beige hallway. His destination was marked by a small sign over the door: CRISIS REACTION UNIT, OFFICE OF THE DIRECTOR.

"It's nearly eight o'clock, Dr. Ryker. You've got to move it."

"Good morning to you, too, Serena. I brought you a coffee," he said holding up both barrels.

"Thank you," his assistant said impatiently. She was wearing her usual black tapered business suit. Her Afro was cut short, highlighting her strong jaw. "On your desk in the red folder are the overnight cables. I've highlighted Priority One, all the places on our watch list. In the blue folder are cables I pulled for your eight a.m. with Mr. Parker."

"I got you the one you like. With the extra espresso." Judd set down one of the coffees on Serena's desk. "A red-eye."

"In Iraq we called it a MOAC."

"Okay, I'll ask. What's MOAC?"

"The mother of all coffee."

"Of course."

"You've got six minutes," she said, and shooed him away.

Judd retreated into his office and sank into

his chair. Just as Serena had promised, on his desk sat two colored folders. He opened the blue one to find diplomatic reports on Egyptian politics, which he flipped through:

SECRET: CAIRO1342 — Special Envoy warns Foreign Minister Elhaddad
UNCLASSIFIED: CAIRO1346 — Media reporting on jailed journalists
SECRET: CAIRO1351 — Election polling projections
SECRET: CAIRO1352 — Disruption of Jihadist cell targeting voting stations in Alexandria
CONFIDENTIAL: CAIRO1356 — Embassy Cairo planning for election monitoring

At the back of the folder was a hard copy of Judd's PowerPoint presentation for Landon Parker, the Secretary of State's chief of staff. Judd was speaking again about disputed elections and the Golden Hour — his theory about the need for quicker crisis response. The Golden Hour had been the inspiration for S/CRU and Judd's ticket into the State Department. But this time the presentation wasn't about the Golden Hour itself but about a related concept, which he'd reveal for the first time that morning.

Judd set this folder aside and opened the

red one, which was stuffed with printed diplomatic cables, the steady stream of messages into headquarters from the State Department's 305 overseas posts. Serena had marked several with a bright yellow highlighter.

CONFIDENTIAL: ULANBATOR91 — Mongolian mining dispute threatens government coalition

SECRET: RIYADH234 — Health update for Saudi Royal Family

SECRET: BAGHDAD1945 — Prime Minister concerned about potential for new Kurdish rebellion

CONFIDENTIAL: PORTAUPRINCE133 — Embassy protests turn violent after rice price increase

UNCLASSIFIED: JAKARTA242 — Indonesian election official jailed on corruption charges

CONFIDENTIAL: ABUJA319 — New evidence of top party bosses involvement with Nigerian fuel import racket

CONFIDENTIAL: HARARE185 — Risk of organized violence low as Zimbabwe election approaches

SECRET: TRIPOLI772 — Support for rebels surging in eastern Libya

"Serena, I don't see any cables in from Ethiopia."

"No, Dr. Ryker, there's no overnight reporting in from Embassy Addis."

"Can you double-check? And please look for anything going on in Lalibela. It's a smaller city up in the north. Anything at all over the past month."

"Lalibela? What are you looking for?"

"Nothing. Just check for me, will you?"

"Of course, Dr. Ryker."

He hated checking up on Papa and Jessica, but he wanted to make sure there was no danger. His wife and a close friend were working on a project in a remote corner of Africa, and he had access to a vast web of information. It seemed only prudent.

Judd set aside any worries about what he would do if Serena did find something dangerous. Or highly classified. Being forced to keep secrets from your most trusted loved ones was a common source of stress. He'd been warned that diplomats often struggled at home to maintain a separate life, and always had to keep track of what was classified and what was not. It was becoming even harder as the lines between the two worlds blurred. Classified reporting relied on "open source" or publicly available information, while secrets leaked into the press all the time. *Who could possibly keep track?* If Judd read a secret cable about a terrorist threat against the U.S. embassy in Kenya or the declining health of the Cuban president, and then the very same news was reported on CNN, could he talk about it with his wife?

The common reaction was just to keep quiet. Judd could feel himself shutting down, changing the subject, feigning ignorance, even when it wasn't strictly necessary. But he knew this was creating distance from his family.

Now that Jessica was working in Africa again, they were even more likely to cross professional paths. How to maintain a healthy marriage while keeping Jessica at arm's length? Especially when she was his best advisor?

"Are you okay, Dr. Ryker?" Serena interrupted.

"Yes, of course," he said, wincing.

"You don't seem yourself this morning. Off your game, I think."

"I'm fine Serena. I'm ready."

"Good, because they're waiting."

"Good morning, everyone. I've asked Dr. Ryker from S/CRU to join us," said Landon Parker, addressing the senior staff of the

40

State Department's Bureau of Near Eastern Affairs. "The Secretary is very worried about the upcoming Egyptian elections. We need them to go well. I think everyone here is highly aware that the White House has made Middle East peace talks the cornerstone of the President's foreign policy. Our legacy hinges on a successful election in Egypt. I know NEA is working this hard. The Secretary thanks you for your efforts."

Parker paused to let the staff accept his appreciation. It wasn't every day that these people had a special audience with the Secretary of State's chief of staff.

"I asked you all to come here this morning because Dr. Ryker has been doing some special analysis on elections which may be relevant for your planning in Egypt. After the unfortunate events in Turkey, Azerbaijan, and Venezuela, we all need to be cognizant that elections, even those we support, are potential flashpoints for instability. The elections themselves have become action-forcing events that too often spark riots, violence, and political instability. We obviously can't have this. We certainly can't have it in Egypt. That's why Dr. Ryker's insights will be useful for you. Dr. Ryker, the floor is yours."

"Thank you, Mr. Parker," said Judd,

standing up. "Some of you may have heard about the Golden Hour. In emergency medicine, it's widely accepted that the chances of saving a trauma patient rise significantly if they receive medical care quickly. The human body can withstand a lot of force, but it can only maintain itself for so long. The rule of thumb is sixty minutes. That is the Golden Hour. Conversely, if medical intervention is delayed beyond that hour, the chances of survival decrease rapidly. In other words, waiting too long can kill the patient."

Judd had given this talk dozens of times. To keep his energy high, he paced in the front of the room.

"My work, analyzing data on wars and coups, has shown the Golden Hour phenomenon also applies to international crises. If there is a quick response, such as military intervention or active diplomacy, chances of success are high. A slow response usually means failure. The Golden Hour is the basis for the creation of the Crisis Reaction Unit about a year ago. It's why I came to the State Department."

"Yes, I think everyone knows about S/CRU, Dr. Ryker," interrupted Landon Parker. "Tell them about Minute Zero."

"Right. Minute Zero. In analyzing cases

of major political shock, there's another critical moment. Immediately after an upheaval, there can be a very short period of breakdown. In the minutes after a coup d'état, the death of a leader, a highly disputed election, or even a natural disaster, there is often a brief moment of extreme uncertainty. A window of chaos. No one knows what comes next, anything can happen, and the entire political system, even one that seems highly stable, is suddenly up for grabs. I call this window of chaos Minute Zero."

Judd checked his audience for signs of recognition. A few nods, but some blank faces, too.

"Okay," he continued. "Has anyone here read *Leviathan*?"

An eager young woman, Judd guessed probably a first tour desk officer fresh from grad school, put her hand up. "Hobbes, the state of nature."

"Correct. Thomas Hobbes wrote about what life would be like without a government, without order."

"Nasty, brutish, and short," said the desk officer.

"Exactly," said Judd. "Hobbes believed that, without government, there was total freedom but also total chaos. And without some order imposed by a political system we would all die quickly and violently. Nasty, brutish, and short. Without a strong government, *bellum omnium contra omnes.*"

"The war of all against all," the young woman said, nodding.

"Precisely. The war of all against all. Chaos."

"Excuse me," interrupted an older man at the back of the room. "But what does Hobbes have to do with the Egyptian election? That's why we're here."

"Good question," Judd said. "It's true Hobbes wrote *Leviathan* in 1651. But he was right about what happens when order breaks down. Everyone turns on each other. The war of all against all. Now, this is relevant to Egypt because a moment can arrive after a political shock. Egypt could reach Minute Zero. That's what I'm trying to convey."

"I don't get it," said the man at the back. "I've been in the Foreign Service for twenty-eight years and I haven't seen anything like that."

"What would happen if Egypt's president died suddenly and the elections were canceled?"

"The army would take over," he responded.

"No, I don't think so," said a woman at the table.

"Yeah, neither do I," said someone else. "I would expect the parties to regroup and form an alliance."

"No chance," said the older man at the back. "That failed before. They won't try it again."

"The Muslim Brotherhood would rise up and take advantage. I think it'd be a bloodbath," said another staffer.

The room suddenly erupted in debate as the Near Eastern Affairs staff argued over what might happen next.

Judd sat back and smiled.

"Okay, people," interjected Landon Parker, quieting down the room. "Let's save the hypotheticals for later."

"See? There's great uncertainty," said Judd. "If the Middle East experts in this room have no idea what would happen next, then there's probably plenty of uncertainty among the Egyptian political class, too. *That's Minute Zero.* That's your opportunity."

"That's NEA's opportunity," added Parker, hitting his fist on the table.

"So Minute Zero is a good thing?" asked the staffer at the front.

"It could be," answered Judd. "In most

situations, we want to prevent Minute Zero from arriving. If we prize stability over everything else, then no, Minute Zero is a bad outcome. In most situations we never want a window of chaos to open. We want to be prepared to close the window as soon as possible."

"To be ready to kill the baby in the cradle," said Parker, hitting the table again.

Judd winced, then continued. "However, on the other hand, if U.S. policy is to shake things up, if we want to instigate change, then some creative destruction might be a good thing. There are instances where we might want to spark Minute Zero."

"Regime change," said the desk officer in the front.

"Perhaps," said Judd. "There are places where we need Minute Zero to move forward. Or at least we need to create the perception of it."

"You're talking about deception. PSYOPs."

"Psychological operations might be part of the strategy. It depends. The point is that if we want to break a logjam, we need enough people to believe that the world is ending. If they believe it, then it becomes true."

"Deception becomes reality," a staffer said.

"Like we did in Libya," said another.

"Exactly. Once the Libyan people were convinced that Qaddafi's reign was over, he was dead," Judd said. "But here is the critical thing about Minute Zero: It's only a minute. It's fleeting. It doesn't take long for events to sway in one direction and then realignment happens in an instant. People quickly choose sides and then a new equilibrium is established. The opportunity, and the challenge, is to influence events *during Minute Zero.* That means being ready and willing to act quickly to shape history. If we wait too long, the window closes. Preparation and speed are everything."

"Two things the United States government is not very good at," Parker said.

"We can do better," Judd said.

Someone at the back guffawed. Several heads shook.

"So what exactly does this mean for our preparations for the Egyptian elections?" asked the veteran.

"If we want to shape events in Egypt, we should first be looking for early warning signs of Minute Zero."

"Which are?"

"Politicians suddenly changing sides. Or

47

asking us what outcomes the American government might find acceptable. Anything that hints things may be turning and no one knows what is going to happen next." Several nods around the table.

"And then what, Dr. Ryker?" Landon Parker asked.

"And then you prepare. If Minute Zero arrives, who's the ambassador calling first? Who's on our side? Who's untouchable? You can't wait for the crisis and then expect to have time to answer these questions back here in Washington."

"If you were advising NEA on Egypt, Dr. Ryker, where would you start?" Parker asked.

"I would start mapping the actors, the potential hotspots, and the leverage points. I'd have at least a dozen contingency plans in place and locked down. This should all be happening now, months ahead of the vote. You can't wait for the last minute. The worst position for the U.S. is to sit back and watch and then just pronounce judgment on the outcome."

"Why?"

"That only gives us a thumbs-up or thumbs-down option. If we do that, we would be just witnesses, not shapers of history."

"What about the voting?"

"If we believe there's serious cheating, we need to act before the vote. *And definitely before election results are ever announced.* Afterward it's just too late."

Judd paused to let people take notes.

"One thing we've learned from reviewing events during Congo's civil war and after the Haitian hurricane," he continued, "is the U.S. embassy is in a unique position. If there are riots on the streets, or no one knows who is in charge, then the public looks to the foreign embassies for signals."

"Or refuge," added Parker. "We've got over a hundred people camped out right now on the grounds of our embassy in Jordan."

"Yes, that's true. Refuge, too. But if Minute Zero arrives, the ambassadors of the big powers can influence events. And no one is bigger than the United States. It's a platform we don't use nearly enough. If the United States ambassador goes on the radio with a declaration, we can make it true by just saying so. The streets are under control. There is no fuel shortage. The president has lost the election and will step down. The message to the army, to the police, to the politicians can be clear: The tide is turning and you better get on the right side of his-

49

tory. This is how the United States can shape events if we know what we want and are prepared to act swiftly. Otherwise we are just bystanders."

Landon Parker glanced at his watch. "Okay, people. Thank you for coming. Thank you, Dr. Ryker. I think your Minute Zero concept is a useful one and I hope it will inform NEA's planning for Egypt. Meeting closed."

Parker grabbed Judd's arm. "Thanks, Ryker. Very interesting. Can I have a word?"

"Of course."

"Walk with me, Ryker," he said, gesturing for Judd to follow.

The two left the conference room and strolled down the long hallway, illuminated with flickering fluorescent light.

"You know I've always been a champion of S/CRU, right?"

"Yes, sir. I appreciate your support," Judd said.

"You know I stuck my neck out to create your whole goddamn office in the first place, right?"

"Yes, sir. I know that."

"I did it because I want the Secretary to have a legacy. I want to be able, when we are all done here, to point to a few things

50

and say: *We. Did. That.* Do you understand?"

"Yes, of course. That's why I'm here, too."

"Then we are on the same page."

"Yes, sir."

"So I need you to help me."

"Of course."

"Actually, Ryker, to be precise, I need you
to help me *to help you.*"

"Sir?"

"The Mali coup worked out a few months
ago. President Maiga is back in power,
Senator McCall has his daughter home
safely, and we've been able to restart our
counterterrorism operations in the Sahara
Desert. It's a good outcome all around. As
far as I'm concerned, our success in Mali is
a credit to you and to S/CRU."

"Thank you."

"But not everybody agrees with me on
that, as I'm sure you know. There's been
blowback right here inside the building.
People are complaining to the Secretary
about S/CRU, about your office encroach-
ing on their issues. No one wants that."

Judd nodded.

"To put it bluntly, Ryker, *no one wants
you.*"

"I realize S/CRU is still new and some

people are resistant to a new way of doing things."

"It's the goddamn State Department, Ryker. Of course they are going to resist. It's part of the DNA of the bureaucracy. It's just part of the culture. It's in their blood."

"So what do you want me to do, sir?"

"We need a win for S/CRU. Something big that no one can ignore. We still have to prove the concept. It's been, what, a year?"

"Coming up on fifteen months."

"Okay, fifteen months. The budget is up for review, and if we are going to keep S/CRU afloat, I've got to justify it to the Secretary. She's supportive, don't get me wrong. But she's got a lot of requests on her plate, and the budget office is desperate to cut something. It doesn't help to have her senior staff bitching about your office. It puts a big fat target on your back."

"What you're saying is S/CRU is facing its own Golden Hour."

"Exactly, Ryker. I knew you'd get it." Parker placed a hand on Judd's shoulder. "And that's why I wanted you to brief the NEA team on the Egyptian elections. To get them to seize the initiative. To get them excited about Minute Zero. It'll help make the case to give S/CRU more time. Got it?"

"Yes. So you'd like me to join the Egypt team and help them with election planning."

"Hell, no, Ryker!" Parker withdrew his hand with a laugh. "The NEA Bureau won't let you anywhere near Egypt. It's too damn important. The White House is breathing down their necks. I'd be all for it. But, frankly, it's not a fight I want to have right now. More importantly, if you wait for Egypt, I don't think S/CRU will still exist by the time the election rolls around. I've got a budget meeting in *ten days.* We need a big win for S/CRU *right now.*"

"How about Cuba? I've been doing some new analysis on weak links in the Cuban communist party. I have a new approach that could blow it wide open."

"No, not Cuba."

"So what exactly do you have in mind, sir?"

"You're about to find out. I need you to clear your schedule and get to a task force meeting that starts in" — Parker paused to check his watch — "nine minutes. Can you do it, Ryker?"

"Of course, sir."

"Good."

"But what's the issue?"

"Saving democracy."

"What country?"

"Zimbabwe."

4.

Just as the Westminster chimes antique clock struck three, the president's tea arrived. For as long as anyone could remember, it had been this precise ritual every day. At that very hour, Winston Tinotenda, President of the Republic of Zimbabwe, sat in his tapestry-upholstered chair by the window. At exactly three o'clock a butler would appear with a silver tray bearing a silver pot of Earl Grey tea, a small silver pitcher of heavy cream, and a bowl of local cane sugar crystals. The president would assemble his favorite concoction and stir it daintily with a matching silver spoon. He would then gaze out the window at his garden, watching for the Goliath herons his official bird keeper had brought from the Zambezi river valley. After a few moments he would take a healthy sip.

"Oh, that's a lovely cup of tea," he would declare to the assembled staff, who always responded with enthusiastic agreement. At 3:15 the president would be refreshed and ready to accept visitors.

President Winston Tinotenda was known to everyone as simply "Tino." No one called him that to his face, of course. Within earshot he was addressed only by his official name: His Excellency, Father of the Nation, and Warrior of the People, President Winston H. R. Tinotenda. Soon after becoming president, Zimbabwe's parliament passed a law forbidding public speculation on the true meaning of his middle initials.

The president's face had begun to sag, long vertical lines pointing from his eye sockets to the end of his chin. His heavy eyes were still scarred yellow from childhood malnutrition. One of his doctors in Singapore had offered an experimental treatment to re-whiten his eyes, but he'd dismissed it as uncivilized. In truth, he worried that the injections might be an assassination plot.

A private barber ensured the president's head and facial hair were kept tight and clean, while abundant moisturizer was flown in from Switzerland to keep his face supple. The newspaper reports of his vigorous daily exercise were, however, mere plants by the Ministry of Information. The president had long ago given up the battle with his waistline. For special occasions, such as state dinners or his annual four-hour address to the nation, he had taken to wearing a slimming girdle. Mentioning this in the press was also punishable with a lengthy prison sentence.

One thing Winston Tinotenda had certainly not given up was a taste for fine men's clothing. A great irritant of his diplomatic jousting with Her Majesty's Government in London was the curtailment of his shopping trips to Savile Row for hand-tailored suits and Jermyn Street for silk shirts. Several years earlier the British government had revoked his travel visa after complaints about one thing or another.

Human rights? Vote fraud? Elephants? He could never remember.

It nevertheless irked him every time he was forced to send one of the few serviceable Air Zimbabwe jets to London to fetch his tailor. "The Prime Minister has lost his bearings," the tailor assured him. "The Queen never would have allowed it in my day."

On this day, just two days before he stood for reelection for a historic seventh term, President Tinotenda was pondering the past. With the weight of history on his shoulders, he was reflecting on those great leaders who'd created the nation of Zimbabwe. The names of the Shona kings of the Monomotapa Empire and Great Zimbabwe had mostly been lost in oral history, but their ruins remained standing.

The Matabele people in southwestern Zimbabwe, his country's largest minority, knew their ancestors well. A Zulu warrior named Mzilikazi had fled the powerful Shaka Zulu in the early nineteenth century, crossing north over the Limpopo River to create Matabele-land. Tinotenda had mixed feelings about the pesky Matabele. They were unwilling to cede authority to his government, so he was periodically forced to send in his troops. But he respected the Matabele's plucky resolve.

He held no such ambiguity about Cecil Rhodes. The British imperialist, through trickery and military force, had stolen the land of Zimbabwe from its rightful African owners and claimed it in the name of Anglo commerce. In his early days as president, Tinotenda had sworn to erase, as much as possible, any memory of Rhodes: streets and towns were renamed, memorials torn down, his accomplishments — if not the details of his treachery — carefully expunged from school history books.

A better precedent for the Tinotenda legacy, he believed, was Mbuya Nehanda. She was a famous spirit medium who had led the First Chimurenga, a revolt against the British in 1896. An old woman, she'd been fierce and brave. She even managed to capture the British native commissioner and cut off his head. *Oh, if only I could have been there!* wished Tinotenda.

Mbuya Nehanda was eventually captured and hanged by the British army, but Winston Tinotenda could feel her alive within his body. Her spirit was one reason he, too, had risen up against the British to fight the Second Chimurenga, the war for independence. A fight he was proud to have won. But he was always on the watch for new plots. For the return of his enemies.

This day, his first post-tea visitor was the head of the army and his personal national security advisor. His name was, by no coincidence, General Simba Chimurenga. Tinotenda had discovered Simba long before he became president. The small boy had grown up not far from Tino's home village, an orphan raised by a family friend. The young Simba had shown a knack for killing things swiftly and covering his tracks. Tinotenda had noticed.

After independence, the boy who had grown up on stories of the glory of war couldn't wait for military service. He longed to prove he was a true patriot. When Simba joined the army at the age of sixteen, he formally changed his last name to Chimurenga in honor of his predecessors. Tinotenda had approved of his nom de guerre and taken the promising young man under his wing. The president had then guided Simba through the army ranks, providing discreet but unmistakable orders to the military promotion boards. Simba was selected for special training in Romania and Ethiopia. After he had been handpicked by the president to command a particularly sensitive mission and performed marvelously, Simba Chimurenga was promoted yet again, becoming the youngest general in Zimbabwe's history.

He'd further burnished his reputation when, just after his ascendance, he stood before his men and bit the head off a deadly green mamba snake. In a country where snakes are feared as spirits of evil, this was an extraordinary show of bravery and — his men believed — magical powers.

General Simba Chimurenga now stood, in full military dress and a chest covered in medals, waiting outside the president's parlor. He tapped his feet with impatience.

"His Excellency, Father of the Nation and Warrior of the People, President Winston H. R. Tinotenda, will see you now," said the butler, with a dramatic bow at the waist.

"My dear Simba," the president greeted him.

"Thank you, Your Excellency. I am not interrupting your tea?"

"Of course not."

"I have come to brief you on preparations for Saturday."

"Yes, yes, I want to hear. I have been worried about the voting in Matabeleland and the central provinces. They are a stubborn people. They cannot be reasoned with."

"Your Excellency, I agree." Simba gestured toward the butler, whom the president then ordered to leave.

Once they were alone, the general continued, "I want to assure you we have taken measures to ensure security. The army and police are already positioned in enemy territory and we have our networks deployed to watch for troublemakers. I am confident the outcome will be satisfactory."

"Good, good. That is very good, my Simba."

"We are also watching the foreigners. The embassies are once again attempting to interfere with our election, but we will not allow any threat to our sovereignty. That is also taken care of. I beg you not to worry, *Sekuru.*"

The younger man's usage of the Shona title of "Grandfather" to address the president of the republic was technically illegal. But an exception was made for Simba Chimurenga.

"I have confidence in you, my son."

"Thank you, *Sekuru.*"

"But one thing is troubling me. If the unthinkable should happen . . . if the forces of evil succeed and convince our own people to turn against the nation . . . if somehow the people are weak and they vote for the sellouts and the traitors . . . what will become of everything we have built?"

"Do not worry, *Sekuru.* I will never allow that to happen," Chimurenga said firmly.

"I will not worry," said the president. "But I am an old man and I am getting tired. I have fought my whole life. But I am not sure I have another war within me."

"You need not fight. Leave it to me. *That woman* will not win."

"Perhaps an old man who has given so

much to his country deserves a quiet ending?"

"Your Excellency, no! If you need quiet and a peaceful rest, you can do that when the time is right. When we decide. We can never concede to the stooges and turncoats. Retire when you wish. But lose — never!"

"Very well, Simba."

"If we must fight a third Chimurenga, Your Excellency, then we will fight. We will never lose. We will never surrender."

"Simba, *you* are the Third Chimurenga."

5.

U.S. Department of State, Washington, D.C.
Thursday, 9:18 a.m. Eastern Standard Time
Judd had gone straight to the Zimbabwe task force meeting hoping to catch Bill Rogerson before it started. He knew Rogerson would be pissed off to see him. Judd couldn't be sure he had gotten Landon Parker's message — that the Secretary of State personally had requested that Judd's unit get involved — and he knew with certainty how the news would be received.

Zimbabwe was now his best and perhaps last chance to show what S/CRU could do, and he didn't want to fail before even getting started. But Judd knew that Rogerson wasn't going to just let him interfere, no matter what Landon Parker said. Instead, his more likely conclusion would be that Judd had committed one of the most egregious fouls of bureaucratic gamesmanship: an end run.

But Rogerson was nowhere to be found. The room was full, but the chairman was already nearly twenty minutes late. There would be no time for an explanation. To avoid an embarrassing confrontation with the Assistant Secretary in front of two dozen colleagues, Judd abandoned his post near the door and took a seat in the corner at the end of the room, as far as possible from where Rogerson was likely to sit.

A low murmur of idle chatter filled the room, people mostly making small talk or checking their BlackBerries. A video screen projected a dozen more staff sitting quietly in another room. "Embassy Harare" flashed in the lower corner. Judd turned to his phone, thumbing through the news clips, searching for anything on Zimbabwe.

Judd's phone buzzed with an urgent text from Serena:

> WH Situation Room, 10am.
> Don't be late!

The White House? What could they want? His heart raced and he pounded a quick reply with his thumbs.

> Got it. What happened?

After a few seconds, Serena replied:

Don't know. Orders from
Landon Parker.

Just as Judd was about to respond, Bill Rogerson, now a full twenty-three minutes late, walked through the door. Without making eye contact with anyone, he took his seat, mumbled an apology about the tourism minister from Sudan talking too much, and opened his briefing book.

"Okay, folks. This meeting is about Zimbabwe's election," he said, reminding himself more than anyone else. As Rogerson belatedly scanned the room, he paused for a barely perceptible moment, when he noticed Judd. "I see we've got all the bureaus here," he said. "So let's save time by skipping introductions." *Straight poker face.*

"The embassy is with us. Welcome, Ambassador Tallyberger." Rogerson waved at the screen. After a three-second delay, those on the screen waved back. "Why don't you brief us first, Ambassador?"

"Thank you, Assistant Secretary Rogerson," said the oldest man in the other room. He wore round spectacles and had a white mustache, which was hard to see against his ashen skin. He looked exhausted. "It is now just after two p.m. Thursday in Zimbabwe. The polls open on Saturday at eight a.m.

66

local time."

Judd glanced at his watch. *Forty-two hours away.*

"We have launched the AEEOMZ, the American Embassy Election Observer Mission in Zimbabwe. We will have embassy teams deploying across the capital city," the ambassador continued. "They will be checking poll sites and monitoring campaign rallies. We've concentrated our AEEOMZ teams in Avondale, Highfield, and Mufakose. We are coordinating closely with the regional observers from the United Nations and the African Union, which are blanketing the major towns around the country, especially Mutare, Bulawayo, Gweru, and Chitungwiza. There are approximately six hundred international polling monitors now in-country, so I think we'll be pretty well covered. We should be very proud to have AEEOMZ participate in this historic event. As of now, everything is peaceful and all seems to be going smoothly."

"Thank you, Ambassador Tallyberger," said Rogerson. "I have the Zimbabwe desk officer here with me. Anything to add, Brad?"

"It's Brian, sir. No, nothing to add at this time."

"Well, Brian, you are very lucky to be

working with Arnold Tallyberger," said Rogerson, turning to face the table. "We are all very lucky to have Ambassador Tallyberger out there at post. He's an experienced diplomat. One of our best. He knows Africa and he will be our point on all matters related to Zimbabwe's elections. I have full confidence in him."

"Thank you, sir," said the ambassador.

"Well deserved, Ambassador. I don't have any questions from headquarters," Rogerson said. "Anyone else?"

Several hands went up around the table. Rogerson called on a young woman. "I'm with the Bureau of Democracy, Human Rights, and Labor. Most Zimbabweans live in the countryside and that's where election violence has been the worst. So why are the monitors concentrated in the cities?"

"Let me take this one," interjected Tallyberger. "Yes, that's correct. First, we assess the likelihood of major outbreaks of violence during or after the election to be low. Second, yes, we would have wanted to deploy more observers at rural polling stations, but it is a matter of limited resources. We only have so many people. And the local authorities specifically requested we keep to the main towns. We are here at their invitation."

Local authorities? thought Judd. *Since when do you ask those you are observing where to observe?*

"Thank you. Next question?" asked Rogerson, pointing at a middle-aged man sitting near Judd. "I'm with Political-Military. How close do we expect the results to be? Do we have any polling data?"

"Polls are very unreliable in this part of the world," the ambassador responded. "People here are just not used to answering questions about their political preferences. They aren't like us."

"Excuse me, I've got a two-hander," said a woman in the outer ring.

"Yes, young lady, go ahead," said Rogerson.

"I'm with Policy Planning," she said, with a wince. "I think we need to step back here for a moment. Many of us are new to Zimbabwe and haven't been following closely. What exactly are our objectives here? Do we have clear instructions from the Secretary? Where is the White House?"

"I'll take this," Rogerson said, sitting up straight. "The United States is very clear about our objectives this weekend. Our first priority is to ensure a safe, peaceful vote for the people of Zimbabwe. They are expressing their democratic rights and we want to prevent any unseemly behavior that could lead to violence or even a breakdown of order. Our primary task is to promote stability throughout the election and the post-election period."

Rogerson scanned the room, glancing past Judd, looking for signs of recognition.

"I also need to share," Rogerson continued, "that I've had a call from the Secretary this morning." He paused to let the importance of his announcement sink in. "She informed me that people at the highest levels are paying attention to Zimbabwe and they expect a good outcome. We may be in the spotlight on this more than we think. No bodies on the streets. Everyone got that?" Rogerson nodded to himself. "Our goal is to keep the seventh floor and the White House happy by maintaining calm. Our bar of success here is keeping Zimbabwe off the Secretary's desk and out of the President's Daily Brief. Everyone got that?"

Heads around the table nodded.

"No bodies in the streets. Is that clear?" he added.

More nodding.

"I'm sorry to ask again," said the middle-aged man. "I realize we have no firm polling numbers, but you haven't mentioned the candidates. Could the opposition actually win this thing?"

"Ambassador, do you want to take that?"

"Pleasure," said Tallyberger. "President Tinotenda has won six straight elections. He has the party bosses lined up in all the major towns and the governors of each of the provinces. He controls parliament. He also has the firm support of the military, police, and intelligence services. I don't think he is facing a serious challenge."

"The lawyer lady. Gigi something. She can't win?"

"No, I don't believe so," the ambassador said. "Gugu Mutonga is the candidate for the opposition Democracy Union of Zimbabwe. They have the youth vote and support in parts of Matabeleland in the south, but the DUZ hasn't really penetrated the Shona heartland. So, no. I don't believe she can win."

"Let me share my perspective," Rogerson interrupted. "I've been speaking with the South African government. As you know, they are the regional power and they currently sit on the UN Security Council, so we are in close and regular contact with the South Africans. Zimbabwe is their neighbor. This is their backyard. They have a strong interest in keeping things quiet. Like us, they can't have chaos."

"Does that mean we are active or not?" asked a man at the back.

"We have to maintain a robust presence to prevent unrest and ensure American interests are pursued. But the United States cannot be the world's policeman," Rogerson declared.

"Which means we will do what, exactly?"

"Luckily, the South Africans don't appear too worried about Zimbabwe," said Rogerson, ignoring the question. "But they are keeping a close eye on the parties, including the DUZ."

"The South Africans have surveillance on the DUZ?" asked a staffer.

Rogerson grimaced. "I cannot speak to any specific South African intelligence operations. But there is concern in Pretoria about suspicious financing of Zimbabwe's political parties. Money coming from private actors in South Africa and from places like Lubumbashi in the Congo. Gugu Mutonga may be under the influence of these outsiders. At this stage we just don't know. We will continue to dialogue with the South Africans on these concerns, but I believe they have it under control."

"President Tinotenda is now eighty-eight years old and running for a seventh term. Aren't the South Africans worried about his age and durability?"

"He's a strong old ox," said Rogerson. "I've known him for many years and think he's still got a few more to go. Do you concur, Ambassador Tallyberger?"

"I do. He was on television last week addressing the nation. He stood and spoke for over two hours. I don't think he's lost a beat. He doesn't look like he's ready to retire."

"What's the instability risk?" asked the Pol-Mil staffer.

" '*Après moi le déluge*,' " Rogerson said.

"Excuse me, sir?"

"Tell them, Ambassador," said Rogerson, pointing to the video screen.

" '*Après moi le déluge*. After me, the flood,' " Tallyberger said. "It's one of Tinotenda's favorite lines. It was actually Louis XV who said it first. Then Mobutu used it in Congo. It's a warning. You may not like me, but beware of what comes next."

"We *should* beware of what comes next," said Rogerson. "Louis XV and Mobutu were both right. After they were gone, we had the French revolution and the Congolese civil war. I don't think anyone wants another revolution in Zimbabwe."

"What are the succession scenarios?" asked a staffer who was biting her nails.

"There is still jostling within Tino's party to be next in line," answered the ambassador, "but we in the Harare diplomatic corps now believe Simba Chimurenga, the army chief and national security advisor, is the most likely successor. He's not yet fifty years old and by far the youngest general in the country. But he and the president are very close."

"Can we live with Chimurenga? Will he keep the lid on?" asked Pol-Mil.

"I think so. He's a career military man and very capable," Rogerson said. "Any more questions before we close?"

A hand went up at the back, a young woman with short black hair and bronze skin. "Does the embassy have any information about the whereabouts or activities of Solomon Zagwe?"

"I'm sorry, who?" asked Ambassador Tallyberger.

"General Solomon Zagwe," she said. "Former President of Ethiopia. The perpetrator of the Red Fear. He's been in exile in Zimbabwe since he fled Ethiopia twenty years ago. He is living in Harare under the protection of President Tinotenda. Do you have any new information about him?"

"I'm afraid we don't have resources for that kind of thing," said the ambassador.

"If you do come across anything, please let us know. We have a strong interest in General Zagwe," the woman said. Rogerson, distracted by a staff member handing him a note, didn't reply.

"Who precisely is 'we'?" Tallyberger asked.

"The Justice Department. I'm Isabella, Isabella Espinosa, a special prosecutor with DOJ on assignment to the war crimes unit here at State. Zagwe is one of our primary persons of interest."

"Well, we'll let you know if we hear anything, Ms. Espinosa," replied Tallyberger, pursing his lips.

"Okay, if there isn't anything else," Rogerson said, passing the note back to his aide, "I need to get to another meeting. Before we adjourn, I want to clarify how this will work over the next two days. My office is going to run everything on Zimbabwe. We will coordinate across all State bureaus and the interagency. This is going to be whole-of-government and I'm running it strictly by the book. All decisions come through my office. I don't want anything to come out of the U.S. government without the ambassador and me being fully informed. Everyone is going to stay in their lane. Brad here —" Rogerson looked to the young man sitting next to him.

"Uh, Brian, sir."

"Right. Brian here is your point of contact."

Judd's phone vibrated with another message from Serena:

> Your car to the White House is ready.
> You need to leave now.

"Brian won't be sleeping for the next two days," Rogerson continued. "So let's keep him busy. Anything at all on Zimbabwe goes to my office. I won't tolerate anyone off the reservation . . ." declared Rogerson, before noticing Judd's hand raised. "Well, I see we have one last question. Make it quick."

"Do we know when election results will be announced?" Judd asked.

"Why *exactly* are you asking?" Rogerson sneered.

"If there's a moment when things will go wrong in Zimbabwe, it'll likely be after the polls close and before the results are announced. That's the window of opportunity for the military or the opposition or anyone else trying to sway the final outcome. If we want influence, that's *our* window, too. We have until the official announcement of the results. So, when that will be?"

"I don't agree that the United States'

influence ends so easily, but I'll answer that question," said Ambassador Tallyberger. "Election results will be reported to the commission throughout the day. It will take until early the next morning to tally the final votes. Then the election commission has to certify the results, the court has to sign off, and finally the election commissioner will hold a press conference to announce the winner. The press conference is scheduled for noon on Sunday, Harare time."

Noon Sunday, thought Judd. He stood to leave and checked his watch again. *Seventy hours away.*

6.

Molweni Hotel, Cape Town, South Africa
Thursday, 3:45 p.m. Central Africa Time
Mariana Leibowitz promised herself, for the second time that day, just one last cigarette. The seasoned Washington lobbyist was used to the commotion of a campaign, but she needed a moment to clear her head.

Mariana slid open the glass doors, stepping from the cramped racket of her hotel suite onto the temporary serenity of the terrace. Perhaps it was the jet lag, she thought. *Or, good Lord, age.*

Her room, one of Cape Town's most expensive, boasted a wide vista of Table Mountain, the majestic flat-topped mesa that dominated the skyline and hugged the city against the sea. Off in the distance she could just make out Robben Island, the former prison in Table Bay that once held Nelson Mandela. It was now a museum and memorial to all who had suffered in the fight against apartheid. She had seen the ticket stand for the Robben Island ferry next to the souvenir shop at the Victoria & Albert Waterfront, a tourist mall at the city harbor. She swore to make time to visit the island. *Or maybe next time.*

By no coincidence, her top-floor suite was the very same room she had stayed in years ago on a very different kind of trip. The champagne and lobster tails were replaced this time with laptop computers and banks of cell phone chargers. Instead of an attractive young man, she was sharing the room this time with a dozen volunteers, all from neighboring Zimbabwe, working nineteen-hour days to resolve the reason for their exile. The campaign team had thrown themselves at Mariana in the idealistic hope that they might be able to soon return home. Even their names — Blessing, Lovemore, and Happiness were the three that Mariana could most easily remember — appropriately represented their aspirations. Instead of a honeymoon suite, on this trip Mariana Leibowitz was living in a war room.

She stubbed out her cigarette, snatched one last guilty glance at the view, and returned to work. Back inside, a huge map of Zimbabwe was tacked on one wall, with multicolored pins stuck in the main towns. Red pins — the color of Gugu Mutonga's campaign — identified solid friendly territory, while dark green pins marked enemy strongholds, the towns firmly under control of President Winston Tinotenda and his ruling party. Neither of these zones were problems. In these places, everyone knew where they stood.

The trouble lay with the yellow pins, the places of unknown loyalty, *the battlegrounds.* These yellow areas, where votes were still up for grabs and where a professional political operator could tip the balance, were the reason Mariana was there.

She poured herself another cup of coffee and scanned the map. The yellow areas were shrinking for sure. But rather than turn red, as was her objective, they were increasingly marked either green or bright fire-orange, the most worrying color pin: locations of violent attacks on Gugu Mutonga's supporters.

Happiness was also pacing the room, speaking quietly in a mix of English and Shona, the main language of Zimbabwe, into a headset attached to her cell phone. *"Ehe, ndino nzwisisa.* Yes, I understand. . . . How many? . . . Have they been taken to the hospital? . . . *Ehe,* please hurry. . . . I

will notify the nearest defense patrol. . . .
Go safely. . . . *Fambai zvakanaka.*"

Mariana eyed Happiness as she took careful notes and logged them into the laptop. Oblivious she was being watched, Happiness plucked a yellow pin from the center of the country and replaced it with a fire-orange one.

"Shit!" Mariana hissed. She spun around to face the opposite wall. A poster declared FREEDOM! PROSPERITY! VICTORY! GUGU! stamped over the smiling face of a handsome middle-aged African woman. Next to the poster, a large whiteboard listed target towns, task assignments for the team, and the names of newspaper reporters. She checked the board and crossed out several names. As always, Mariana kept the most important agenda for that day in her head.

She slid open the glass doors again and stepped out on the terrace to make a private phone call. After four rings, just before she was ready to hang up, the phone was answered.

"Hello, Mariana."

"Judd, darling, it's so good to speak with you. I know you are busy, but it's urgent. And it's very important. I promise."

Judd gazed out the tinted window as his black government SUV was nearing Pennsylvania Avenue, approaching the White House.

"I only have three minutes. Are you still in Congo?"

"No, South Africa. But I'm calling you about *Zimbabwe.*"

"Zimbabwe? How do you know about that? I only just found out."

"That's cute, Judd. You know I can't tell you that. But I know you are working on Zimbabwe. And you're just in time. I need you."

"You need me?" Judd was impressed with Mariana's sources.

"The election is two days away. This is crunch time, baby. Gugu Mutonga has a real shot at beating Tinotenda, but Washington is missing its chance to make history here. The administration is completely asleep at the wheel."

"We aren't at the wheel, Mariana."

"Okay, bad analogy. But that's precisely the point, Judd. Where is the United States on the election?"

"You know how these things work, Mariana. Have you talked to the ambassador?"

"Tallyberger? He's fucking useless, Judd. You should know that. Arnold Tallyberger is exactly why I need your help."

Judd's car was now one block away. "Why

are you calling me?"

"Judd," she barked. "You realize Tino has been president for six terms already? Six! That's thirty years. And he's running again!"

"Yes, I know. It's a long time."

"Zimbabwe finally has a chance to make a fresh start. We can help Gugu Mutonga win."

" 'We'?"

"Yes, Judd. You and me. I am working with her party, the Democracy Union of Zimbabwe. They're a longtime client. I'm sure you know that. I want your help to get the United States on board and help us win."

"You know the U.S. doesn't pick sides in a foreign election."

"That's bullshit. You think they aren't picking sides in Egypt?"

"I don't know, Mariana. But they aren't picking sides in Zimbabwe as far as I know."

"Believe me, I know that. It pisses me off! What I want the U.S. government to do is to just stand up for the truth. No hiding behind diplomatic protocol and all this neutrality crap. Just keeping things quiet isn't good enough, Judd."

"What are you suggesting?"

"Gugu is going to win this thing."

"She is?"

"I don't work for losers. You should know

that by now. I'm not going to work for a candidate I can't help win. You know I always do my homework."

"Yes, Mariana. You always do your homework."

"Always a deep dive, Judd. Always a deep dive. That's why I'm working for Gugu. And now I've got private polling showing we are going to take the election on Saturday. We're winning this fucking thing."

"You're winning? You have the data?"

"I can't show you any numbers yet, but I've got it. And Tino is going to do everything he can to stop us. He'll cheat, lie, and steal if he has to. He's already sent out his goon squads to suppress the vote. I'm documenting all the election abuses and intimidation. I'm going to need the U.S. to push for a speedy announcement of the election results and then to stand up for the winner. *The real winner.* When it comes to a head on Sunday, I need to be able to count on you."

"Have you spoken with Landon Parker? Is that why you're calling me?"

"I always speak with Landon. He's a dear, but he's being cagey on Zimbabwe. I don't understand it. He should know what's right, what's in the interests of the United States, but he says it's complicated and won't commit. I'll keep working on him, but *I need you,* Judd."

"What about William Rogerson?"

"You must be joking. Bill Rogerson's got his head so far up South Africa's ass, he has no idea what's going on anywhere else. All he cares about is keeping Pretoria happy. He doesn't give two shits about Zimbabwe."

"I can't make any promises, Mariana."

"I know you only do crises, Judd. That's your thing, right? Crisis reaction? Zimbabwe could easily blow up. So how about getting ahead of this? How about *preventing* a crisis? How's that for your Golden Hour?"

"Maybe."

"So you're in, then. Good."

"That's not a yes, Mariana," Judd said, stepping out of his ride and onto the cobblestone path leading to the White House. "The politics here are . . . complicated."

"That's what Landon said! What's wrong with you guys? Has the United States government completely lost its balls?"

"I've got to run, I'm sorry. I will look into it. That I promise," Judd said as he approached the visitors' security gate for the West Wing.

"Do you know about Motowetsurohuro, Judd?"

"What?" he said, stopping to listen.

85

"Moto-wet-suro-huro. In Shona it means the Great Rabbit Fire."

"Okay, what is it?"

"To hunt rabbits in Zimbabwe, people burn a field using the flames to chase the rabbits into a trap so they can be killed, skinned, and eaten. Well, back in the 1980s, in a remote part of the country, a group of kids — you know, teenage boys — got into a fight with a policeman over a girl or a goat or something, I don't know. But the policeman was killed. When the police came, the families hid the kids. So they called in the army on trumped-up charges that they were rebels or something. The army flooded the area with troops and attack helicopters. They went on a rampage. They burned down the villages. They killed hundreds of people."

"That's horrific, Mariana."

"They called it Operation Motowetsurohuro. They hunted down the people like rabbits. They trapped them and killed them. Can you even imagine?"

"Awful."

"It was a massacre, Judd. A slaughter."

"Why are you telling me this, Mariana?"

"Guess who tried to help those people?"

"I don't know."

"Well, the United States and Britain

didn't say shit. Not a fucking word, Judd. The only person who tried to help those poor people get justice was a young attorney who was barely out of law school. She fought for those families, taking their cases to the courts, even to the United Nations. And she never accepted a dime."

"And?" Judd asked, flashing his ID badge to the security guard, who released the White House gate.

"The Zimbabwean courts took up the case, but once the lawyer began to present evidence of the deaths and the army's role, the witnesses started disappearing. And then the government removed the judge. Tinotenda appointed a new judge, whose first act was to throw out the whole case. He put pressure on the UN to bury it, which they did, claiming lack of evidence."

"Mariana, hold on for a second." Judd set down his phone on the X-ray belt and walked through the metal detector. Once through to the other side and cleared by the marine guard, he picked up his phone.

"So, Mariana, are you asking me to raise this case with the Justice Department?"

"No. I'm telling you this story because that young lawyer is Gugu Mutonga."

"Your client."

"This woman is the real deal. And this

election isn't just about politics. It's a mission for justice. This could be Zimbabwe's fresh start. A chance for redemption."

Judd walked up the path toward the West Wing and had nearly arrived at the door, where another guard stood at attention.

"It's a chance for redemption for the United States, too," she said. "That's why I need your help."

"I'll look into it, Mariana," said Judd just as the marine opened the door for him. "I'm still getting up to speed on Zimbabwe."

"That's why you need my help, too. I'll be calling you again soon."

"I know you will, Mariana."

Click.

Mariana set down the phone and returned inside to the hubbub of the campaign war room. "Where are we, Happiness? What's the latest?"

Happiness glanced up at Mariana from her laptop, pursed her lips, and shook her head. Then she stood up, walked over to the map, and replaced one more yellow pin with an orange one.

7.

Judd entered the West Wing, cleared another security post, and then took a short flight of stairs down into the secure complex. He dropped his BlackBerry in a cubbyhole, swiped his ID card one more time, and then entered the Situation Room.

Every seat at the cramped conference table was taken, so he slipped into an empty chair in the outer perimeter by the door. All six of the flat panel screens were off. He scanned for a friendly face but didn't see anyone he recognized. He still didn't know why he was in this meeting, and he dearly wanted to catch his breath. Parker had told him to get on a plane to Zimbabwe *tonight,* and he had a lot to do beforehand. But if Parker wanted him here . . . Suddenly, the room went quiet as a tall man in a crisp white naval uniform marched in and stood at the head of the table.

"Good morning, everyone. I'm Admiral Hammond, special assistant to the President and National Security Council coordinator for arms control and weapons of mass destruction."

The admiral was interrupted by the release of the sealed door as all eyes turned to see the late arrival. A young black man with a wide face and a short goatee slunk into the room. "Sorry . . ." he muttered, with an apologetic bow of the head. Judd's face brightened as the man sat down next to him.

"Sunday!" he whispered, with a paternal pat on the back.

"Hello, Dr. Ryker," Sunday whispered back. Sunday was a CIA analyst who'd been a big help with Mali. Maybe he knew what —

"We've brought together this specific mix of DOD, State, and the Intelligence Community here today," said Admiral Hammond. "You in this room are considered experts in countries with known deposits of uranium."

Uranium? thought Judd. *Am I in the right meeting?*

"The White House, under advisement from the Office of the Director of National Intelligence, is increasingly concerned about the security of radioactive materials. Here are our target countries."

A screen lit up with a map of the world. About two dozen countries were highlighted in bright red. "Mali," sighed Judd, finally understanding why he was there. *Am I being pulled off Zimbabwe already?* he wondered.

"Nearly two-thirds of all uranium comes from just three countries: Kazakhstan, Australia, and Canada. We've established high-confidence monitoring systems in those locations. But there are a growing number of new discoveries. Estimated reserves are low, and these new sites are typically not large enough for commercial mining companies. So governments have been inviting small, lesser-known prospecting companies to conduct seismic studies and carry out test drilling. We have concerns that several of these unknown wildcat miners may be connected to international criminal cartels or extremist networks seeking high-grade uranium. They won't care about the price or commercial viability. They only need access to enough material to create a weapon."

Yikes. I see where this is going.

"I won't pretend to fully understand the physics," the admiral said. "But we have reports from a British intelligence source

91

about the possible discovery of a new and highly dangerous variant of uranium with unusually high levels of the U-235 isotope. This is still unconfirmed, but it's alarming enough that we called you all here today. The British memo is still being assessed by science teams at CIA, DIA, and a special unit at the Department of Energy. But if it turns out to be correct, this could be a naturally occurring form of highly enriched uranium. That means raw ore capable of being weaponized without complex processing."

Admiral Hammond leaned forward and placed both hands on the table.

"I don't think I need to tell the people in this room how serious this is. If such material exists and falls into the wrong hands, it would be our worst nightmare."

The room buzzed with nervous energy.

"You were all asked to come here this morning to assist with our urgent risk assessment. Here are our immediate countries of interest." The screen flashed as he read out the list: "Pakistan, Somalia, Mali, Chad, Papua New Guinea, the Philippines, Venezuela."

Shit. Some list, thought Judd.

"In each of these countries, we are taking steps to upgrade the monitoring of mining zones and, as of this morning, we are establishing Intelligence Community task forces to assess the risks. This is a new classified program code-named UMBRELLA ROSE. As part of this program, you will each be asked to work with the assessment teams to provide political, economic, and other analyses. We want to ensure we consult across the interagency with country experts to make sure we aren't missing anything. You will all be contacted by your team leaders based at Langley in the coming days. They can fill you in on more details. Any questions?"

"I'm with OSD Special Projects. What kind of monitoring are you talking about?" asked a young woman.

"UMBRELLA ROSE will deploy a combination of human intelligence, existing overflight capabilities, plus new technological advancements that are being field-tested now by DARPA. Next?"

"DIA, Western Hemisphere. Are you involving local intelligence and military services?" asked an older man.

"Negative. The existence of UMBRELLA ROSE is classified as TOP SECRET NO FORN. No foreign intelligence sharing. I repeat, this is TOP SECRET NO FORN. To the extent we notify the authorities of overflight, it will be under alternative civilian-use cover. Next?"

"I'm with State, S/CRU, the Crisis Reaction Unit," Judd said. "How will this work with zero local participation?"

"It's suboptimal. But operational security dictates we keep it close hold. Outside of the ambassador, CIA chief of station, and required military staff, no one in the embassies will be aware of UMBRELLA ROSE. In several of our target countries, we have reason to believe there may be high-level government collusion. We can't afford any leaks on this one. With nuclear security, there's no room for error, people."

Sunday raised his hand, "CIA, Africa Issue. What about Zimbabwe?"

"Zimbabwe?" asked the admiral, turning to an aide, who just shook her head. The admiral shrugged.

"There's a defunct uranium mine in Kanyemba. It was closed years ago, but we have signs of new activity. If we are tracking new uranium sites in unstable countries, Zimbabwe should be on the list."

"Very well. Have Langley send over any information and we'll look into adding Zimbabwe to UMBRELLA ROSE."

After a few more technical questions that the admiral couldn't answer, the meeting was adjourned.

As they retrieved their BlackBerries and departed, Judd put his hand on the shoulder of the CIA analyst. "Good to see you again, Sunday."

"Aaay, good to see you, too, Dr. Ryker."

"You're not working on West Africa anymore?"

"At Langley they like to move us around, keep us fresh." Sunday glanced over his shoulder and whispered, "Plus I don't think they want someone with Nigerian parents working too long on Nigeria."

"But why Zim?"

"I must have irritated my supervisor."

Judd cocked his head. "What's the problem with Zimbabwe?"

"Don't get me wrong," Sunday said. "Zimbabwe is fascinating analytically. There's a lot going on. Their election is this weekend."

"Saturday," Judd said.

"Right, Saturday. But Zimbabwe's not exactly the best way to get into the President's Daily Brief."

"I hope you're wrong."

"Why's that?"

"Because I'm working Zimbabwe, too."

"Aaay." Sunday covered his mouth, his eyes wide. "I'm sorry. I didn't know you

95

worked on Zim."

"I haven't. Not until this morning."

"What a coincidence."

Or maybe it wasn't. Was *this* why Parker had sent him to this meeting?

"We need to talk, Sunday. Right now."

8.

Harare, Zimbabwe
Thursday, 4:32 p.m. Central Africa Time
"Where are the cherry-red Jimmy Choos?"

"I'm sorry, madam," said the assistant, bowing her head.

"Those aren't cherry-red!"

"I'm sorry. They only sent Jimmy Choos in pink and teal. I have a pair of red Manolo Blahniks, if that may suffice."

"Tsaaah! No!" The woman tsked. "Those are the wrong ones. That won't do at all. Call Hong Kong and have them send the shoes I asked for!"

The First Lady Harriet Tinotenda, disgusted with the sloppy attention to detail by her staff, threw the shoe box across the room and crashing into a tall pile of white department store boxes.

"Yes, madam. I'll call them right now."

"Make sure they understand I need them by Sunday morning. The president's

97

swearing-in is in the afternoon, so the shoes must be here in time."

"Yes, madam."

"I cannot go to the inauguration in the wrong shoes. I won't have it."

"Yes, madam."

"Is this everything?" the first lady asked, waving her arm at a rainbow mountain of discarded boxes from Louis Vuitton, Tiffany & Co., Cartier, and Prada. "What is that one?" she demanded, pointing to a flat unopened black box in one corner.

"Ascot Chang. They sent a hand-tailored suit for the president. As a gift."

"Tsaaah, no. My husband doesn't wear Italian suits. Send it back."

"Yes, madam."

"Where is the rest of my shopping?"

"I'll get it now, madam," said the assistant, who collected the suit box, bowed submissively, and then backed out the door.

Harriet surveyed the room. She clicked her teeth. This was no way to shop properly, she thought. After her husband won another term, she would persuade her friends in Hong Kong to open a branch in Harare. She knew *plenty* of women who could keep a designer shop open for business. Yes, she would ask Winston about this after the election. Maybe she'd even become an investor.

If a sufficient designer store wasn't possible, perhaps she could befriend the British ambassador's wife and convince her to allow an occasional shopping trip to London. Just one day at Harrods each year would be enough. They could take an Air Zimbabwe jet and load it up. These petty political games had become such a nuisance. The ambassador's wife would surely understand, she thought. *These old men and their egos. So predictable.*

"Tsaaah. Where is that useless girl?" she hissed to herself.

Bored of waiting, she wandered over to the window. It was two hours past sunset, but her garden was well lit.

Beyond the walls, the city was pitch-dark, no doubt because the nation's main coal power station was missing spare parts again. Winston had complained about this problem ahead of the election, but his cabinet had pleaded that the fault lay with the Americans and British. Their devious sanctions prevented the national electricity company from buying the necessary replacement parts. *Hypocrites and racists,* she thought.

Within her compound walls, the lights were on, thanks to a diesel generator imported from China and running on fuel trucked in every week from South Africa. Because of these special arrangements, she could gaze at her garden even at this late hour.

Maybe she could meet with the Chinese ambassador's wife and help with the power station problem? *Yes, after the election, I'll raise that with Winston, too,* she decided. Such contributions to the nation would help seal her husband's legacy. A power plant and a department store.

As she watched heavily armed military guards pace through her grounds, she cast aside her frustrations and allowed herself a moment of pride. *Look at me,* she thought. *A poor village girl from the lowlands, sitting here in the Presidential Mansion. Living here as the wife of the most powerful man in the country.* How far she had come! She prayed to God for her blessings and thanked her ancestors who brought her such good luck.

Of course, she didn't believe her circumstances had really materialized from sheer luck. *I am not lucky — I made this happen,* she thought. Through her own cunning and quick wit, she'd stood out among the hundreds of students at the Saint Catherine's Mission School for Girls. She secured a scholarship to the prestigious Kwekwe Secretarial Academy. Then a strategic relationship with the headmaster — an alliance the old women of Kwekwe had unfairly scorned as immoral — was parlayed by her into a job in the Ministry of Public Works. When her moment arrived, the day the President of the Republic was due to visit the ministry, she bribed a security guard with Marlboro cigarettes for a position near the front, where she was sure her shapely red business suit would catch the president's eye.

Their first encounter didn't go as she'd hoped. She had shaken President Tinotenda's limp hand and gushingly expressed her sincere appreciation for his leadership of the nation. But she wasn't sure he'd noticed her. It was only the next day, when her supervisor arrived with a written notice of her transfer to the office of the president's chief of staff that she knew her gambit had worked. From there, she needed only a few weeks to begin a romantic relationship with the old man, and only a year more to extract a marriage proposal. *Old men and their egos. So predictable.*

Her wedding was the grandest affair in Zimbabwe since independence. The marriage ceremony was held in a private church, but the reception had to be moved to the national stadium to accommodate all the well-wishers. It was a glorious event, she recalled, despite the newspapers' petty grumbling about the cost to taxpayers. And the tabloids made a fuss about their age gap. *What difference should fifty years make when you are in love? Jealousy is an ugly sentiment for small people,* she thought.

Those same small people were also no doubt envious of what she had now. Twenty-two bedrooms, fine English furniture, the latest in Japanese televisions, the best designer clothing flown in from East Asia. Perhaps it was *better* to have the shopping brought to you, she suddenly wondered.

Her thoughts were interrupted by the return of her assistant. "This just arrived by courier for you, madam," she announced, holding a black velvet box about the size of a Burberry hand purse.

"Set it down and leave me."

"Yes, madam."

"Did the courier say who it's from?"

"No, madam. I'm sorry, madam. Shall I have the boy chase him and ask?"

"Tsaaah. *Aiwa.* No," she said emphatically and waved the girl away.

She walked over to the mysterious gift. She took a deep breath and then gently opened the hinged box as if it were a giant oyster shell. Inside the silk-lined box lay a diamond necklace, twelve large-carat stones on a delicate gold chain.

"Naka!" she exclaimed. "So beautiful!"

There was no note, no explanation. The only hint of the jewelry's origin was a small gold label: CHAKRI DIAMOND COLLECTION, BANGKOK. *Old men and their egos.*

She unfastened the necklace and draped it around her neck. She walked over to the mirror to admire herself. It was the most beautiful thing she had ever seen in her life, she thought. *Perhaps I am lucky after all?*

Her elation came to a screeching halt with the realization she might never wear this necklace in public. She didn't care what the press might say, or even about the vapid chatter of the political classes. She didn't care where the jewels came from. She could never wear her new gift because her husband, President Winston Tinotenda, would know it was not from him.

9.

White House, Washington, D.C.
Thursday, 10:38 a.m. Eastern Standard Time
Judd led Sunday out the White House gate and across Pennsylvania Avenue to Lafayette Square. They weaved through a swarm of high school students in matching orange T-shirts and skirted a dozen protestors holding signs about illegal government eavesdropping. They walked past the statue of Andrew Jackson to find, on the far side of the park, an empty bench away from the crowds.

The two men sat for a moment in silence, scanning the area. Once Sunday was satisfied they were alone, he asked, "What do you need?"

"To get up to speed on Zimbabwe damn fast," Judd said. "I'm leaving for Harare tonight."

"Where should I start?"

"I'll read my briefing book on the plane,

but it's all new to me. I need the context. Tell me what's most critical."

"The place to start is with the British. The sting of colonialism, the psychological trauma of being dominated by a foreign power — all that's still raw."

"Still?" Judd asked.

"Zimbabwe's not like Nigeria or even Kenya. My grandparents are still living in Nigeria. They remember British rule, but they've come to terms with it. It's not part of their lives anymore. My parents barely remember the British. I don't think my father interacted at all with Europeans until he went to college. And now most of my family are American citizens. There's no issue.

"It's not like that with the men running Zimbabwe. They are the same ones who fought the British and won. They think about the war every day. It's part of their identity. It's the core of their legitimacy as a government. So they are highly sensitive to what the British or Americans might be up to."

"Is that what's driving Tinotenda? Fear of the British?" Judd asked.

"Fear and paranoia. He sees plots all around him. He keeps his cabinet in a state of ignorance. They never know when a shuffle is coming or where they're going. It helps him maintain loyalty and disrupt any factions within the party from growing too strong."

"An old Mobutu trick."

"Aaay. Mobutu Sese Seko was the master. He used to sleep with the wives of his ministers, just to show them who's boss. I don't think Tino's got that kind of stamina left in him. But Tino has been accelerating the rotation of his security detail. This suggests he is worried about internal plots. The only constant has been his national security advisor, General Chimurenga. He's the only one Tino seems to trust."

"So what's Tino's game plan?"

"My assessment is that Tino is stuck. He still views himself as the father of the nation. He wants to defend the country from all of the forces he spent his whole life fighting. But he's lost the fire in his belly. Maybe it's age. Maybe it's fatigue. No one knows. But he isn't showing any signs that he's ready to quit. My hunch is that he just can't imagine Zimbabwe without himself as president."

"What about the rest of the party?"

"They're locked in, too," Sunday said. "The party bosses have all spent so many years manipulating each other, building their own little empires, repeating the same propaganda. No one even knows what the truth is any longer. They long ago started believing their own lies. Everyone is frozen. They're all stuck in ice."

"So how do we crack the ice?"

Sunday tilted his head and gave Judd a mischievous smile.

"What exactly do you mean, Dr. Ryker?"

Judd leaned forward. "If the United States wanted to break up the ice, to help create a whole new system, something better, how would we do that?"

"Do we *want* to do that?"

"Consider it a hypothetical, Sunday. If I wanted to do this, what would I do first?"

"Isn't regime change a bit above the pay grade of a State Department office director?" Sunday's grin grew wider.

Judd nodded, accepting the challenge. "Is the CIA supposed to be providing objective analysis or second-guessing civilian officials?"

"Is that what's happening here? Am I an analyst briefing a policy maker, or is this just two friends chatting in the park?"

"You're right," Judd said. "Let me re-phrase my question. Between friends, of course. If the President of the United States determined it was in the interest of American foreign policy to shake things up in Zimbabwe, the best way to do this would be to —"

"Kill President Tinotenda," said Sunday, with a casual shrug.

Judd sat back in the bench and exhaled.

"Obviously," added Sunday.

"Okay, okay," Judd said. "If we don't want to do that —"

"Technically, that would be illegal."

"Yes, of course," Judd said. "If assassination is off the table, what other steps might be taken?"

"You could attack their business interests. You could try to break up the support base. You could try to lure some of Tinotenda's allies into challenging him. The key to these tactics is all the same. You have to convince people that change has arrived, that Tinotenda is on his way out. As soon as people believe it, they'll jump faster than you can say 'Every man for himself.' No one wants to be the last rat on a sinking ship."

"What about leaking rumors that Tino is dead or dying?"

"Sure, but how long would it last? Only until he got on TV."

"What about supporting the opposition?"

"Nope."

" 'Nope'?" Judd leaned forward again.

"No," Sunday said.

"Why not? That seems like the logical thing to do. Lend support to Gugu Mutonga and help her win a democratic election. What's wrong with that strategy?"

"Won't happen. Simba Chimurenga would never allow it."

"Chimurenga," Judd said flatly. "He's the national security advisor?"

"That's his official title, yes. And army chief. But his real power comes from his personal relationship with the president."

"Are they family?"

"We don't think so, but Tino treats him like blood. Not quite a son, but maybe a nephew. They either have some special bond or they have dirt on each other. Probably both."

"Are they in business together?"

"I don't know. Wouldn't surprise me." Sunday shrugged.

"What can you tell me about a massacre many years ago. Moto . . . something."

"Motowetsurohuro," Sunday said. "In the north, not far from the Kanyemba mine, actually. We don't know what happened exactly, but there used to be villages there, and now there aren't."

"They're just gone?"

"Yes. Erased from the map."

109

"How does that happen?"

"The government denies it *ever* happened. The record has been totally expunged. They claim it was always propaganda from local troublemakers. Our ambassador inquired about it at the time in a meeting with their foreign minister and they nearly expelled him from the country."

"My God, Sunday. We didn't do anything?"

"A local church recorded the names of those who disappeared. They have a list of several hundred people. But no living witnesses and no bodies."

"No bodies?"

"Nope."

"No case."

"Aaay."

"The trail's gone completely cold?"

"As far as I can tell."

"So that's what Simba has on Tino? The massacre?"

"Plausible. Or maybe that's what Tino has on Simba. Ever since, Chimurenga has been treated almost like Tino's son. And that's what brings us back to this weekend's voting. If Tinotenda somehow lost the election, then Chimurenga would make sure, one way or another, it never happened. Just like Motowetsurohuro."

"How could he do that? There are hundreds of election observers."

"Good question. Since I was put on Zimbabwe, I've been watching how they operate and where they draw lessons. Chimurenga visited Gabon and Angola to see how they run elections, plus he's run election security for the past two voting cycles at home. Based on what I've gathered, I assess that Chimurenga's built three layers of protection."

Sunday paused to check they were still alone. He then leaned in and whispered, "Phase one is to intimidate the electorate. That usually works. With some money and guns, it's not hard to bribe the right people and frighten the rest into voting for the Big Man."

"Incumbents don't always win."

"True. 'The people who cast the votes don't decide an election, the people who count the votes do.' You know who said that?"

"Tinotenda?"

"Joseph Stalin." Sunday smiled again.

"So that's phase two?"

"I think so. If intimidation doesn't work, then Chimurenga can steal the election by vote rigging, ballot stuffing, and, if it comes down to it, falsifying the results."

"How can they get away with that? Aren't the ballots counted at local stations and posted outside so all the people can all see the local tallies?"

"Control the computer network, control the result. Even if the local counting is accurate, they can change the numbers in the aggregation. There are always discrepancies in an election. One constituency here and there where you get some odd results. They can just fix the numbers. Even if the opposition could get their hands on the raw data, it would take months to challenge the final results in court. And by that time it's too late. Once the final election results are announced and the new government is sworn in, it's very hard to reopen the books."

"The opposition needs real-time data."

"Sure. But how are they going to get that? The election commission is run by Judge Makwere. Do you know who he is?"

"I'm guessing he's close to Tinotenda?"

"Bingo. Makwere is the uncle of Harriet Tinotenda."

"The First Lady."

"Right."

Judd sighed. "Does the Agency have polling numbers?"

"We always do."

"Well, what do they say?"

"It's a small sample size, but the numbers are pretty clear that, in a truly free and fair election, Gugu Mutonga would take it in a landslide."

"A landslide? Really?"

"Most voters were born after independence. The ruling party is a bunch of greedy, out-of-touch old men. Most voters get that. Even people in the countryside have relatives in the city. Zimbabweans know what's happening."

"Assuming Mutonga can make it through the vote and somehow finds a way to get through the counting, you said there were three layers. What's next?"

"Chimurenga just refuses. Phase three is declaring a state of emergency, probably on trumped-up claims of a national threat."

"Walk me through that scenario. What happens?"

"The election and the constitution are suspended, the opposition arrested, and the army deployed into the villages. We've got plenty of evidence that the Green Mambas — those are the party's youth militias — are already fanning out, just in case."

"You're talking about a total police state."

"Total police state," Sunday repeated.

"But South Africa and the other neighbors

wouldn't accept that. Neither would the United Nations, right?"

"Probably not. But it only takes a few weeks to dismantle the opposition and squeeze their supporters. Then Tino can announce an amnesty and a new election. All he really has to do is promise a transition plan, make some noise about reconciliation, and drag it all out. He knows everyone will back off."

"Is Tinotenda involved in this?"

"Probably not. He tries to stay above the fray. I find it hard to believe he's unaware of what Chimurenga is doing to keep him in power. But I think he's happy to feign ignorance and keep his hands clean."

"This is a lot worse than I thought, Sunday."

"It's not pretty."

"How likely is it to get really ugly?"

"Like what?"

"Like real violence?"

"I don't want to put a number on it, Dr. Ryker. But the stories are pretty chilling. The Ministry of Agriculture is run by Chimurenga's cousin. Last month he imported truckloads of machetes for a farm extension program. But we did some analysis at Langley and the pattern of machete distribution is more aligned with opposition votes from the last election than with food production. So I'm fairly certain the machetes are intended as weapons, not farming tools."

"Shit."

"That's exactly what I said when I figured it out!"

"What did Rogerson say when he heard about the machetes?"

"I don't know. I was told the analysis was passed to State. I never heard anything. The embassy has been funding a farming initiative, so they probably thought machete deliveries were a good sign."

"We have to stop this," Judd said.

"The embassy is cautious. They don't want to be blamed for inciting violence. Ambassador Tallyberger doesn't want blood on his doorstep."

" 'No bodies on the streets.' Those were Rogerson's words this morning."

"See? The embassy isn't going to take any risks of creating chaos."

"But doing nothing can't be the only alternative."

"If I may, Dr. Ryker?" Sunday asked. "Nothing will change while everyone in Harare and in Washington is convinced they already know what's going to happen. If we want an outcome that doesn't reinforce the

115

status quo, the only way is to break confidence in the whole system."

"Minute Zero," whispered Judd under his breath.

"Excuse me?"

"Minute Zero," Judd said. "It's the moment you're talking about. When certainty breaks down and no one knows what's going to happen next. We need to create Minute Zero in Zimbabwe."

"I don't understand."

"You ever watch the Discovery Channel?"

"Sure," Sunday said.

"So a few months ago I'm watching Discovery with my kids. It's a program about ant colonies. The narrator is explaining how this one anthill is rock solid. The anthill is strong enough to withstand a tropical storm. A hurricane, even. And hidden inside is a complex city, with all of the ants moving in organized teams through tunnels to reinforce the walls and bring food and everything else needed to sustain the colony. And most of all, to protect the queen ant. If one of the teams breaks down, fails to do their job, then the whole city would be under threat. But as long as everyone works, the colony survives.

"Then all of the sudden, the anthill is crushed" — Judd clapped his hands to-

116

gether — "by an aardvark. The aardvark sticks his snout into the hole he's just punched and starts eating ants. Most of all, he creates total chaos. The ants all abandon their jobs, the teams disperse, no one knows where to go. It's total mayhem. They even start attacking each other. And in the frenzy after an aardvark attack, the queen ant is usually killed.

"But what happens next is fascinating. After the aardvark leaves, the ants naturally reorganize themselves into new teams, and order is restored. It's organic. Out of chaos, new teams form, and a new queen ant rises. But for that moment of chaos, their stable world is gone and no one knows what comes next."

"Minute Zero," Sunday said.

"Right. Watching that show was when I came up with the concept. Now imagine it was the Cold War and we found out the queen ant was a communist."

"We'd be the aardvark."

"Exactly. We'd punch a hole in the walls, eat a few of the queen's minions, but our main objective would be to break up the existing order and try to start anew."

"Or like Iraq," Sunday said.

"Sure, like Iraq. Except if we *expected* the chaos just after Saddam fell, we would have been ready to shape events. If we had anticipated Minute Zero, we would have been prepared to alter the outcome. At least I'd hope we would."

"Dr. Ryker, can I ask you, as two friends just talking: Why are you suddenly working on Zimbabwe?"

"I'm not sure, Sunday. I'd like to think the Secretary believes that S/CRU can help. Maybe we can make a difference. Can I ask *you* something, Sunday?"

"Sure."

"How did you know about Kanyemba? I mean, how did you know even to be in the Situation Room to add Zimbabwe to UMBRELLA ROSE?"

"It's my job. Did you know that the uranium for the original Manhattan Project came from Africa?"

"I didn't."

"From Congo. A mine called Shinkolobwe. A British prospector discovered rich uranium deposits at Shinkolobwe in 1915 and then worked with a private company, probably a front for the Defense Department, to bring it to the United States. That uranium was eventually used in our first atomic bombs."

"I never heard that before."

"I hadn't, either, Dr. Ryker, until I started

digging. But I think there's more."

"More uranium in Congo?"

"No. During the height of the Cold War, DOD began a search for high-grade uranium all over Africa. They were looking for another Shinkolobwe. As far as we know, they never found anything. But there were always rumors of a second super-uranium mine. I think that might have been —"

"Kanyemba."

And right then, Judd knew who he had to call next.

10.

"Sir, you've got a phone call."

Simon Kenny-Waddington set down his umbrella on his secretary's desk and frowned.

"Tell Cairo it's time to go home."

"It's not Cairo, sir," she replied. "It's America."

Simon cocked his head to one side and pressed his lips together. It was one of his odd gestures, one of the many quirks the British Foreign Office official had displayed since he was a child growing up in Kent. His secretary knew this particular expression meant favorable curiosity.

"Name?"

"A Dr. Ryker. From the American State Department."

Simon's eyebrows leapt up to the top of his forehead, another positive sign.

"Judd Rykaaah," he sang, nodding to himself.

"Shall I put him through, then?"

"Yes. I'll take it in my office," he said. "Won't be long."

Simon plucked his umbrella off the desk and pranced back into his oak-paneled office. Despite the grandeur of the Foreign Office building and the prestige of a Whitehall address, the inside of Simon's office was appropriately austere. A colonial map of India hung on the wall, the only décor. His desk was entirely clear, a sign he had completed his workday and was prepared for the commute home. The only items sitting on his desk were a black telephone and a single photo in a simple brass frame.

As Simon picked up his phone, he made eye contact with the middle-aged woman in the photo. She was pale but very pretty, with a Cleopatra-style bob haircut, sitting under an umbrella at the beach. On her lap sat a little girl, just five years old at that time, with the same haircut. Simon noticed the clock, realizing he was going to miss his train.

"Judd, my boy. Nice to hear from you. How aaaare you?"

"Hello, Simon. Have you got a moment?"

"For you, of course."

"I know you've got a lot on your plate."

"Nothing out of the ordinary. Just the usual. But that's the life we've chosen, haven't we, Judd?"

"Yes, it is."

"I know it's not politically correct to say anymore, but noblesse oblige is alive and well, I'm afraid."

"I've got something important, Simon."

"You calling about the Sudan? Just terrible what's going on in Khartoum. It's a real dog's breakfast."

"Not today. I'm calling about Zimbabwe."

"Ahhh, of course you are. Zimbabwe. The election this weekend."

"Exactly."

"Well, Zimbabwe is a tricky one for us. We've got to be cautious, you know. They're still sensitive about the whole colonial power business. Our travel sanctions against the president haven't bought us any friends in Harare, either, have they? It's best for everyone if we keep a low profile. It's tedious, I know. I am sorry. But it's probably for the best."

"Yes, I know that's the British position. But I also know you're paying more attention than you let on. Come on, Simon. I know you have a view."

"What's the sudden American interest in

Zimbabwe, of all places?"

"We want a free and fair election."

"Of course you do!" laughed Simon. "Free and fair! We all want that. What is your real interest here, Judd?"

"That is our real interest. Africa is booming and we can't have Zimbabwe, sitting in the heart of southern Africa, going down the drain and dragging down the others. Some old men just don't know when it's time to quit and turn the keys over to the next generation."

"You're mixing your metaphors, my boy." Simon was still chuckling. "I should have asked, what's *your* interest, Judd? Aren't you supposed to be the State Department's crisis man? Where's the crisis in Zimbabwe?"

"I'm keeping an eye on it."

"If you say so. What can I do for you?"

"Do you have a view on Gugu Mutonga's chances of winning?"

"Unlikely, I'm afraid. We are making our peace with President Tinotenda and his cronies. I'm supposed to review the travel policy after the election. At least until the old crank dies, we're strictly hands-off."

"What about Simba Chimurenga?"

"Ahhhh, General Chimurenga. Well, funny you should ask. He's quite the blue-eyed boy, isn't he? The twinkle in Tino's eye."

"So you think he's the chosen one. That seems to be the consensus here, too. Do you have any dirt on him? There's no way he rose that quickly through the army ranks without doing something extraordinary. I'm hoping you and Her Majesty's Government know what it is."

"I'm afraid not."

"Well, you may be sitting this election out, but I'm sure you're still plugged in. I bet you have a man in close on Chimurenga."

"Perhaps."

"Well, we don't. If it comes down to something serious, I may call on you. Pardon my French, but if the shit goes down, Simon, I'll need your inside man."

"If you say so, Judd."

"You know anything about a British memo on" — Judd lowered his voice — "uranium?"

"Ahhhh, Judd, that's what I've been waiting for! I *knew* you had another interest in Zimbabwe. Uranium. Of course, my boy."

"Do you know about the memo?"

"There is no memo."

"And unofficially?"

"Unofficially, I don't know."

"Well, then if I'm keeping you at work late today, it's partly your fault. That non-memo is one reason there is heightened interest here in Washington."

"I see. I should have guessed that. My fault."

"But do you believe it? Is there something suspicious going on with uranium in Zimbabwe?"

"I can't answer that. Plus I told you: We are sitting this one out. Zimbabwe is on your plate."

"What can you tell me about the mine at Kanyemba?"

"I think I should be asking *you* that question, Judd."

"It was a British company, right?"

"I don't know about that, Judd."

"Come on, Simon. A British company hunting for uranium in Zimbabwe. There's no way Her Majesty's Government wasn't involved."

"If there was a British company involved — and I'm not saying there was — then it would have only been on paper. The real owners most certainly were not subjects of the Queen."

"They're not? Then who are they, Simon?"

"Judd, I'm terribly sorry. I have to run."

"Simon, it's your bloody memo sending me on this wild-goose chase. At least tell me what you know."

"Ha," laughed Simon again. "Too true. Too true."

"Help me on this and maybe I can help you with one of your problems? What else are you working on?"

"You . . . have anything on Egypt?"

"Like what?"

"It would be jolly useful to know if you Yanks are ever going to put an ambassador in Cairo. It's been vacant for six months and your embassy is acting like time is frozen. We don't have anyone to work with."

"I'm sure we will send someone before the elections. Egypt is too important."

"Can you tell me who?"

"Not yet, but I'll try to find out."

"I bloody well hope you're right! And I hope it's a real ambassador and not just another rich friend of your president."

"I'll get you a name, Simon."

"I just don't understand you Americans sometimes."

"I'll get you a name."

"Do you know who your last ambassador to Cairo was? The Winnebago king of Oklahoma. Or maybe it was Ohio. For ambassador to Egypt, Judd!"

"Simon, what can you tell me about the mine at Kanyemba?"

There was no response, and for a moment

126

Judd thought the line had gone dead. Simon had set the phone down and moved to close his office door.

"Simon?"

After a few seconds more, he came back on the line and whispered.

"The main investor in Kanyemba was Arabia Sunrise Investments, a private equity fund managed out of Jeddah and linked to a member of the Saudi royal family."

"Saudis?"

"They had a silent minority partner who was the real player. A fixer who made things happen."

"Okay, who was that?"

"The partner was hidden behind multiple layers of front companies in Jersey, Mauritius, and the Isle of Man. Someone was trying to cover their tracks."

"And?"

"And we think the end of the trail leads to a firm called Royal Deepwater Venture Capital."

"Royal Deepwater? Should that mean something to me?"

"It should. It's American."

11.

Most strangers assumed Tinashe and Tsitsi were siblings. The young couple was in love, but they dared not show it in public. That would be inappropriate of course. And, most importantly this evening, it would invite unwanted scrutiny.

Tinashe was tall and too skinny, but he knew how to protect himself. That was one of the first things he learned growing up running around the streets of Mufakose, one of the poor neighborhoods encircling Zimbabwe's capital city.

Officially, Mufakose was designated a "high-density suburb." To Tinashe, the one-room brick-and-aluminum-roof house on Mbizi Road, where he lived with his parents, grandparents, four siblings, and two cousins, was just like every other house on the street. The crowded living conditions were normal.

Mufakose was just home.

Tinashe never thought much about it until, once he was a little older, he visited Borrowdale, one of the leafy northern "low-density suburbs" where the government officials and foreign expatriates lived in grand houses behind high walls and barbed wire with signs that read HAPANA BASA — NO WORK. He couldn't believe it when his friend insisted that just three or four people lived in one of those enormous houses.

"*Aiwa!* No! You are lying, *shamwari!*" We could fit one hundred in that house!"

That was when Tinashe understood what "high-density" really meant. It wasn't in his nature to be envious. Tinashe's grandmother, his *ambuya,* read him the Bible every Sunday, and she would never have allowed him to covet. Instead he promised himself he would one day own one of those big houses. And he would invite everyone from Mbizi Road to live there with him.

Tinashe's plan began with skipping school to sell gum and fruit by strolling in between cars stuck in traffic or hawking his snacks to the riders in emergency taxis, the ancient station wagons that plowed the bus routes picking up passengers and cramming them ten, twelve, sometimes fourteen to a car. "High-density customers," he called them.

Tinashe made enough money to eat every day and, usually, bring home some extra cash to his family. He knew the real profits were made not by the street sellers like him and not even by neighborhood bosses who controlled the most lucrative intersections. The real money was made by the Big Men. Those who lived behind the walls of the low-density suburbs.

Every time Tinashe managed to save some money, the bosses would take a bigger cut or the police would arrive to beat the boys and steal their goods. Whenever Tinashe started to get a little bit ahead and begin to imagine a better life for his family, someone above him would stop it. Back to square one. Back to Mufakose.

Tsitsi had been the one to introduce Tinashe to Gugu Mutonga. In reality, neither had ever met the Big Woman. But he felt he knew her intimately. And that Gugu knew him. When she spoke on the radio or at rallies about the frustrations and unmet hopes of Zimbabwe's youth, it was like she was talking directly to him. She knew exactly what he was thinking. She knew who Tinashe was. Gugu Mutonga knew what Tinashe wanted.

Tsitsi was the pretty young girl who'd grown up a few houses down. Both families

130

came from the same rural home village, their *kumusha,* several hours' bus ride from Harare.

Tsitsi's father had once been the village chief. Although the government had long ago taken away any formal duties, her *baba* continued to command respect among the people. Although her family never spoke of it, Tsitsi had pieced together what had happened. In the weeks before independence, her father had mediated a land dispute and ruled in favor of a poor family against a richer one. The loser retaliated by reporting to the advancing guerrillas that Tsitsi's father was a snitch for the hated colonial police. Tsitsi never learned if it was true. But from that day, her family was blacklisted.

As a child, Tsitsi was unaware of her family's political problems. She was just like any other kid on Mbizi Road. She attended Rusununguko Primary School and then Mufakose No. 4 High School. Like all the other girls, she spent her early mornings fetching water and firewood for her mother while the boys played soccer in the streets. In the late afternoon, after her schoolwork and chores were complete, she was allowed to join the boys.

She was always drawn to a tall one who

smiled at her. Tinashe and Tsitsi hid their friendship at first, but as they grew older, they also grew closer. Hiding their affection became harder.

Once they reached the age of sixteen, the parents, fully aware of their relationship, began negotiations for marriage and the *lobola,* or bride price. When Tsitsi caught wind of it, she was secretly relieved. Some of her friends had already been arranged to marry much older men. She was pleased Tinashe was her age and she already had feelings for him. But she resented having her husband chosen by her parents. And that her family was exchanging her future for cash and cattle. That was the old village way, not how she believed things should happen in the city. But despite her love for Tinashe, she refused to marry him.

Tinashe was oblivious to the brewing rebellion and how his fate was being negotiated by others. He was smitten with Tsitsi, but — like every boy in Mufakose — he was also obsessed with Manchester United.

One evening, when the two of them found some privacy, he confided in her. He was frustrated. He wanted a better life, to escape the bonds of the local bosses, to create his own opportunity. He wanted a big house for Tsitsi, for them to raise a family. That was when she conceded to the marriage. And soon after their wedding, Tsitsi introduced Tinashe to Gugu Mutonga. Not the person, but the idea that a better future was possible.

On this evening, the couple slipped down one of the alleys running between the houses. Tsitsi was careful not to step in the open canal of raw sewage and trash. They rounded a corner to find a gang of young boys smoking cigarettes. One was wearing a white T-shirt with a black fist, the symbol of President Tinotenda's party. The gang eyed Tinashe and Tsitsi as they crossed the street, the couple averting their eyes. The boy in the T-shirt blew smoke out of his nostrils, and then called out. "You! Where are you going after curfew? It is past midnight."

"Not yet midnight," replied Tinashe, noticing the boy wasn't wearing a watch.

"Don't be clever, cockroach! Where are you going?"

"I'm sorry, *baas*," Tsitsi said. "This is my brother. We are going for *muti* for our mother. She is sick."

The boy took a long drag on his cigarette again and blew the smoke in their direction. "Where is your party card?"

133

"We are going for medicine for *amai.* We don't have our card."

"To pass by here, you must have your card. We don't allow traitors and sellouts to be in this place. You understand?"

"Yes."

After a long pause, the boy released them. "Go for your *muti,*" he scoffed.

"Thank you, *baas.*"

The two slunk down the street, then took a sharp turn into a narrow alley. At the end was a small shop with the windows locked and the lights out. Tsitsi rapped softly on the metal shutter three times.

"We are closed."

"We are here for *muti,*" she said.

"Malaria or diarrhea?"

"No. We need *muti* for our hearts."

The door click-clacked and opened a few inches. "Ahh, Tsitsi! We've been waiting for you!" a woman whispered.

They entered the small store and the door was locked behind them. "We are nearly ready for tomorrow," she said, and turned on a single lightbulb.

"Tssss!" hissed Tsitsi, her eyes wide with excitement.

The room was stacked from floor to ceiling with posters and T-shirts, all emblazoned with the smiling face of Gugu Mutonga.

12.

U.S. Department of State, Washington, D.C.
Thursday, 7:15 p.m. Eastern Standard Time
"Dr. Ryker, there's still nothing out of Ethiopia."

"Excuse me, Serena?"

"You asked me this morning for anything out of Lalibela. There's nothing. The only report I could find was about a mid-level embassy official visiting the archaeological sites a few weeks ago."

"Oh, right. Thank you."

So, Lalibela is quiet. Phew.

Judd turned his attention back to the stacks of paper on his desk. Since returning to the office from the White House, he had immersed himself in intelligence reports and diplomatic cables on Zimbabwe. It was the usual minutiae about visiting foreign officials from Angola and Venezuela, tedious details about the opening of the Chinese-built Winston Tinotenda College of Nursing, and unsubstantiated reporting on missing workers from a voter education drive. Judd turned to the next cable, which contained a sterile list of deficiencies in the voter list. "A key challenge for democracy in Zimbabwe is weak capacity within the Election Commission" was the cable's conclusion. *No shit,* he thought.

On its own, each document was typical reporting by a political officer who spent too much time behind the walls of the embassy compound playing the Foreign Service's game of CYA. *Cover your ass.* Judd had gotten used to reading between the lines on these cables. But when taken together, the reports left Judd uneasy. *Am I reading too much into these? Or am I missing the bigger picture?*

Judd had spoken to Sunday again to ask the analyst to look into Royal Deepwater Venture Capital, the name given to him by Simon Kenny-Waddington. Judd was feeling pleased with himself that he had exploited his personal network to unearth clues. And that his contact in the British Foreign Office had come through. This was often how he found the best information: backchannel.

He was also grateful for Sunday. It was useful to have a private line of communication with a CIA analyst with access to all of the Agency's resources. And he was glad that it was someone he could trust.

That was the good news. He was wheels-up in a few hours and still had little idea of what he was flying into. Even if Judd figured out a plan in Zimbabwe, would he be able to act? S/CRU was still an experiment.

It had all happened so fast. The early phone call on a Saturday morning, a State Department seminar on his Golden Hour theory on Monday, and a job offer that same day from Landon Parker before he was on the plane back to Boston. A few weeks later, the whole family had moved from Massachusetts to Washington, D.C. The transition had been so quick, Judd's new colleagues could hardly believe it. Some even whispered it was "highly suspicious."

Judd's old colleagues, the other professors at Amherst College, also couldn't believe it. After all his hard work, Judd had given up his own research — and tenure — for what? A temporary assignment in the belly of a government bureaucracy. What was he thinking? they sighed. Judd often asked himself the same question.

He knew Professor BJ van Hollen had

been an influence, perhaps even the decisive one. BJ had always encouraged Judd to apply his skills to real problems and not just sit back and milk the comforts of academic life.

"Inquiry for its own sake is virtuous but indulgent," BJ had told him over one of their long dinners. "Inquiry for the real world is imperfect but consequential." Judd had even quoted this saying at BJ's funeral.

Imperfect but consequential. That was a laudable goal.

Jessica had also encouraged him to take a chance with public service. His wife had been less emphatic, more subtle, than BJ had been, but probably more persuasive in the end. That's how Jess always did it: discreet influence.

Judd's concentration was broken by a knock on his office door.

"Hello, sweetheart" came the soft, familiar, if unexpected voice.

"Jess?" He forced his look of confusion into a happy facial expression. "Uh, what are you doing here?"

"I came to take you to dinner. I've been working so hard on my Ethiopia water project and you've been in the office late almost every night. So I called the babysitter. We haven't had a date in weeks."

"Yeah, I know. I'm sorry about that."

"And I get the sense you will be traveling again soon."

"I *am* traveling soon. Tonight, in fact."

She raised her eyebrows. "I'm that good."

"But how did you know I wasn't coming home? I, um, I was going to send you a text . . . Actually, how did you get up here? How did you even get into the building?"

"Let me close this door and give you some privacy, Dr. Ryker," interrupted Serena. "And nice to see *you* again, Dr. Ryker," she said to Jessica before slipping out and shutting the door.

"Serena, of course!" said Judd. "That's how you got up here."

"Girls' secret," Jessica replied, pressing an index finger to her lips. She had put on bright red nail polish, Judd noticed.

Then she approached Judd and gave him a delicate kiss. He closed his eyes to accept and relaxed his shoulders.

"Very nice. Now let me take you out of here," she said, waving her hand dismissively at his messy desk.

"I've got a lot of work before my flight."

"It'll be good for you to clear your head for an hour. Plus you've got to eat."

Judd nodded his assent.

"Where do you want to go?" he asked. "There's not much choice around here. Foggy Bottom is a food wasteland."

"Well, we're not having dinner in this place," she said emphatically.

"So, you've eaten at the State Department before?"

"No. But I've heard . . ."

The couple walked out the employees-only back door of the Harry S. Truman Building, which deposited them onto Virginia Avenue. "If we walk north toward the World Bank, the restaurants get better."

After a few blocks, they found an intimate Italian bistro and took a quiet table at the back, out of sight. Once they had settled into their seats and ordered a bottle of red wine, Judd began, "So, any news from Papa?"

"Nothing more than what you heard this morning. He's still laying the groundwork for the project."

"Which is . . . ?"

"Clean water retention systems. You remember I told you about it yesterday? We are infiltrating the underwater aquifers and installing new polymer tank and piping systems to enable OCSWP."

"Oh, right."

"You have no idea what I'm talking about,

140

do you?"

"Remind me. What's OCSWP?"

"Off-grid concentrated solar water purification. See, you don't remember. Or maybe you weren't listening."

"No, no, I remember. Just too many acronyms, Jess. I'm really interested. I promise. OCSWP sounds pretty cool."

"Uh-huh," said Jessica warily. "Let's change the subject. I came here to talk about you. Where are you flying to?"

"Zimbabwe. The midnight flight to Johannesburg, then I'm catching an early connection into Harare."

"I see."

"You aren't surprised?"

"Nope. I saw on the news about the dead tourist. An American jumped from the bridge at Victoria Falls. How terrible. I figured that would have the State Department in a tizzy. I guess Rogerson came to his senses. The old goat finally realized he needed you."

"Not exactly."

"What do you mean, 'not exactly'?"

"The Secretary's office air-dropped me on Rogerson's team for this one. I'm going to Zimbabwe over his objection."

Jessica laughed. "That'll teach him."

"I doubt he sees it that way."

"Look on the bright side: The Secretary of State must be genuinely worried about Zimbabwe blowing up and she knows you can be helpful. That's great news, Judd. Powerful people are seeing the value of S/CRU. They see the value in *you*." She raised her wineglass. "Let's celebrate."

"Or someone thinks Zimbabwe is going down in flames and they want to lay this disaster on me," Judd said. Jessica dropped her arm. "There's a good chance this is a cover-your-ass disaster dump," Judd explained.

"So own the disaster." Jessica shrugged. "Show them. I don't see you have much choice. Seize it."

"I know. I need a big win. The budget is being cut and the Crisis Reaction Unit is vulnerable. Zimbabwe could be do-or-die for S/CRU."

"So it's sink or swim," Jessica said.

"Yep."

"Fish or cut bait."

"Yes, that's it."

"Shit or get off the pot."

"All right already! I get it, Jess."

"Are you sure?"

"I've been working on some new cutting-edge data analysis. I've got radical ideas for transforming U.S. strategies in places like

Cuba and North Korea where the politics are stuck. And I think I can apply the same principles to help the U.S. government shape volatile transitions, like in Egypt and Iran. I know I could make a real contribution to increasing the leverage of U.S. policy in those places. Yet the survival of S/CRU now hangs on . . . Zimbabwe."

"Judd, you are looking at this all wrong. *This is an opportunity.* It's a *good thing* the Secretary is forcing you into a corner."

"It is?"

"Absolutely. Fuck Rogerson."

"Fuck Rogerson?"

"You do your thing, Judd."

"I know. You've told me."

"You're getting frustrated, but this is your chance. And if something really terrible starts to happen again in Zimbabwe, then you have to stop it."

Judd wrinkled his brow. "Again?"

"Yes, Judd. The last time something horrible happened there, no one did anything. *No one gave a shit.* You can't let those poor people get slaughtered again."

"Who's getting slaughtered, Jess?"

She stopped and took a deep breath. "Judd, you have a chance to make your mark and to do the right thing. How can you not seize this?"

143

"What horrible things? What are you talking about?"

"You have to do the right thing, Judd. That's all I'm saying."

"Since when are you emotional about Zimbabwe? I've never heard you talk about it before and suddenly you're an expert?"

"I've been reading."

"Even if I want to help, I don't have much time. Or leverage. You know that. I'm flying in there the same day the election starts, and it's just me."

"Didn't you just say you have new ideas for leverage?"

"Yes. But what am I supposed to do?"

"Win."

"No one cares about Zimbabwe. Landon Parker wouldn't have given it to me if anyone did. I have no political top cover, no time, no tools."

"Then turn those all to your advantage. Fly under the radar, be quick, use what you have. And fight to the death, Judd. That's what you did in Mali and it worked. You really have no other choice."

"No choice . . ." Judd mumbled, and rubbed his temples.

"You just have to win."

"I *do* have to win this one, Jess."

"So stop feeling sorry for yourself. It's

unprofessional."

Judd dropped his hands and relaxed his shoulders. Then he looked right into Jessica's eyes. *God, she is beautiful. And smart. I am lucky,* he thought. "You're right, Jess."

"Good. About time. So, what's your plan?" She sipped her wine.

"I'm working on it," he said.

"You're leaving tonight, sweetheart."

"I know."

"Well, let's start with item one. What's your objective?"

Judd didn't reply immediately.

"Come on, Judd! What are your goals? Who're your allies? Who's gonna block you? These are the basics."

"You are quite the romantic, Jessica. You surprise your husband for a dinner date and you want to talk about strategy for regime change."

"Regime change?" she asked with a smirk. She sat up straighter and pushed out her chest. "Okaaay, good. *Regime change.* At least you know what you are trying to achieve."

"That's not official policy," he said quickly.

"If you say so. Where's Rogerson on this? What's he going to do?"

"He won't do anything. Just the opposite.

He's just trying to keep things quiet. Stability, first and forever."

"Okay, item two: your team. Who else matters?"

"Rogerson's brought the whole building in. Every State bureau plus another half dozen federal agencies. I think his interagency task force has twenty-five or thirty people now."

"That can't possibly work."

"He calls it 'whole-of-government.' "

"Sounds like a circus," she said, scrunching her face in the way she often did when she smelled something foul. "Listen, Judd, this isn't my area of expertise. But from years of running agriculture projects in some pretty crazy places, I've learned one thing: You get things done with *a small team.* No bigger than it needs to be. If you need a team, the smaller the better."

"Okay . . ."

"And everyone has to be clear on what skills they bring to the mission. You know about the great literature on this, right?"

"More Emily Dickinson?"

Jessica shook her head.

"Shakespeare?" he asked.

"DC Comics," she said.

"What?"

"The Justice League, Judd. You know:

Superman, Batman, Wonder Woman, the Flash. The team of superheroes. Didn't you read comic books as a kid?"

"Yeah, sure. I loved Iron Man."

"No," she scoffed. "Iron Man was the Avengers. That's Marvel Comics." Jessica took another sip of wine.

"I obviously don't know my superhero teams like you do," Judd said.

"No, you don't."

"What's your point, Jess?"

"Did Batman try to fly the invisible airplane?"

"What?"

"No, he didn't. That was Wonder Woman's plane. You get it?"

"I think so."

"They each brought something special to the team. They knew their role. They did their jobs."

"They stayed in their lane," he added.

"Exactly, Judd," she said.

"You sound like Rogerson."

"Forget him. You need to find *your team*. Each member brings a special skill and does their job. You need your own powerful team."

"I need my own Justice League?"

"Precisely. You have to know your allies and what they can do."

147

"Right. Okay, I get it."

"And, item three, don't forget you are fighting supervillains. You need to know who they are. You need to be very clear about who is really working against you. Who in the U.S. government is on your side and who is making trouble? You need to figure that out right away. Same goes for Zimbabwe once you get on the ground. Who's on your team and who's not?"

"I don't know yet," Judd rubbed his temples again. "Everyone is lying. The national security guys, the State Department's old boys' network. I'm sure when I get to Harare the Zimbabweans will do the same."

"What about the ambassador?"

"Tallyberger? He's an old friend of Rogerson's. I don't expect any help from him."

"Do you have any leverage on this guy Tallyberger?"

"Like what?"

"I don't know. Anything you can find out that might be useful later. You're going to need him at some point. Doesn't hurt to do some homework."

"You're cold-blooded, Jessica Ryker."

"Don't say that. You know I hate that," she snapped.

"You're right. I take it back. I'm sorry."

"I'm trying to help you," she said.

"You're right, Jess."

"Judd, dear. Look at me." Jessica placed both hands on the table and stared directly into his eyes. It was her *I'm serious* glare. "Suck it up."

"Suck it up? That's your advice?"

"Yes. You are being thrown into the deep end on this. If you think about all the problems, and what you don't know, and who's lying to you, then you will lose. Don't focus on what you don't know or can't control. Determine your goals, figure out who you can trust, build your team. Then use what you have and scrap it out."

Judd nodded. "That's all?"

Jessica lifted her wineglass, and her face relaxed. "That's all. Cheers. To your Justice League."

"To my Justice League," Judd said.

"And to regime change."

Clink.

13.

U.S. Ambassador's Residence, Harare, Zimbabwe
Friday, 1:35 a.m. Central Africa Time
"No, Bill. You haven't woken me," Arnold Tallyberger lied. "I'm always happy to hear from you."

"I know it's late, Arnold. I'm sorry to call at this hour. How is Bernice?"

"She's fine. She misses Helsinki."

"Those were the days, Arnie. You still owe me for that one. You might still be sitting in a Finnish jail if it weren't for me."

"I know, I remember, Bill. Pass Bernice's regards to Valerie."

"I will, Arnie, thank you. I'm calling you so late to give you a heads-up."

"Okay, I'm listening."

"I just found out you'll be getting a visitor from State."

"You're coming for another visit? How wonderful! I can call the hunting lodge.

They'll be thrilled to have you back again. They love VIP visitors."

"No, Arnie. It's not me. His name is Judd Ryker. And I want to be very clear that I did not send him."

"Who?"

"Ryker. He's not coming to hunt lion. This Ryker is running some newfangled crisis response unit. It's an experimental plaything of Landon Parker's. They got it in their heads that we might need some help on Zimbabwe. I tried to talk Landon out of it, but you can't argue with that guy."

"We don't have a crisis in Zimbabwe, Bill."

"Exactly my point, Arnie. I knew you'd get it. But there's nothing I can do now. Someone's convinced Parker this unit can be a problem solver and help the Secretary, but this Ryker kid is a menace."

"I see."

"Good. Go ahead and be nice to him. We don't want anyone crying up to the seventh floor. But keep Ryker's nose out of our business. You got that?"

"Yes, Bill. What exactly is he coming here to do?"

"Beats me. But I've been told he's flying out tonight and will be landing in Harare early Saturday morning. The first flight from Joburg. You should be getting the country

151

clearance request soon."

"I could deny him clearance. That would stop him."

"No, don't do that. Too obvious. It'll just raise eyebrows and you'll be forced to explain. Better you just let him come and poke around. Maybe give him something to distract his attention. Just don't let him get in your way. And for God's sake, Arnie, don't let him stir up any trouble."

"I'll take care of it."

"You've got everything under control over there, right?"

"Yes. I don't think the election will bring any surprises. Our expectation is continuity."

"Good. The last thing we want is Zimbabwe on A1 of the *Washington Post.* Nothing more than a short paragraph in the back about low turnout or too much traffic or something like that. Nothing on the goddamn front page, Arnie. Let's keep a lid on it."

"Yes, sir."

"Is there anything I need to know, Arnie? Are you picking up any signs of trouble?"

"The CIA chief of station doesn't think so."

"Who's your COS?"

"New guy on his first COS post. Only

been down here a few months, but seems on the ball. Maybe a bit over-caffeinated. Came down from Morocco."

"Morocco? Don't tell me they sent you Brock Branson."

"Yes, that's him."

"Brock's a hothead. A real yahoo. Don't you know what happened in Marrakesh? Jesus, how the hell did Langley promote Brock Branson to be a station chief already?"

"I don't know, Bill."

"Can you trust him?"

"I think so. I'll ask him to keep an eye on this Ryker."

"Good. You let Brock keep an eye on Ryker. But you better keep an eye on Brock."

14.

U.S. Department of State, Washington, D.C. Thursday, 10:22 p.m. Eastern Standard Time
"Dr. Ryker, your car will be ready in ten minutes. They'll have you at Dulles Airport by eleven and you'll have plenty of time to make your flight. Don't worry."

"What about my connection, Serena?"

"You arrive at Joburg/O. R. Tambo International Airport just after midnight tomorrow. You can sleep at the airport for a few hours in the diplomatic lounge and then get the first morning flight to Harare. You'll be wheels-up at seven and on the ground in Harare at eight."

"Saturday morning at eight a.m.?" *That gives me just twenty-eight hours before results are announced.*

"Yes."

"That's the same time polls open. There's no quicker way?"

"Not unless you have your own plane."

Judd, annoyed he was cutting it so close, flipped through his papers, deciding which to take with him on the flight. "Where's that Zimbabwean history book the CIA sent over?"

"It's right here, Dr. Ryker," she said handing it to him. "Your travel go bag is by the door. It has enough clothes for a few days. The embassy will give you toiletries. Is there anything else you need?"

"Actually, yes," he said, giving Serena a serious look. "Can you do me a big favor?"

"Of course, Dr. Ryker."

"Can you find out who is going to be our next ambassador to Egypt?"

"Could be tough. I do know a staffer on the Deputies Committee. Or maybe I could ask —"

"Don't tell me how," Judd interrupted. "I'd rather not know. Deliberate ignorance is sometimes for the best. Just find out. I'd be extremely grateful."

"Consider it done. You have anything more difficult for me to do? I'm up for a challenge."

"There *is* something else."

"Yes?"

"I'd need you to be very discreet."

"Aren't I always?"

"Yes, of course you are, Serena."

"I have top secret clearance, just like you. For all you know, Dr. Ryker, I may have higher clearances than you."

"You do?"

"If I did, I couldn't say," she said, deadpan.

"Of course, Serena. But this request is different. Please close the door."

"No one else is here. It's after ten o'clock."

"I know. Close the door anyway."

Serena did as she was asked and turned to face Judd.

"If you are uncomfortable doing what I'm about to ask, Serena, you can say no. I'll respect your decision."

"Yes, sir."

"I need you to look into Arnold Tallyberger's personnel record."

"You need dirt on Ambassador Tallyberger?"

"I didn't say that."

"But that's what you mean, right?"

"I just need to know if there's anything in there that's . . . relevant."

"I understand."

"Don't you want to know why, Serena?"

"No. Actually, I don't. Deliberate ignorance is sometimes for the best."

They were both startled by a knock on the door. They looked at each other, then back to the door.

Knock, knock, knock. "Hello? Dr. Ryker?"

Serena opened the door and standing there was a woman, late twenties, with short brown hair and olive skin. She was wearing a tailored business suit, and a leather portfolio was tucked under one arm. Despite her diminutive size and lawyer-like attire, her tight facial features and aggressive posture suggested she could handle herself in a street fight.

"It's Isabella Espinosa, from the meeting this morning. From the Zimbabwe task force."

"Yes," replied Judd. "You're FBI, right?"

"Justice Department. I'm the special prosecutor seconded here to State. I hunt war criminals."

"You're the one tracking the Ethiopian general."

"Zagwe. Solomon Zagwe. Yes, he's the one."

"I haven't heard anything more about him, I'm sorry."

"Yes, that's what everyone's told me for years."

"Years?"

"I've been chasing Zagwe for a long time. Every time we get close, the Zimbabwean authorities protect him."

"What exactly did he do?"

"We're preparing a sealed war crimes indictment against Zagwe. As his dictatorship was weakening, he started attacking provinces that were sympathetic to the rebels. We've been building an evidence base to prove that he wiped out an entire village. On his orders, all the adults were rounded up and shot. Then, as a warning to the others, he deployed the army to barricade the roads and prevent any food from being brought into the province."

"The Red Fear," Judd said.

"Right. Zagwe called the campaign the Red Fear. He threatened to bring it to other provinces if they challenged him, too. Several thousand people were killed with bullets in the first few weeks. And then the bastard murdered another half million people by creating a famine. There was plenty of food in the country. He just wasn't allowing any of it to move. That was the Red Fear. This guy should be in a prison cell. But instead the *cabrón* is living in a luxury villa in Harare."

"Jeeesus," said Judd. "What can I do?"

"I've been working for years to gather the evidence and take witness statements. The only thing missing is the target in custody. If Tinotenda falls, I want to make sure someone grabs Zagwe. This may be my only chance to get him."

"I'll talk to the embassy, maybe see if they can put someone on it."

"Not good enough. I've tried before to get the embassy to cooperate. They always say they're too overstretched and can't spare the bodies."

"So, Ms. Espinosa, what do you want me to do?"

"Take me with you."

Serena interrupted, "I'm sorry, ma'am. There's no way we can get country clearance for you before Dr. Ryker's flight. He's wheels-up in ninety minutes. I'm sure he'd normally be happy to assist —"

"It's okay, Serena. I want Ms. Espinosa to come along. Go ahead and tell the Operations Center that a member of my team was accidentally omitted from the clearance cable request. Just have them add her name."

"*Gracias,* Dr. Ryker," said Isabella, bowing her head in appreciation. "You're the first one in quite a while to help me."

"The only problem is we are leaving for the airport now. I mean right now."

"I'm ready."

"Good. Serena, can you let the embassy know Ms. Espinosa will also be accompanying me as part of the S/CRU delegation and she'll require a room and a change of clothes on arrival?"

"Anything else, Dr. Ryker?" Serena asked.

"How long is the flight to Joburg?"

"Eighteen hours. Then you have a layover before your connection to Harare."

"Too much time lost," he mumbled to himself. "Serena, keep pressing the embassy to get me a high-level meeting."

"Ambassador Tallyberger already reported back that a meeting with President Tinotenda is out of the question on election day. They said there's zero chance he will make time to see a foreign official. And definitely not an American."

"What about General Chimurenga? Ask the embassy for a meeting with him."

"Tallyberger said no to that, too."

"I'll ask him myself. If we can't see Tinotenda, then we have to see Chimurenga."

"You're talking about Simba Chimurenga?" Isabella asked.

"Yes. You know him?"

"He's the national security advisor," she said.

"We can ask him about Zagwe, too."

"Chimurenga's not going to help us. He and Zagwe have history. My intel suggests they know each other from way back.

Chimurenga was sent to Ethiopia just before Zagwe fell, as part of his military training. It's not confirmed, but the timeline fits for Chimurenga to have participated in the Red Fear."

"If they're close, maybe you can use that?"

"I doubt it. Everything I've read on Chimurenga is that he's pure macho. All male, all military. I don't think he's going to be inclined to help a Mexican-American woman lawyer and — no disrespect intended, Dr. Ryker — a skinny white professor."

Judd laughed.

"What you need is a big ugly guy from the Pentagon with medals pinned across his chest," Serena suggested.

"A big ugly guy in military uniform . . . Yes . . . you're right, Serena," Judd said. "And I know just the one."

■ ■ ■ ■

PART TWO:
SATURDAY

■ ■ ■ ■

15.

Winston Tinotenda International Airport,
Harare, Zimbabwe
Saturday, 8:04 a.m. Central Africa Time
Colonel David "Bull" Durham was already waiting for Judd on the tarmac. He hadn't seen or spoken with his friend since their adventure in Mali three months earlier. The colonel was itching to get back in the field, but he was waiting for medical clearance. The sudden order yesterday to report for a short-term civilian liaison assignment in Zimbabwe had come as a total surprise.

It was no surprise once he learned the true nature of the mission.

Fortunately, Durham caught a U.S. Air Force C-140 supply plane already heading from Stuttgart, Germany, to Gaborone, Botswana. From Gabs, he caught a short commercial flight into Harare, arriving just thirty minutes before Judd's South African Airways connection from Johannesburg.

"Bull!" shouted Judd when he spotted the burly bald-headed man in jeans and a crisp golf shirt. The two embraced with slap-hugs, then backed up to a professional distance.

"You look well, Bull. Back in fighting shape, I see."

"I've got full use of the old shoulder." He flapped his elbow like a chicken. "And this little souvenir," he said, pulling up his sleeve and circling a finger around a pink bullet scar.

"You'll always have something to remember Timbuktu."

"Lucky for you, my medical clearance came through just in time for this latest little excursion of yours. You aren't going to get me shot again, are you?"

"No, sir, Colonel Durham!" said Judd, with a mock salute.

"At ease, soldier!"

Dropping the joke, Judd turned to his companion. "Colonel Durham, meet Isabella Espinosa from the Justice League —"

"Department," Isabella interrupted.

"Right. Sorry," Judd said with a chuckle. "Isabella Espinosa from the Justice Department. She's joining me for a few days on special assignment. We'll brief you on the details later."

Isabella reached out, her petite hands

swallowed by Durham's beefy palms. "Isabella, this is Colonel David Durham from Special Operations Command in Stuttgart."

"Call me Bull."

"He's a career Green Beret with some unusual skills," Judd said. "He'll tell you he just flies Black Hawks. But his real calling is diplomacy. His specialty is dictators."

"I have no idea what Judd's talking about," Durham said.

"Don't believe him, Isabella."

"So, you two are friends?" Isabella asked.

"We were together in the Sahara Desert not long ago," Judd explained. "We managed to pull the rabbit out of the hat. I'm hoping we can do it again here."

"Judd likes to have me around, Ms. Espinosa," Durham joked. "I'm Robin to his Batman."

"You're not Robin, Bull. You're the Hulk."

"See, I'm the big ugly guy."

"That's exactly what I said."

"I'm just here for show."

"And in case we need airlift," Judd added.

"When I saw my orders were to report for an unarmed diplomatic mission in Africa requiring full formal dress, I knew immediately it had to be you, Judd."

"That's right. You're welcome," Judd replied with a smile. "In all seriousness,

Bull, I appreciate you getting down here on zero notice. I hope I didn't pull you away from something important."

"I was preparing for deployment to the Korengal Valley in Afghanistan. But I figure playing your sidekick in Zimbabwe, where there's no war of any kind as far as I can tell, must be more critical for national security. Right, Judd?"

"I'm glad you learned something from your civilian friends, Bull. And I don't think we'll be here for long."

"I hope not."

"If the war in Afghanistan ends while you're stuck here with me, I'll get you deployed to Yemen. Or maybe Somalia."

"That's the kind of stand-up guy you're traveling with," Durham said to Isabella.

"Speaking of a stand-up guy, where's the ambassador? Isn't he supposed to meet us?" Judd asked.

The three scanned the area, but no one from the embassy was anywhere in sight. With no other options, they moved to the back of the line at passport control.

After twenty minutes the line had barely moved. Eventually an arrival party of suits arrived, surrounding a gaunt white man with small spectacles, a silver mustache, and wavy gray hair.

"Terribly sorry to be late, Dr. Ryker. I'm Ambassador Tallyberger. You've arrived on the most hectic of days. You know it's election day, right?"

"Hello, Ambassador. Yes, we know. That's why we're here."

"I told the Operations Center that meeting you at the airport would be a problem, but they insisted you had to arrive this morning. So I'm here. We're extremely short-staffed, so let's move."

After quick introductions and handshakes with Bull and Isabella, the ambassador flashed an ID card at the security guard and their entourage was led through a side room, their passports were checked, and they were escorted out to a waiting limousine.

Once safely inside the car, Tallyberger asked Judd, "So, please tell me. Why exactly are you here?"

"Wasn't it all in my clearance cable?"

"Yes, but I still don't understand. There's no crisis here. I'm not sure why the Secretary's office has sent their crisis envoy."

"Crisis prevention. Disputed elections can often be a flashpoint, so Landon Parker wanted me to be here to see what I could do to help the embassy."

"Help the embassy . . ." Tallyberger repeated, rubbing his mustache. "Well, I don't expect the elections to be disputed. So far all the voting procedures seem to be aboveboard. Our field reports are coming in and most polling stations have already opened on time. The lines are long, but that's always the case in Africa. People don't mind waiting here. I certainly don't expect an outbreak of civil war or anything like that. This is *Zimbabwe,* Dr. Ryker. It's not the Congo."

"I appreciate that, Ambassador. And thank you for making time on such a busy day to collect us from the airport."

"What kind of embassy resources will you require while you are here, Dr. Ryker?"

"A car and a driver should be plenty. And I'd like to speak to the chief of station as soon as possible."

"Yes, we can arrange that. I'm afraid we probably don't have spare hands to escort you. Will you be all right getting around the city on your own?"

"I brought my own security," said Judd, gesturing toward Bull.

"We could use you as election observers. We've already got teams posted in all the major neighborhoods of Harare. But we need one in Rusape."

"Rusape? Where's that?" Bull asked.

"About two, maybe three hours east. It's a

lovely town, on the road to Mutare and the border with Mozambique. We could have you there by lunchtime."

"That's a generous offer, but I think we'll stay in the capital," Judd replied. "We'll stay out of your hair, Ambassador."

"You are no trouble at all, Dr. Ryker," said Tallyberger as he crossed his arms.

"Actually, one thing, Ambassador," Isabella added. "Is there, by any chance, someone — perhaps from diplomatic security or the marine guard — who could keep an eye on Solomon Zagwe's villa?"

"You are asking me to deploy embassy resources for a stakeout?"

"Yes, sir. Just for the next forty-eight hours."

"Ms. Espinosa, I would love to help with your little project, but I've already told you we're down on manpower. This isn't like the old days when we had a full political section and plenty of consular support. I'm afraid I just can't spare the bodies."

16.

CIA Headquarters, Langley, Virginia
Saturday, 2:30 a.m. Eastern Standard Time
Sunday rubbed his eyes and checked the clock. No point in going home now, he thought. Satisfied that decision was made, Sunday rolled his head in a wide circle, stretching his neck muscles, then reversed direction until he could feel his neck bones crack.

Sunday had been hunting down Royal Deepwater Venture Capital since Judd Ryker had called him several hours ago. He wanted to have a lead by the time Dr. Ryker landed in Johannesburg. But so far he was coming up empty.

He'd found old tax records that reported Royal Deepwater was a hedge fund investing in mining and rare commodities and had once had an office in downtown Washington, D.C. That was consistent with a connection to Kanyemba. But according to

172

the IRS, Royal Deepwater had closed years ago.

Sunday also found, buried deep in the CIA's archives, references to a firm called Royal Deepwater with offices in northern Virginia, Delaware, Beirut, and Dubai. But they all had long been closed and the trail had gone cold. The company seemed to have vanished. Or it was hiding.

Sunday refocused his eyes on the computer screen, worrying that maybe he was looking in the wrong place. Company registers, tax records — those were easy to forge. Or erase. He needed another angle. He needed to clear his head.

Sunday left his cubicle and power walked around the perimeter of the Africa Issue office, his usual way of getting some exercise during all-nighters and for problem solving. As he passed by a window he noticed, through the trees to the north, lights in the distance, flying low. An aircraft following the Potomac River on its course into Washington, D.C. It was too late for an airplane landing at Reagan Airport. Must be helicopters heading for the Pentagon, he guessed. The rules don't apply to the Defense Department.

At that thought, Sunday stopped, spun on his heels, and ran back to his cubicle. He quickly logged into a database of sensitive Defense Department procurement records. He typed into the search field: Royal Deepwater.

The reply: No records found.

He typed: Kanyemba.

No records found.

Next, he tried: Shinkolobwe

No records found.

Nothing? This wasn't right. Sunday knew for sure that Shinkolobwe was an old DOD project. Why wasn't it in the procurement records? Sunday stood up again to continue his pacing and to figure out what to do next.

As he passed the adjacent cubicle, where his brilliant but slovenly colleague Glen sat, he scowled at the messy workstation. Glen had left coffee cups and plates on his desk, stacked on top of piles of papers. Newspapers, reports, and books were scattered over everything. *How does Glen work like that?* Sunday wondered.

A clean desk was a clean mind. That was something Sunday's grandmother had taught him at an early age. That was why Sunday was all digital, all the time. Everything he did was electronic. He only read newspapers and books online. If someone gave him a hard copy of a research paper, he would have it scanned and stored so he could always find it later.

Scanned and stored, he thought.

Sunday returned to his computer and searched again: Uranium.

Thousands of records were listed. He sorted them by date, then opened the most recent record, a contract with a private security company. Nothing out of the ordinary. He jumped down to 1945 and opened another random document. On the screen was an out-of-focus page, a low-quality scan of a contract that had been originally written on a typewriter. Sunday could read the address of the company as Reno, Nevada. He typed into the document search field: Reno.

No records found.

Huh? He was staring at the word "Reno" and the computer wasn't seeing it? Didn't the Pentagon run optical character recognition on all its old records? Or did it not bother with the oldest ones?

Sunday narrowed the search dates for uranium-related contracts to 1980–1984, the years he believed the Kanyemba mine was being explored. This produced 214 records. Sunday opened each, one at a time, scanning with his own eyes for key words: Zimbabwe, Kanyemba, Royal Deepwater.

After nearly an hour, he hit the jackpot. A 1981 contract for an exploratory survey of the Zambezi river valley, starting in Kanyemba, Zimbabwe. The contract listed:

Primary contractor: Kanyemba Mining
   Company
Approved partners: Allied Surveyors,
   Global Logistics Inc., Royal Deepwater
   Venture Capital

At the very bottom of the contract was a scrawled signature. Sunday squinted to make out the rolling letters of someone named Max O'Malley.

17.

Bangkok, Thailand
Saturday, 1:43 p.m. Indochina Time
(Eastern Standard Time + 11 Hours)
Max O'Malley outfitted his office in a corner room on the eighty-first floor of the Baiyoke Tower with the same care and precision he brought to all his business deals. He'd chosen the location for its stunning views of downtown Bangkok and the anonymity of a busy commercial hotel. Sitting up so high also gave him a sense of omniscience, watching all the little ants below move in their cars and *tuk-tuk*s while he pulled the strings from the heavens. Plus this room was close to the rooftop cocktail lounge.

When he'd moved in a few weeks earlier, he replaced the bed with a large desk made of Burmese rosewood that was more appropriate for his purposes. And a bar stocked with ice and rare single-malt scotch,

177

an essential part of doing this type of business. O'Malley also removed the hotel room art to make way for his own celebrity wall. He hung photos of himself: posing in the Rose Garden with the President of the United States; with Dean Martin at a black-tie Americans for the Future fund-raising gala; at the Waldorf Astoria Hotel with a Saudi prince; and on the steps of the Grand Palace with the king of Thailand. Also on the wall, prominently displayed, was a framed certificate from the chairman of the President's Reelection Committee, honoring him as a "People's Defender," the highest level of achievement for the party's fund-raising bundlers. Above the photos were his diplomas, a BA from Notre Dame, an MBA from Wharton, and an MSc in nuclear engineering from Virginia Tech. He was most proud of his science degree, an edge which repeatedly proved an advantage in his commercial ventures.

The one photograph missing from his wall, his most cherished of all, was of him standing with the Secretary of Defense on the deck of the aircraft carrier USS *Theodore Roosevelt*. The SecDef's personal inscription was his favorite part. That was exactly why this particular photo was kept, not on the wall for visitors to admire, but in a safe deposit box at the HSBC branch in central Bangkok. It pained him to keep it stored in the dark, but he couldn't take the chance the SecDef's words of thanks and encouragement might one day be misinterpreted by an inspector general or a congressional committee of inquiry.

O'Malley was sitting at his desk, waiting for the call, when his phone finally rang. The caller ID showed a name he recognized, his contact at Suvarnabhumi Airport. He answered with a simple grunt.

"It's here."

"I'm on my way," O'Malley replied.

Twenty-five minutes later, his car pulled through the gate at the executive jet arrivals hall. Waiting in a private hangar at the far side of the airport was an all-white Dassault Falcon 7X. The eight-seat ultra-long-range business jet had only one passenger today: a locked steel case. The pilot, a former South African special forces lieutenant with short hair and a thick neck, silently handed the package to O'Malley. The American accepted the case, examined it briefly, then retreated to a table at the other end of the hangar. He punched in a PIN code, held his thumb to a biometric reader beside the lock, and heard the sweet click-click of the release.

O'Malley's heart rate accelerated as he opened the case. Inside, surrounded by black foam, were three small velvet purses. He gently plucked one pouch from its nest and poured the contents into his palm. He angled the handful of small rocks to see them against a different light and judge their weight. Satisfied, he dumped them back inside, replaced the pouch, and slammed the case shut. He flashed a thumbs-up to the pilot, who turned and departed.

Once O'Malley and the case were safely inside his car, he fished out his phone and placed a call.

"This is Romeo Delta Victor Charlie One. Password six four nine Bravo November Tango six. Yes, confirmed. The payment is one hundred and fifty million, as previously arranged. Correct, one five zero million U.S. dollars. Confirmed. Send it now."

18.

U.S. Embassy, Harare, Zimbabwe
Saturday, 8:50 a.m. Central Africa Time

"Get your fucking game on!"

"Excuse me?" Judd asked the CIA chief of station, who had just jumped out of his chair. Isabella Espinosa had finished explaining to Brock Branson that her mission to Zimbabwe was to hunt General Solomon Zagwe.

"I said, 'Get your fucking game on!'" Brock was becoming even more excited. "I knew that Red Fear fucker was living here in Harare," he said, jabbing a finger at Bull Durham for no apparent reason. "But I didn't know anyone from Washington gave a shit."

"Well, I do," said Isabella, pointing back at Brock. In contrast to his loud personality, there was nothing distinct about Brock's appearance. He was in his late thirties, Caucasian, with a medium build and brown hair, and wore a full, almost shaggy beard, which, Judd assumed, was an attempt to look older in a country where seniority was often respected above all else.

"I didn't know anyone *anywhere* gave a shit," said Brock. He was pacing back and forth in tight circles in his cramped office on the top floor of the embassy. Bull and Judd were squeezed into chairs, and Isabella was sitting on a small couch near the window. In the morning African light, Isabella's hazel skin glistened, softening the tough mask of determination on her face.

"I've been chasing this target for three years. I've spent months poring over witness testimony, legal archives, and banking records," she said, narrowing her eyes. "And that's why I've dropped everything to be here right now. If President Tinotenda loses today, I can't let Zagwe get away."

"Well, I don't think Tino is going to lose the election. But I'm in, sister! What do you need?" Brock's eyes darted back and forth.

"A local car to stake out Zagwe's villa."

"Done. What else?" Brock licked his lips.

"Really?" asked Isabella, looking at Judd, dumbfounded.

"Yep. Done. What else do you need?" He drummed a rapid beat with his fingers on the desk.

"It would help if you could bring down Tino," Judd offered.

"Believe me, I'd be more than happy to oblige. I'd pull the fucking trigger myself. Or push the old man down the stairs. But the CIA doesn't allow us to do that kind of thing anymore. You know, Congress and all," he said, with a wink at Isabella. "I'm here to help you D.C. boys. So, what else?"

"I've already arranged face time with Gugu Mutonga," Judd said.

"You're ahead of the game. How'd you manage that?" Brock asked.

"Through a friend."

"Okay, I get it," Brock raised his hands in mock surrender. "So what do you need from me?"

"How about a meeting with President Tinotenda?"

"That's a tough one, amigo. He's not gonna waste time meeting you. Nothing in it for him. You're all downside, Dr. Ryker."

"How about General Chimurenga?" Judd asked.

"You wanna meet old Simba, eh? All the charm of a rattlesnake in heat, that one! It'll be tough to get him today with the election and all." Brock grimaced. "But . . . old Simba owes me one or two."

"So, is that a yes?" Judd asked.

"Special Agent Espinosa, what do you think?" he asked, turning to face Isabella.

"What do I think about *what*?"

"Should I burn a valuable favor to help Dr. Ryker get a meeting with General Chimurenga?" Brock Branson was rubbing his head.

"Yes," she said quietly. "Definitely."

"Then it's a yes, amigo!" Brock slapped Judd on the back. "What time do you want to see him?"

"How about right now?"

"You might be pushing your luck, Dr. Ryker! But let's see what the bastard says." Brock shrugged and picked up his phone. After a few seconds he shouted, "Simba! It's me! *Makadii! Ndiripo makadiwo!* I want you to meet someone! Today. No. . . . No. . . . No, it has to be today. I know . . . I know . . . Okay . . . Yeah, sure. Yeah, that will be fine. *Ndatenda, shamwari. Fambai zvakanaka.*" He hung up the phone with a loud clunk.

"Okay, we're on."

"Now?" Judd asked. "Just like that?"

"Nah. He's tied up with security for the election. Plus he said he has to go to his home district to vote. Can you fucking believe that? Chimurenga has to *go home to vote*! Sometimes these Zimbos crack me up." Brock shook his head, as if remembering an old joke.

Then, snapping back to the conversation, Brock continued. "Simba will give you five minutes this afternoon. Five o'clock. At the Meikles. It's a sweet hotel, right downtown, old-school. Good gin and tonics. It's full of spies and all, but that's where the Harare elites like to meet."

"Don't you think somewhere more, I don't know, *discreet* might be better?" asked Isabella.

"Nah! It'll be fine. The safest place is wide out in the open," said Brock, holding up his hands again. "It's, like, 'Fuck you, I have nothing to hide.' "

"If you say so." Isabella shrugged.

"I would like nothing more than to play host to you D.C. boys, but if there isn't anything else, I've got work to do."

"One last thing," Judd said. "What do you know about the Kanyemba uranium mine?"

"Good question!" Brock said, squinting. "I've been trying to get a man in there for weeks. They won't let me get in close. They've got troops manning checkpoints on all the roads into Kanyemba. It's tighter security than the fucking diamond mines in the Eastern Highlands. I don't get it. It's damn suspicious. But I don't yet know what

185

they're up to."

"What about UMBRELLA ROSE?" Judd asked.

"What do you know about that?"

"I was fully briefed by Admiral Hammond at the White House on the operation. If it's a uranium mine and it's potentially danger-ous, then you should be receiving some help."

"I'd love a surveillance drone. But my sta-tion wasn't on the original list. Unless I've got evidence of an imminent threat, I'm just going to have to wait my turn."

"Zimbabwe was added to UMBRELLA ROSE," Judd said. "Doesn't that mean you get a drone?"

"Zimbabwe's low-priority. I'm used to it. I don't expect a UAV overflight anytime soon."

"The United States is short on Preda-tors?" Judd shook his head.

"Not Predators. For this kind of mission, we need a Global Hawk," Brock said.

"You need an RQ-4 UAV?" interrupted Bull.

"Yup."

"I might know a guy," Bull said.

"You can get me a Global Hawk?" the sta-tion chief asked. "With geothermal sen-sors?"

"I can make a call back to Stuttgart," said Bull, without breaking his poker face. Judd and Isabella looked at each other with raised eyebrows and suppressed smiles.

"He might know a guy," Judd smirked.

Brock Branson was impressed, too. "Get your fucking game on!"

19.

Papa Toure strolled slowly in the searing heat. He walked along the dirt path, following the directions he'd been given. It was impossible to see his destination. As he came up and over a large rock, however, suddenly there it was: the Church of Saint George. Rather than build the church up high on the ground out of stone as they did in Europe, the twelfth-century Ethiopian Orthodox Christian monks had carved the cross-shaped church out of the rock, deep down below the ground.

Papa stood at the edge of the hole, admiring the craftsmanship, the intricate detail around the windows, the careful use of light and shade to keep the church cool.

He descended the stairs to the lower level, where he circled around the church. The outer walls had dozens of small dark caves, a watchman napping inside one. Once he returned to the main entrance of the church, he stepped inside.

An elderly monk approached him. He was dressed in a purple robe, with a white turban-like hat and a large silver cross hung around his neck. "Welcome, my brother."

Papa bowed his head and returned the greeting.

"Are you here to pray, my brother?"

"I am not," answered Papa.

"Are you a Christian?"

"I am not. I am Muslim."

"You are very welcome. You may still pray here. But you are not Ethiopian, I am sure."

"I am from Mali. From the Sahara."

"What brings you all the way to Ethiopia? Are you with the United Nations?"

"No. I am here because of water. My work is water."

"*Inshallah,* my brother. We need water here. You are very welcome to Lalibela. To Bete Giyorgis, the Church of Saint George."

"*Inshallah.* This is a very beautiful place."

"Yes, this is the new Jerusalem."

"You live here, yes?"

"Yes. Here and at the orphanage in town."

"You are the caretaker for the church and the orphanage, yes?"

"Yes."

"I have brought you this for the orphans," Papa said, bowing his head and handing the monk a thick roll of local currency.

"Thank you, my brother. The children will thank you. Praise to God."

"Praise to God," Papa repeated. "Can I visit the orphanage? Will you show me?"

The monk led Papa out of the church, up the steps, and onto a path toward the center of town.

They crossed through a small marketplace with women sitting in rows, selling yellow beans, bright red chili peppers, and tall pyramids of brown grain. Large pots of dark red stew bubbled on open flames. Papa stopped to watch a woman pour batter on a wide, flat stove, just like one of the many creperies he had visited in Paris.

"Injera," said the monk. "She is making injera, our national bread." The steam of the stove rose, and the savory sour smell tickled Papa's senses. The woman pulled the spongy bread off the stove and stacked it on a pile. "You are hungry, water man?" asked the monk.

"No, brother. I am here to see the orphanage."

"We are here," he said, pointing to a dilapidated concrete building with peeling orange paint on the walls.

Inside, groups of children sat quietly reading books or writing in small notebooks.

"How many children are here now?"

"Two hundred and six," said the monk.

"It is many."

"Yes. We always have many."

"How do you manage?"

"Generous donations. Like yours."

"This is the same orphanage that raised Solomon Zagwe, yes?"

"You are from the United Nations!" gasped the monk, backing away from Papa.

"No, brother. I am not from the UN." He handed over his business card, which read PAPA TOURE, DIRECTOR, WATER ENGINEERING INTERNATIONAL, A PROJECT OF THE HAVERFORD FOUNDATION with a logo of a blue raindrop and phone numbers listed for New York, Geneva, and Bamako.

"Why, then, are you asking about Solomon?"

"It is not every day I meet a holy man who lives in a church and raised a former president. I am interested in history."

"Solomon was a good boy." The monk shook his head. "I don't know where he went wrong, but *he was good.*"

"I see. I also have a son. It is so difficult to raise them, you give them everything."

"Yes, we do."

"And then you have no more control. We do our best. But we can't be held responsible for what they do as adults. Isn't that true, brother?"

"Yes."

"It can be painful, yes?"

"So painful."

"What was Solomon like as a boy?" asked Papa.

"Always working to get ahead. He never liked to rest. Never satisfied."

"How did he ever rise from this place to become president?"

"He was clever. He worked hard. He joined the army and was sent to Saudi Arabia for training. He made many friends there and was very powerful when he returned. On a very bad day, he killed the emperor and became president. I should have been proud. One of my charges became the most powerful man in the country. But it did not feel Christian."

"I understand."

"I am ashamed," said the monk.

"I understand, my brother," said Papa, placing a hand gently on the monk's shoulder.

"I am a humble servant of the Lord. I know of the word of God. I don't know these games of power. These games of big men."

Papa nodded his head in sympathy.

"Something went wrong," continued the monk, tears welling in his eyes. "Something terrible. Something unbearably un-Christian. I cannot speak of what he did."

"I understand. No more questions."

After a few moments of silence, Papa asked, "My brother, are you still in contact with Solomon?"

"No!" he insisted. "He cannot return to Ethiopia. He can never return to this place."

"He doesn't write? To the man who raised him? I don't believe that."

"No, he does not write."

"He has forgotten you? Despite all that has happened, despite all you did for him, he has forgotten the place that raised him?"

"I did not say that. You asked if he writes."

"So, what does he do?"

"He has not forgotten the Church of Saint George or the orphanage."

"What do you mean?"

"Those books," he said, pointing to a crooked shelf holding several dozen dog-eared volumes. "The soccer balls, the clothing, even our new television. He has sent them all. He does not write, but he has sent us these gifts. I know they are from him."

"I see. He sent you a television?"

"Yes."

"May I see it, brother?"

The monk led Papa into a side room. A flat-screen television was in one corner, a crowd of young children sprawled in front, focused intently on the soccer match on the screen. The game commentary was very loud and in Italian.

"Solomon Zagwe sent you this television?"

"He is still a good boy deep down. He has not forgotten us."

"Yes. I see. It is a fine television, yes."

In the upper corner of the screen a blue sticker announced SAMSUNG, THE NEXT BIG THING. Behind the TV, a cardboard box lay propped up against the wall. Papa walked around the back to examine it. In one corner of the box was a shipping label:

PATTANAKARN ELECTRONICS, SUVAR-NABHUMI, BANGKOK 10250, THAILAND.

"Yes, brother, it is a fine television," Papa repeated.

20.

Harare, Zimbabwe
Saturday, 9:44 a.m. Central Africa Time
General Simba Chimurenga was feeling confident. He watched the lines of new recruits for the Green Mambas, most of them young boys no older than fifteen or sixteen years old, conscripted from the villages. They were all wearing new dark green jumpsuits, but few had shoes. Those lucky enough to have anything on their feet wore ratty sandals made from old tires. They appeared strong. And angry.

Chimurenga called over the unit commander, who arrived with a sharp salute.

"How many today?"

"Two hundred here, sir. We have another fourteen recruitment sites around the country, sir."

"Why aren't these recruits wearing shoes?" demanded the general.

"I'm sorry, General. Only uniforms were

delivered from headquarters."

"I want these boys to have proper shoes. The Green Mambas cannot attack barefoot. Buy them boots," he said, pulling a fat wad of U.S. dollars from his pocket.

"Yes, sir."

"I want them to have the boots *today*. Before they deploy."

"Yes, sir. I know where to get boots for the men," he replied, shoving the money into his pocket.

"Are the trucks ready for them?"

"Nearly, sir."

The general's phone rang, a sign the commander took to depart. Chimurenga eyed the caller ID. He had been waiting anxiously for this call from his business partner.

"The package has been delivered," said Solomon Zagwe on the other end. "I have just spoken with our man in Asia."

"Very good," said the general. "Just in time. Have the funds arrived as well?"

"Yes. I spoke with the bank. They will have the cash on hand. Your man can pick it up."

"What is the total?"

"One fifty."

"One fifty? That is less than our agreement."

"I know. That is the discount for our urgency. I told you we could get more if we waited for full production, for the full order. But you insisted we needed the money today."

The general watched as the recruits marched in straight lines, holding pipes or knobkerries, the short Zulu sticks with a heavy ball on one end. They swung their sticks in unison, smashing them on the ground with a loud thud.

"Yes, we need the money today."

"So the number is one fifty."

"It is enough," said Chimurenga, flipping the phone closed.

He beckoned the commander back.

"How much are we paying the boys?"

"The new recruits are paid ten dollars for the day. Plus food and a uniform."

"And boots."

"Yes, sir. And boots."

"I want to address the Green Mambas. Call them over." Within a few seconds the two hundred boys lined up nervously in front of General Chimurenga. The commander directed them to sing a revolutionary song about the bravery of their ancestors and the glory of fighting imperialists. When they were finished, the commander shouted, "Forward with the revolution!"

"Pamberi!" was the chorus reply with raised fists.

"Forward with the people!"

"Pamberi!"

"Forward with Zimbabwe!"

"Pamberi!"

"Forward with President Tinotenda!"

"Pamberi!"

"Forward with the Green Mambas!"

"Pamberi!"

"Forward with General Chimurenga!"

"Pamberi!"

The commander then bowed and backed away, leaving the floor to the general. The recruits stood at attention in tense silence.

"Yesterday you were village boys. Today you are men."

"Yes, sir!" they shouted in unison.

"Yesterday you were children. Today you are Green Mambas."

"Yes, sir!"

"Yesterday you were nothing. Today you are part of the Revolution."

"Yes, sir!"

"Yesterday you had nothing in your pocket. Today you will be paid fifty dollars."

"Yes, sir!"

"Yesterday you served your mother. Today you serve your nation."

"Yes, sir!"

"Yesterday there were traitors and sellouts

among us. Today you will destroy them."

"Yes, sir!"

21.

Georgetown, Washington, D.C.
Saturday, 5:54 a.m. Eastern Standard Time
The kitchen was a perfect aromatic brew of fresh coffee, sizzling bacon, and French toast. The sun had just risen over the trees in her back garden. Jessica had been up for only ten minutes but she was wide-awake. And she was ready.

"Juice!" shouted one of her boys.

"Noah," she scolded, waving a spatula, "how do we ask?"

"Juice, *please,* Mommy!"

"Toby, you're six years old. You can pour your brother a glass of orange juice," she directed her other son. "Not too full."

As she flipped the French toast on the stove, she checked the time. Nearly six o'clock.

Jessica nudged the bacon strips around the griddle and was watching the clouds of bubbling fat sizzle when her phone rang.

She hooked on an earpiece, instructed her children with a "Boys, let Mommy take a phone call," and pressed the button.

"Good morning."

"This is two four one Zebra Charlie," said Sunday on the other end.

"Yes, it is a good morning," she responded, taking a gulp of coffee.

"Ma'am, we need to scramble."

Jessica set down the spatula and punched a string of digits into her phone. After a few seconds she heard a static signal and then three beeps in ascending pitch.

"We're now secure on Purple Cell protocols. Shall I proceed, ma'am?"

"Yes," said Jessica.

"Thank you, ma'am. I've been working on our case throughout the night and making headway, but we've got a problem."

"Yes?"

"I learned just a few minutes ago that the British memo on uranium threats is under suspicion. There is now doubt within the Intelligence Community whether there was any threat at all. It may be that naturally occurring, highly enriched uranium doesn't even exist. The DNI is launching an after-action investigation into the memo's sources and methods. Until that is complete, they are putting all uranium surveillance operations on a stand-down."

"Doesn't exist?"

"I don't know, ma'am. I only know the current assessment is no longer an imminent threat from uranium proliferation. UMBRELLA ROSE is on hold until further notice."

Shit. "And our target?"

"Kanyemba is no longer considered a potential risk. Just when we got Kanyemba added to the list, they've suspended the program. Does that mean Purple Cell is on stand-down?"

"Hold," she said. Jessica plucked the bacon from the pan while she thought about her next move. She scooped up the French toast and placed two golden brown slices on each Cookie Monster plate.

"Eat up," she instructed as she set down breakfast in front of her children.

"Ma'am?" asked Sunday.

"Not you," she said, turning her back. "Is the stand-down order for UMBRELLA ROSE relayed yet?"

"Not yet. Should be official later today. But I have it from a good source, so I called you right away . . ."

"Keep this close-hold."

"Shall I inform our field operatives?"

"Negative. Is that clear?"

"Yes, ma'am."

"Keep looking for connections. Focus on the banks. The money trail will lead us where we want to go. That's our window. That's all for now."

"Yes, ma'am."

Jessica hung up the phone. "Syrup, boys?"

"Yes, Mommy."

She opened the fridge, pulled a small jug of Vermont maple syrup, and drizzled it over the French toast.

How long can I keep this up? she thought.

The strains of her double life were weighing heavily on Jessica that morning. *How had it come to this?* Twelve years ago, she'd been a young agronomist, fresh from graduate school and fortunate to be placed on a research team with the eminent Professor BJ van Hollen. Her mentor had dragged her to Kidal, a remote city in northern Mali, to work on an exciting new water project. Or so she thought.

She now knew the real purpose of the project was to recruit her into the Central Intelligence Agency. Van Hollen didn't know at the time she would wind up marrying the other student on the Kidal team, a fresh-faced data nerd from Vermont named Judd. They were opposites in almost every way, so how could BJ have known?

As Jessica's romance with Judd had progressed, so too did her career in the CIA. Everything changed one day when she was pulled into a "red cell," a special analytical unit assembled outside the normal structures and isolated from everything else. The purpose of a red cell was to get out of your normal team, to take an unconventional view of a tough problem.

She loved it. Her memory of that first secret project was of total exhilaration. It probably helped that the day her red cell assignment was complete was also the very day that Judd proposed. Heady with love and the adrenaline of a clandestine job, she accepted.

Her red cell experience had convinced her that small, capable teams given total freedom could be highly valuable at problem solving. Jessica started thinking about how a similar independent cell might be effective on the operational side of the Agency. She shared her new idea with BJ van Hollen, who took it right to the CIA's deputy director for operations. Purple Cell was born.

The upside was Jessica could pick her teams and operate with total independence, outside normal reporting channels. As she'd won recognition and racked up operational successes, demand for Purple Cell had grown among the very elite policy makers who knew about the top secret unit.

The downside was she could never tell her family about any of it. To run the covert team, she had to maintain her cover as an agronomist and soccer mom. Judd's long hours at Amherst College and then at the State Department allowed her ample space to run both her family and Purple Cell.

But it wasn't the physical demands that were wearing on her. It was the psychological stress of living a double life, of lying every day to those she loved. She could handle the deception and political games at work. She thrived on that. It was the lies at home that were becoming the problem. It was one thing to keep her emotions in check when ex-filtrating a hostage from Bolivia. Or to remain cold and calculating when destroying the personal life of a corrupt Jordanian politician.

Maintaining the deceptions with her husband was taking its toll. She had held it all together so far. Judd knew little about her true background and was in the dark about her real job. But he was analytical by nature and she knew he would eventually figure out the truth. She was pushing the limits — and violating the rules — by working on projects that overlapped with her husband's. The recent assignment in Mali had been an especially close call. Now she was testing her luck again. Actually, she was doubling down on the risks to both work and life. *Maybe Judd already knew?*

Jessica dialed another phone number. As it rang, she dropped two slices of bacon on each son's plate.

"Go," answered Brock Branson on the other end.

"Confirm, please."

"This is seven six six Zebra Charlie."

"Are we secure?"

"Affirmative, ma'am."

"Where's my bird?"

"Ma'am, we were so far down the list, I didn't think we'd see any goddamn birds for months, but we've had a stroke of luck. A resourceful bastard landed right in my lap. We'll have a bird up and out of the nest later today. The first pictures from Kanyemba should be back tonight."

"With eagle eyes?"

"Yes, ma'am. With geothermal sensors."

"Very good."

"Anything else, ma'am?"

"No one kills my bird except me. I don't care what you hear from Langley. Is that clear?"

"Roger that."

"No. One. But. Me. Kills. My. Bird."

"No one but you kills your bird, ma'am. Got it. Game on."

Jessica hung up the phone and turned back to breakfast.

"Who's killing a birdie, Mommy?"

"No one, Noah. No one is killing any birds. Your mom would never allow that. More bacon?"

22.

The line of people wound all the way down Mbizi Road, past the roadside shops hanging dried meat, the tall pyramids of oranges, and the rolling mounds of fresh tomatoes and onions.

Tinashe fidgeted with two stones in his hand and danced in place. He craned his neck to try to see the front of the voting line. He couldn't. Only hundreds of people waiting patiently in the midday sun to cast a vote.

"Ah! Tssss! Calm yourself," urged Tsitsi, who was holding an open red-and-white-striped umbrella. "Our turn will come."

"I want to vote," he replied. "I am ready."

"Be patient, Tinashe. You are always in a rush."

Tinashe ignored her scolding but he knew she was right. Tsitsi was always right. He paced back and forth and scanned up and down the line again.

"I don't see any Tino boys. Only Gugu's people. Only our people," he said.

"*Zvakanaka,* very good." She spun the umbrella handle between her fingers.

"*Ehe, zvakanaka.*"

"Police?" she asked.

Tinashe gestured toward a hill in the distance. A small crowd of uniformed policemen with batons stood under an acacia tree.

"*Zvakanaka,* very good."

"Perhaps, Tsitsi, the police are with us today?"

She shrugged.

"I have to see," he said, ducking away.

A few moments later an old woman in a red and purple wrap dress approached. "Little Tsitsi! Yesterday you were running down Mbizi Road, playing with the boys. Today you are a woman! You are old enough to vote?"

"*Ehe.* Yes, *ambuya,*" she said, bowing her head and averting her eyes in deference. "I am a woman."

"How is your day?" the old woman asked.

Tsitsi clapped her hands in the polite form of Shona greetings. "My day is well if your day is well."

The old woman clapped her hands in response and nodded. "My day is well."

"Then so is mine."

"*Zvakanaka*. Very good."

"*Zvakanaka.*"

"How is your father, Tsitsi?"

"He was sick, but now he is better."

"God willing, he will recover," the old woman said.

"Thank you, *ambuya*. How are your sons?"

"All down south. They all are in Johannesburg. They send me money. It's the only way I survive."

"Survive. That is good," Tsitsi said.

"Now you are a woman, little Tsitsi, why no children?"

"Not yet, *ambuya*," she replied, hiding her annoyance out of respect.

"God willing, soon."

"Yes, God willing," Tsitsi said, scanning the long voting line, which hadn't moved during their conversation.

"How long have you been queueing, Tsitsi?"

"All morning, *ambuya*."

"I am too old to stand in queues like this."

"*Fambai zvakanaka*. Go well, *ambuya*."

"*Fambai zvakanaka.*"

As the old woman shuffled off, Tinashe

returned excited. "No Tino boys, Tsitsi. Only Gugu's people. I don't see how Gugu can lose!"

"The people are with her."

"We are ready. I am ready!" he said quickly.

She looked up again at the long, unmoving line and, against her better judgment, allowed herself a brief moment of delight. "Our turn will come."

23.

Lucky Magombe peered over his reading glasses, out the window of his office, at a cluster of modern steel-and-glass office towers. Black Star Capital's new headquarters, on the urban edge of northern Johannesburg, was the high-tech hub of his operation.

In the next room was the company's modest trading floor. Five days a week, two dozen young African men and women worked the trading floor, each wearing a headset and staring at a computer screen, watching for tiny movements in share prices to exploit. When Lucky's traders discovered discrepancies of some kind, they would shout their orders into their headsets. These orders would be executed nearly instantaneously by other Black Star employees sitting in Harare or Nairobi or Accra. It wasn't

New York or London, he knew, but it was something. The growth of Lucky's net worth could attest to that.

On this Saturday, the trading floor was empty and money was far from Lucky's mind. Instead he was pondering his options. Despite his wealth and professional success, Lucky was unhappy. His friends and colleagues in South Africa sensed a deep sadness he carried with him. But he never spoke of it.

Lucky Magombe was most comfortable when surrounded by numbers and blinking trading screens. It hadn't always been like this. There'd been no electronic screens at all when he was a young trainee just out of technical college in Harare and ecstatic to have his first job as a runner for the stockbroker Carrington & Cobb.

Back then the Zimbabwe Stock Exchange had been all paper and chalk. Clients would call in their orders by phone or, more often, send a houseboy from the northern suburbs on a bus downtown to the brokerage office. The broker would write down the buy or sell order with a dull pencil on a small pale blue memo pad, tear off the top sheet, and then shout, "Lucky!" His job was to run the order slip down the street, across African Unity Square — around the brokerage, it was still known by its pre-independence name, Cecil Square — to a squat office building over on Union Avenue. Then he'd run up four flights of stairs to the stock exchange floor and hand the paper slip to Carrington & Cobb's floor trader.

The traders — on a normal day there were six or seven of them — sat at a long U-shaped table. At the end of the room was a blackboard with the list of stocks traded on the ZSE, the latest prices, and the current bid-ask prices all written in chalk. After a sale, the floor manager would erase the price with an efficient swipe and scribble the new price. Once the trade was complete, the other broker would countersign the blue order slip and, victorious, Lucky would run the paper back to the Carrington & Cobb head office. That had more or less been the system since the ZSE first started trading in 1946.

But these days there was no paper and no chalk. The ZSE brokers, who had grown to more than twenty, still called out the trades aloud, but the exchange's trading board was a giant electronic screen and the records were all kept on a secure computer network.

Lucky Magombe's big break was seeing the technological changes coming. After only a few months on the job, he'd noticed the paper-and-runner system was full of errors. Sometimes the original order was incorrect or a trader would make a mistake. Occasionally, a runner would lose the slip altogether.

He soon discovered that not all of the errors were accidental. When the manipulation of prices might make someone extra money, he quickly learned, foul play was inevitable. Lucky started keeping track of the mistakes. Eventually, he found patterns and concluded, to his horror, that the fraud was not the occasional slippery work of one or two corrupt individuals. He realized Carrington & Cobb was padding its profits by systematically cheating its own customers.

That was when Lucky had quit and started Black Star Capital. His idea was to turn the old system against itself, to make money by arbitraging inefficiencies. The Black Star model would be leaner, quicker, and especially more accurate than all the other brokers.

Lucky's firm had started small. He was the first to use cell phones as a parallel reporting system to double-check all trades. Then Black Star Capital stopped using runners and instead directed the floor trader by mobile phone and confirmed all activities via e-mail. As an early adopter, Black Star quickly gained a reputation for using the latest technology to get the best price. And with a zero-error guarantee, clients started pouring in.

Black Star Capital was also the first to develop online trading for its clients and to provide analytical data tools on all the listed companies. Then Lucky deployed cloud computing to store records and to run algorithms on all trading data to search for anomalies in the market. Lucky had realized using the latest technology would not only give him a competitive edge but allowed him to police the entire trading system. Which led him to other uses for the technology . . .

As Lucky Magombe pondered the best course of action today, he recognized the irony of his own success: Black Star Capital had been born by eliminating the very job that had given him his start. *Progress often requires destruction,* he thought.

Just then his phone rang. He answered quickly without checking the caller ID. "Magombe," he said, like a punch.

"I am calling for Cannonball," said a deep voice.

"What is it?" Lucky asked.

"Are you ready to join the Canterbury

Cricket Club? Your membership has been prepared. It will be available this Sunday. At noon."

Lucky pondered the question, his mind racing.

"Sir?" the voice asked again.

"Not yet," Lucky finally answered. "Wait for my word."

"Shall we continue with your membership preparations for the Canterbury Cricket Club?"

"Yes," he said before hanging up.

The truth was that Lucky Magombe was sad, because despite all his wealth and apparent success, he could not do the one thing he most longed to do: go home.

24.

As their vehicle crossed over a highway bridge, the driver turned to Judd Ryker and Isabella Espinosa in the backseat and said, "Welcome to Mbare."

Colonel Bull Durham, in the front seat, asked, "What is this place?"

"Mbare is a high-density neighborhood of Harare."

"High-density? You mean it's a slum?"

"We prefer 'high-density.' Mbare is famous. It's the neighborhood where the British put the most rebellious Africans. It became a forward base for the anticolonial struggle. Today it is a base of the opposition."

"It's Gugu Mutonga country," Judd said.

The shops were all closed, since election day was an official holiday, but the streets were filled with people selling biscuits,

218

bottles of Coca-Cola, phone cards, and plastic shoes. As they drove deeper into Mbare, the traffic slowed. Judd noticed Durham adjust the rearview mirror.

"What is it, Bull?"

"Two cars back. They're following us."

"Who?" asked Isabella, spinning around in her seat.

"Don't be alarmed," offered the driver with a chuckle. "They always tail embassy vehicles. When we catch them, they claim it's for our own safety."

'Who's 'they'?" asked Isabella.

"Probably the Central Intelligence Organization," said Durham. "CIO is responsible for tracking the opposition and monitoring foreign embassies."

"Yes, but don't worry," said the driver.

"Well, I don't like it," Isabella said.

"We're almost there," said the driver, pointing ahead to stadium lights. "There is Rufaro."

"Gugu Mutonga is holding her final campaign rally in Rufaro Stadium," explained Judd. "It's right in the heart of Mbare. And it's the same place Bob Marley played on Zimbabwe's independence day."

As they approached the stadium, the crowds grew so thick that traffic ground to a halt.

"Let's walk," suggested Durham. He directed the driver to stay with the car, and the three Americans stepped out of their air-conditioning and into the throng. The crowds all flowed like a giant river in one direction toward the stadium entrance.

As they struggled to stay together, Judd grabbed Durham's arm and pulled him in close. "Are they still tailing us?"

"Yep."

Judd strained to try to spot their pursuers, but it was a sea of unfamiliar faces.

"Mauya, murungu!" a boy yelled at Judd before disappearing into the crowd. Then another shouted, "Hello, *murungu!* You are welcome!"

"Murungu!" yelled a third child, before giggling and running off.

"Murungu?" asked Bull.

"White guy," said Judd. "Brock told me kids would yell that at me when we entered the townships. He says it's not meant as an insult. More matter-of-fact."

"Okay, *murungu,*" Durham said.

Once they reached the stadium entrance, Durham found a side corridor and eventually led them to a door marked PRIVATE. Judd knocked. A large man with thick sunglasses opened the door. "We are from the American embassy. Mariana Leibowitz called ahead," Judd explained. The door slammed closed.

They waited for a few moments, then the door swung wide-open.

"You are welcome," said the guard, with a bow and a sweep of the hand. He led them down a long corridor underneath the stadium. The crowd was cheering and stomping their feet. Judd could feel the vibrations in the floor and wondered if the old stadium could withstand the pounding.

They arrived at another door. "The Americans are here," said the guard, who then pushed the door open. Inside, sitting on a plastic chair, was a handsome middle-aged woman in a well-pressed business suit. Her hair was pinned back tightly and her rectangular designer glasses were low on her nose.

"Dr. Ryker," she said with a warm smile and firm handshake. "A pleasure to finally meet you. Mariana Leibowitz has told me much about you. Welcome to Zimbabwe."

"Thank you, Ms. Mutonga."

"Call me Gugu."

"Thank you, Gugu. I'd like you to meet Colonel Durham and Special Agent Espinosa. They are from the Departments of Defense and Justice."

"You are also welcome," she said with a friendly bow. "When the Democracy Union of Zimbabwe wins this election today and our party has the opportunity to rebuild our beautiful country, we will need your help. Today we have no security. We have no justice. We have neither here in this place. We will need our American friends."

"We are here today to do what we can to try to prevent trouble," offered Judd.

"Very good. You are welcome. We need you to be here to witness what is happening. To ensure the will of the people is revealed. We need you here to do a very simple thing: to tell the truth."

The truth. Seems so simple, thought Judd, *but it never is.*

"How is the voting going?" Isabella asked.

"The government is attacking our people in too many places. But we are confident we can still win. We are optimistic. We are certain if the rules are followed, the DUZ will be victorious. The people are with us. Can you hear them?"

Gugu Mutonga opened her palms and looked up to the ceiling. The tremors of the stomping crowd could be felt through the floor, and the din of the chanting filled their ears.

"My friends, I'm sorry. I beg you to excuse me. I'm expected outside."

■ ■ ■ ■

A few minutes later Gugu Mutonga walked onto the stage and the masses erupted. Judd, watching from the side of the stage alongside Bull and Isabella, instinctively ducked his head, expecting the stadium to collapse from the crowd's exploding energy.

"GU-GUUUUUUUU!" chanted the crowd. Thousands of raised hands formed the letter *G*, as if they were squeezing oranges. "GU-GUUUUUUUUU! GU-GUUUUUUUUU!"

Gugu Mutonga, now pacing the stage, clapped her hands over her head in appreciation, then opened her palms and bench-pressed the sky as if holding the country on her shoulders. This ignited another round of frenzied "GU-GUUUUUUUUU! GU-GUUUUUUUUU!"

When the chanting finally slowed, Gugu took the microphone. "Who is ready for a new Zimbabwe?"

"WE ARE!" shouted the crowd.

"Who is tired of the past built on hatred and fear?"

"WE ARE!"

"Who is ready for a better life for our mothers and our fathers?"

"WE ARE!"

"Who is ready for a brighter future for our sons and our daughters?"

"WE ARE!"

"Who can deliver on a new Zimbabwe?"

"GU-GUUUUUUUU!"

"Who can lead a new Zimbabwe?"

"GU-GUUUUUUUU!"

"Who believes in you?"

"GU-GUUUUUUUU!"

"Who will win today?

"GU-GUUUUUUUU!"

25.

"You're here on the weekend again, S-Man?"

Sunday looked up from his computer terminal to find his colleague leering over the cubicle's half wall. Glen held a Styrofoam coffee cup in one hand and a donut in the other. His hair was standing up on one side as if he had just rolled out of bed. "You need to get a life, Sunday."

"Aaay. That's what my girlfriend says."

"You've got a girlfriend?" Glen chuckled, taking a shark bite out of the donut, leaving a thin mustache of powdered sugar on his upper lip.

Sunday frowned. "You're here on Saturday morning, too, Glen."

"Yeah, but I don't have a girlfriend."

Sunday brushed his top lip with his hand. The other man tentatively copied Sunday, then glanced down at the powder on his fingers, shrugged, and wiped it on his jeans. "Seriously, Sunday, what's going on? What're you doin' here?"

"Zimbabwe. It's election day."

"Oh, shit. That's right! That old fucker Tino's still holding on, isn't he?"

"Yes."

"I remember running tracers on that man's accounts, like, a decade ago. Maybe longer. You sure Tino's really still alive?"

"Yes."

"Maybe they are just propping him up. Like Castro. Or *Weekend at Bernie's.*"

"He's alive."

"Maybe you'll get lucky and it will all blow up this weekend. Yep. Maybe this is the weekend Tino finally kicks it. Boy, that would be something, eh, Sunday?"

Sunday didn't respond and turned back to his desk. After a few seconds Sunday looked up again and Glen was still there, still leering, still grinning.

Sunday exhaled. "What, Glen, are *you* here working on?"

"Somali pirates," he said firing finger guns at the ceiling. "They seized another Korean container ship last night."

"You don't say," Sunday said.

"Yup, that's the third grab-and-go this

month. I can't say any more. So, Sunday, who's this girlfriend of yours?"

Sunday ignored the question and turned his attention back to his computer.

"Okay, S-Man, I can take a hint. I've got pirates to catch anyway. We can talk about your girlfriend later."

Sunday grunted as he logged into the network and clicked through several security screens to access a database. With a few keystrokes he pulled up all financial transactions in or out of Zimbabwean banks for the past month. Long endless lists scrolled on his screen. He opened a data filter and set the size minimum at $1 million. The list shrunk from millions of transactions to a few hundred. One immediately stuck out as larger than all the rest.

Oct07 $150,000,000 ZimBank (HRE)
  1015655 ABC from HSBC (IOM) 786252
  XXX

That's today, Sunday thought. Who is transferring $150 million into a volatile country *on election day*? He opened another screen and logged into another CIA database. He typed in the receiving account information, and the screen reported:

ZimBank Account 1015655
African Ballistics Corporation (ABC)
500 Fidel Castro Avenue, Harare, Zimbabwe
Authorized Holder: Simba Chimurenga

"Aaay!" Sunday said aloud. "Christmas for the general. Who is Santa Claus?" he mumbled to himself. He entered the sender account data and received:

HSBC Account 786252
Anonymous (XXX)
Prevost Avenue, Douglas, Isle of Man
Authorized Holder: Name Withheld

Sunday scratched his head. He picked up the phone. "I've got an anonymous bank account linked to a suspicious transaction I need network mapped. I'm sending over the account information now." A few moments later his screen popped.

HSBC 786252, Anonymous (XXX), Isle of
  Man, Name Withheld
↓
AsiaOne Bank 786252, XTC Trading Co,
  Mauritius, Name Withheld
↓
Barclays 786252, Orca Financial, Jersey,
  M.O. Smith

↓
HSBC 786252, RDVC, Bangkok, Thailand, Max O'Malley

Max O'Malley? Sunday pushed his chair back away from his desk. The same person who had tried to mine uranium at Kanyemba and failed was now bankrolling Simba Chimurenga? And presumably these were campaign funds for President Tinotenda. Elections always brought out dirty money, he thought. But what is an American mining investor living in Bangkok doing in . . . Zimbabwe? It made no sense.

And who was funding the opposition? Sunday returned to the database and searched for any accounts associated with Gugu Mutonga or the Democracy Union of Zimbabwe, but came up empty. He cleared the $1 million minimum filter and searched again. The page began to fill.

Oct07 $9872 ZimBank (HRE) 6764882 DUZ from SunBank (JHB) 786252 BST
Oct06 $9994 ZimBank (HRE) 6764882 DUZ from SunBank (JHB) 786252 BST
Oct05 $9765 ZimBank (HRE) 6764882 DUZ from SunBank (JHB) 786252 BST
Oct04 $9902 ZimBank (HRE) 6764882 DUZ from SunBank (JHB) 786252 BST

229

Oct03 $9881 ZimBank (HRE) 6764882
DUZ from SunBank (JHB) 786252 BST

Sunday scratched his head again. One transaction every day from the same account in Johannesburg to the same account in Harare. DUZ was Gugu Mutonga's party. But what was BST? And why were the amounts so random? And so small?

"Glen!" Sunday yelled.

"You need girlfriend advice over there, S-Man?"

"You've worked on underground money transfers in Somalia, right?"

"Yeah, they're called *hawala.* They're a way for people working overseas to send money home to relatives. But the terrorists started using them to move money, so we've mostly shut all the *hawala* down."

"I've got repeat transactions, one per day, every day, from one account to another. What would that tell you?"

"A hair under ten thousand dollars, right?"

"Exactly," Sunday said.

"And slightly different totals each day, right?"

"Yes! How did you guess?"

"Classic under-the-radar strategy." Glen attacked another donut. Talking with his mouth full, he explained, "Most of the financial tracking software defaults to flag all transactions above $10K. If you were trying to mask money transfers, you'd keep it under that level."

"But why alter the amounts?"

"Precise repeats typically get flagged, too."

"I see."

"Whoever is transferring that money doesn't want the bank to notice," Glen said.

"Or the Zimbabwean intelligence services?"

"Or us," Glen said, wiping his hands on his jeans as he wandered away.

Sunday pulled up the website for SunBank in South Africa, clicked on CLIENT LOGIN, typed in the BST account number, and then ran a PIN search algorithm. After a few seconds he was in. He moved through the system and found account details:

SunBank Account 786252
Black Star Trust (BST)
Millennium Tower, Sandton, Johannesburg
Authorized Trustees: Lucky Magombe

Who in the world is Lucky Magombe? he thought.

Sunday opened a separate screen and searched for Lucky Magombe in the agency's profile database. All that came up was a simple biography about a Zimbabwean stock trader who'd moved his business to South Africa. No known criminal record. No known political affiliations. Sunday pushed his chair back and exhaled loudly. He rolled his head in a circle, cracking his neck.

Winston Tinotenda versus Gugu Mutonga? Or is it Max O'Malley versus Lucky Magombe?

26.

Sitting in his corner office at the headquarters of Black Star Capital, Lucky Magombe studied the blinking screens. One screen displayed a long list of district names with rolling columns of numbers as the votes came in. The other showed a map of his home country, Zimbabwe, broken down by individual voting constituency. The data on the first screen fed into an algorithm projecting final outcome probabilities on the second screen. These calculations were converted into a color-coding for each district on the map. Lucky had written the code himself.

So far, there was little to report. Several obvious strongholds glowed green for Winston Tinotenda and red for Gugu Mutonga. But, only a few hours into voting, most of the map's zones remained black. Too early

233

to predict the result with any confidence.

Lucky zoomed in on the map for his home area, in the far north of the country, just near the town of Kanyemba. It, too, was black. He overlaid the map with satellite imagery and zoomed in to the center of Kanyemba. He began at the old mine compound, the easiest landmark to find from space. He could clearly spot the straight lines of the roads and rectangular shapes of the compound's now-derelict buildings. He followed with his finger the winding snake of a river flowing east. Several miles downstream, the river merged with a small creek to form a familiar triangle. This was the site of the village where he'd grown up. Lucky Magombe, sitting on the fourteenth floor of an air-conditioned office in Johannesburg, was staring at a photo of his home.

Except nothing was there. Just trees and dark red earth. There was in fact no sign at all there had ever been a village on that spot. Lucky's stomach ached as he zoomed in closer to scour for any sign of a house, a well, anything. *Nothing.*

If only he had a satellite photo from before his village was completely erased. When the young lawyer Gugu Mutonga took the village's case to court and then all the way to the United Nations. The government denied a village had ever existed there. There was no proof of a village, so there was no atrocity. No records, no photographs, no witnesses, no bodies ever found.

Of course, everyone knew the truth about Operation Motowetsurohuro, the Great Rabbit Fire. Everyone knew that three villages and their nine hundred residents had lived there for years in peace. And now they did not. Everyone knew about the army and the attack helicopters. And everyone knew the message of Motowetsurohuro: *Silence.*

Lucky also knew that as long as there was proof a village had once been, then the fight for justice would not be over. He knew there was proof that those people lived, that his mother existed. That proof was *him.*

As Lucky stared at the place that denied he was a real person, he wrestled with what to do next. He closed the screen with the satellite map and turned back to the voting tabulations. Satisfied, he picked up his phone and called a number inside Zimbabwe.

A deep voice answered, "Hello."

"Is this the Canterbury Cricket Club?" asked Lucky.

"Is this Cannonball?"

"Yebo."

"Your membership has been prepared. Are

you now ready to play?"

"Is the cricket team there?"

"Yes, everything is in place. The target is in our sights. We are only waiting for your approval."

Lucky longed for revenge. He wanted to taste blood. He wanted to pull the trigger on those who had destroyed his village and killed his mother. But Lucky thought of the woman who had carried him on her back, taught him to read, had made him who he was. He decided she would not want retaliation. She would want *justice.*

27.

"What exactly are we looking for, Isabella?"

Special Agent Isabella Espinosa and Colonel David "Bull" Durham slumped down in the front seat of the battered Mitsubishi Pajero SUV with standard local license plates. They had a clear sight line on the front gate but were parked a safe distance from the villa of former Ethiopian President General Solomon Zagwe. The whitewashed wall of the compound was decorated with flowering vines and the lawn was neatly trimmed.

"Anything," she replied. "Luggage in the driveway. Any signs of flight preparation."

"It doesn't look like the house of a monster."

"Don't be fooled. Zagwe is a war criminal. Thirty years ago he launched the Red Fear. He ordered the massacre of thousands of civilians. And then he starved another half

237

million innocents. He's a certified mass murderer."

"Sounds like Saddam Hussein."

"In a way. Zagwe tried to appear to the world like a gentleman. But underneath, to his own people, he was a total psychopath."

"Yep, that was Saddam."

"You served in Iraq?"

"Yes, ma'am. Three tours. You should've seen the palaces. Makes Zagwe's villa look like an ice-fishing shack."

"Ice fishing?"

"Minnesota. Born and raised," Bull said.

"Los Angeles," Isabella replied.

They both turned their attention back to the front gate.

"So if Zagwe's been in exile here for so many years, why now, Isabella?"

"This is probably our best chance to get him. If Tinotenda loses today, Zagwe will have to make a run for it. If he gets to North Korea or Russia, we'll never be able to extradite him. I've got to grab him in the chaos after Tino falls."

"Why don't we grab him right now?"

"Believe me, I'd love to," she said. "But we've got no authority here. If we handcuff and hood him, the Zimbabweans would never let us leave the country. They'd probably arrest us."

Durham scowled.

"That's why it was fortunate Dr. Ryker invited me along," Isabella said.

"What's Judd's interest in your case?"

"I don't know, actually," she paused. "I guess he just understood that my best window of opportunity will be in the minutes after Tino is down."

"Right."

"Judd agreed that if we wait, even for an hour, it could be too late."

"Minute Zero," said Durham. "Yeah, he told me all about it."

Isabella was about to respond, when there was sudden activity at the front gate. The two ducked down farther. Durham carefully raised his binoculars while Isabella watched through a camera with a long-range zoom.

"Is that him? Is that Zagwe?" asked Durham, watching a tall thin man exit the gate.

"Yes!" she said, snapping away with the camera. Zagwe was wearing a light gray suit, far too big for his skinny frame. Aviator sunglasses shielded his eyes. "I'm going to follow him. You stay here and watch the house."

"I'll do it," offered Durham. "You're a civilian."

"Negative. This is my case. I'm going."

"I see that," he replied. "But you've got

no experience tailing bad guys. I do. And if something goes wrong, better it falls on me than you. We need you to keep the case moving forward."

"It's my case," she insisted.

"You just said Zagwe was a mass murderer. *A psychopath.*"

Isabella dropped her head in concession and Durham slipped out of the vehicle and into the street.

The residential avenues of the lush Gun Hill neighborhood were mostly empty. Bull, a huge bald American in a golf shirt and jeans, stood out, so he kept a healthy distance. Zagwe marched forward at a steady clip, puffing impatiently on a long cigarette.

Durham cut across an empty field, walking diagonally through a patch of burned grasses. The smell of the embers filled Bull's nose, mixing with the sweet fragrance of the jacaranda trees.

The general stopped at a small corner kiosk. Durham hid behind a thick baobab tree. He watched Zagwe make small talk with the proprietor and then hand him a paper bill in exchange for a pack of cigarettes. *Just out for smokes,* thought Durham.

But rather than return to the villa, Zagwe continued his journey away from the house.

He followed a path along the outer edge of another compound, closely hugging the concrete wall. When he came to the end of the block, Zagwe checked over both shoulders before disappearing around the corner.

Bull waited behind the tree for a few moments, then continued his pursuit.

As he peered around the corner of the wall, *whack!* His ears rang and a sharp pain pierced his skull. Durham stumbled back, holding his head. Zagwe hit him again in the face with something sharp. Bull's head snapped back and blood oozed from a gash on his cheek. In the face of a surprise attack, Durham's instinct was to lunge forward, using his weight against the lighter man. He rushed the general, driving him back into the concrete wall. Zagwe yelled in pain as Bull released a forceful punch into the general's stomach. Bull stepped back to regain his balance and cocked his fist for another blow when he saw a 9mm Makarov pistol in Zagwe's hand.

Durham stepped back again and raised his hands.

"Who the fuck are you?" demanded Zagwe. He was waving the pistol back and forth and trying to catch his breath.

"I'm no one," said Durham.

"You're American. Why are you following me?"

"I'm not following anyone. *You* attacked *me.*"

"Do you know who I am?"

"You are the guy who just hit me in the face."

"Do you know what happened to the last American who was caught following me?"

"I don't know what you are talking about," replied Bull. "I don't know who you are."

"I had him thrown off a bridge."

"I don't know."

"I killed that Yankee like a dog," said Zagwe, narrowing his eyes and raising the pistol to Bull's head.

"I don't know —"

"Just like I'm going to kill you —" Which was when Isabella Espinosa's fist collided with the side of Zagwe's head. The gun fired, the bullet sparking as it ricocheted off the concrete wall. Zagwe turned toward his new attacker just as Isabella unleashed another punch to the base of his nose, which exploded in blood. Zagwe howled and covered his face, blood seeping through his fingers. Isabella spun and delivered a round-house kick to his midsection. Zagwe spilled backward onto the dust, his hand releasing the gun as he hit the ground. Durham

242

grabbed the pistol. "Let's go!" he shouted, and the two Americans turned and fled at full speed.

As they ran between two houses, Durham flung the gun over a compound wall. *"Go, go, go!"* he barked.

Once they reached the Mitsubishi, Durham started up the vehicle and drove slowly out of the neighborhood.

"What happened back there?" Isabella demanded, still fighting to catch her breath.

"He got me."

"I thought you were a professional tracker? A Green Beret!"

"I messed up."

"Yes, you did."

"Thanks for saving me back there."

"Mierda, Bull," she hissed, shaking her head.

"I'll bet it felt pretty good to unload on that guy?" asked Durham with a grin.

"It's my case, Bull."

"I know. I'm sorry."

"Now he knows we are onto him. He's going to be even more careful."

"I know. I fucked up. You saved me. We'll still get him."

"My case. . . ."

They drove in silence, making several U-turns to check for surveillance. When

Bull was confident no one was following them, they headed back to the embassy. As they pulled up to the security barrier and waited for the car to be inspected, Isabella said, "Yes."

"Yes what?" Bull asked.

"Yes. It felt pretty good to unload on that *cabrón.*"

28.

U.S. Department of State, Washington, D.C.
Saturday, 8:05 a.m. Eastern Standard Time
"Here again early on a Saturday?" Serena asked.

"Mmm-mmmm. You know how it is," replied the heavyset secretary who had squeezed herself into her office chair. "If the boss has to work, I got to work."

"That's right."

"Why're you here? Isn't Dr. Ryker traveling?"

"Africa," Serena said. "I'm using the peace and quiet to get my work done."

"Tell me about it! I can't get anything done when Mr. Parker is here, either. I'm putting out fires fourteen hours a day."

"Is Mr. Parker here now?"

"Mmm-hummm, he's here. The Secretary's in a breakfast meeting with the Brazilians, so he's in there with her. Munching on bagels and talking about biofuel subsidies

245

or saving the rain forest or something."

"How's your momma?" asked Serena, noticing a Christmas family picture on her friend's desk.

"She's doing better. I hope to have her come back to the house soon. The doctor says maybe next week."

"Oh, that's good. That's real good. Tell me when she's home. I'll bring you all my crab cakes. A welcome-home crab cake celebration. Maybe that'll motivate her to get better faster and come on home?"

"That'd be nice. Momma'd love that."

"I owe her that at least."

"Serena, you aren't here early on a Saturday morning to talk about crab cakes. What're you here for?"

"Research. Dr. Ryker is over in Zimbabwe and there's something funny about the ambassador out there."

"Tallyberger?"

"That's the one."

"With a name like that, how could something not be funny?"

"That's the truth!" The two women laughed aloud. "But I can't put my finger on what's wrong." Serena lowered her voice. "You know anything about him?"

"Skinny white fella. Close to Rogerson. They did some tours together. Helsinki and

Port Moresby, if I remember right."

"His Zimbabwe tour is up soon, right?"

The secretary typed into her computer for a few moments, her long fingernails clacking loudly on the keys. "Yep. He's a short-timer. Due to leave for Embassy London in a few weeks. Maybe he's acting funny because he's got one foot out the door already. I've seen it before."

"Could be. I think there's something else," Serena whispered.

"You know something about Tallyberger?" her friend asked in a hush.

Serena leaned in farther. "Maybe something from . . . Port-au-Prince?" Serena pointed at the computer.

"Haiti? What do you know about what happened in Haiti?"

"That's why I'm asking you," Serena said. "Can you check his file?"

The secretary shuffled in her chair, then craned her neck to look over Serena's shoulder. Satisfied no one was watching them, she shrugged.

"You're not here, right?"

Serena shook her head.

"And so you're not asking me about anything, right?"

Another shake. "So you'll check his file for me?"

"Don't need to. Already know what happened," she said, tapping a long fingernail to her temple.

"You do? I knew I came to the right woman."

"Well, I mostly know. He curtailed Port-au-Prince."

"Tallyberger cut short his Haiti tour?"

"Uh-huh."

"When? Why?"

"About ten years ago. I don't know why for real, but something happened. Something bad. There was an investigation and then some kind of settlement. As part of the deal, he was moved early. That's how he got reposted to Helsinki."

"Helsinki?"

"Yep. To be with Rogerson. That's why he's so loyal. Rogerson saved his career."

"What did he do to have to curtail?"

"Dunno."

"You don't know why he was forced to leave Haiti?"

"Nope. They buried it. Must've been part of the deal. I only know there were no charges. No press. No personnel records. Someone swept it right under the rug. But it must've been something bad for him to agree."

"Wow. That is something. How do you

know about it?"

"Because I was sitting right here."

"I knew I came to the right woman!"

"The question is: How did you know to ask me about Tallyberger in Haiti?"

"I can't say. Girls' secret."

"I just gave you the dirty goods on him and you can't say why you're even asking?"

"Do you really need to know?"

"No," she said, sinking back in her chair. "I shouldn't have even asked. After all these years, I know better."

"Thank you. I owe you one."

"Is that all? You came up here for gossip on skinny old Arnold Tallyberger?"

"Nah. The real favor I need is something serious."

"More serious than asking me to dig into confidential personnel files? What could it be?"

"Can you find out who's on the short list to be our next ambassador to Cairo? The committee hasn't announced anything yet, but I need to know today."

"Is Dr. Ryker working on Egypt, too? I can't keep that man's program straight. No wonder you're here sweating on the week-end!"

"Nah. I just need to know. I know the Deputies Committee keeps these names tight. But it sure would make my life easier to know who will be going to Embassy Cairo."

The secretary clicked away again on her keypad, then scanned the empty room. "I didn't tell you anything."

"Of course not. I'm not even here."

"Sandoval."

"Who?"

"Ruben Sandoval. Fund-raiser for the President. Owns a franchise chain of organic juice bars and yoga studios in Florida."

"Never heard of him."

"No one has."

29.

"He is our father and our grandfather!" screamed the emcee up on the stage. The crowd, a sea of fists raised high in the air, roared its approval. "President Tinotenda is the soldier for the people! The defender of the poor! The protector of the righteous!"

Judd, watching from the back of the cavernous national stadium, had a sinking feeling of regret for not waiting until Bull and Isabella returned to the embassy so they could join him. Ambassador Tallyberger had insisted he wasn't able to spare a security officer. That was no surprise. Brock Branson, the CIA station chief, had offered to send along an escort, but — stupidly, he realized now — Judd refused. "I've been in more dangerous places than a campaign rally. I'll be fine," he had said proudly. At the time he meant it.

251

"Our president is the lion that kills the enemy in the night! He feasts on their fear! He devours their hearts! He is the long spear that pierces evil in the night! He brings death and anguish to those who betray the people!"

President Winston Tinotenda, in the center of the stage, listened patiently to the praise singer from the comfort of an upholstered burgundy throne. He was wearing a dark tailored business suit and a white baseball cap emblazoned with the symbol of his party, a black fist. Across his front, a green silk sash hung over one shoulder as if he were a geriatric beauty contestant.

In a smaller but no less ornate throne next to him sat Harriet Tinotenda, the first lady. Her full-length dress had a traditional African pattern but the sunlight revealed a luxurious twist: encrusted gemstones in a ring around the collar and in long, glistening stripes along the sleeves. She wore a bored expression of disinterest but was clearly savoring the adoration.

"Our Father is the provider of our bounty! The creator of economic opportunity! The deliverer of light! The vessel of truth!" continued the emcee, who was aggressively stomping around the stage as he pumped up the crowd. "Our Father is the sun that shines brighter than all the other stars! The earthquake that shakes the foundation of our enemies!"

Behind the president stood a wall of brawny men in military uniforms, frozen at attention.

Now Judd's regret was turning to concern. The stadium continued to fill, people streaming in from all directions.

"The victor in today's elections! His Excellency, Father of the Nation and Warrior of the People, President Winston Tinotenda!" As the president strained to rise, the crowd shrieked and surged toward the front.

Judd ducked behind a concrete pillar to avoid being swept with the masses onto the stadium's field. As the swelling subsided, he peeked around the corner. Tino was now on his feet but hunched over in front of the microphone. The stadium went quiet in anticipation of the president's speech. He licked his lips and scanned the sea of faces.

Satisfied, he declared, "Today, my children, your Father will be victorious!" The crowd erupted with cheers and fist pumping.

"Today we will mightily defeat the forces that want to destroy the Revolution! We will never allow the traitors and sellouts to rule this country! We will fight them in the ballot box! We will fight them on the battlefield! We will fight them in the streets!"

The crowd roared.

"We must fight the traitors!" demanded the president.

"Fight the traitors!" yelled the crowd.

"Will we allow the puppets to win?" boomed Tino.

"No!" shouted the crowd in unison, punching the air.

Tino raised a fist over his head. "Will we ever give our nation back to the imperialists?"

"No!"

Judd's stomach fluttered.

"Will we allow our Mother's milk to be stolen again?"

"No!"

The crowd's frenzy was escalating.

"Will we allow our brothers' farms to be taken away again?"

"No!"

"Will we allow the British to ever rule this country again?"

"No!"

"Will we allow the Americans to enslave our people again?"

"No!"

Uh-oh. Not good, thought Judd.

"Will you ever have another Father of the

Nation?"

"No!"

The crowd heaved again toward the front. Judd clung to the pillar, but he was pushed from behind and his fingers lost their grip. He gasped for breath as he realized he was helpless to stop the momentum.

The stampede thrust forward. *Oh, shit!* He was lifted off his feet and swept down toward the stadium floor. *I'm going to be trampled!* Just as panic began to swell inside his stomach, firm hands gripped his arm and pulled him up and back against the tide.

Judd turned to face his anchor, a huge African man with thick arms but no expression at all on his face. Like walking upriver in a whitewater rapid, the man towed Judd against the waves of people rushing forward. As Judd limply allowed himself to be dragged, he suddenly wondered: *Am I being rescued? Or kidnapped?*

Before Judd could decide, they reached a sanctuary underneath the stadium.

"You are safe now," said his rescuer.

"Who are you?" asked Judd.

"But you must leave. It is not safe for you to stay here."

"I'm with the American embassy," said Judd, hoping this might help protect him but immediately realizing how stupid it must have sounded.

"Please. You must go," the man said.

"Who are you?"

"I am no one."

"Why did you help me?"

"Brock," he whispered.

"What?"

"I am a friend of Brock's."

"Brock Branson? From the embassy? He sent you?"

"You must go now."

Crack! Crack! Crack! exploded in the air. Judd whipped his head toward the source of the gunshots. Up onstage, President Tinotenda was firing a pistol into the air.

"Forward with the Revolution! Forward with Zimbabwe!" he chanted, pointing the gun at the heavens. *Crack crack crack!*

Judd turned back toward his rescuer, but he was gone.

30.

CIA Headquarters, Langley, Virginia
Saturday, 8:58 a.m. Eastern Standard Time
Sunday rubbed his eyes. He'd been staring at banking records on his computer screen for hours. He didn't want to use his trump card, but he felt it was his only choice. He needed answers. Reluctantly he picked up the phone.

"I've got an urgent Purple Cell request for voiceprints on a target."

The other end of the line responded with several questions, which Sunday answered in rapid response. Then: "Max O'Malley, DOB January 15, 1950, AmCit, last known location, Bangkok, Thailand. Let's start with anything from the past week."

Sunday paused to sip coffee while he waited for results. When they arrived, he nearly choked.

"Nothing? Nothing at all? How is that possible? What about the past month? . . .

Nothing?"

Sunday drummed his fingers on his desk.

"Okay. New target. Lucky Magombe, no DOB, likely Zimbabwean citizen, possibly South African. Last known location, Johannesburg, South Africa. Again, start with the past week."

After a few moments his screen flashed. Four hits, starting with the most recent, a call intercepted less than two hours ago:

SATURDAY OCT07, CALL INITIATED 1.15PM CAT/7.15AM EST. TRANSCRIPT:
Unidentified 1: Hello.
Target: Is this the Canterbury Cricket Club?
U1: Is this Cannonball?
T: Yebo.
U1: Your membership has been prepared. Are you now ready to play?
T: Is the cricket team there?
U1: Yes, everything is in place. The target is in our sights. We are only waiting for your approval.
[inaudible]
[End call]

SATURDAY OCT07, CALL INITIATED
12.24PM CAT/6.24AM EST.
TRANSCRIPT:

Target: Magombe.

Unidentified 1: I am calling for Cannonball.

T: What is it?

U1: Are you ready to join the Canterbury Cricket Club? Your membership has been prepared. It will be available this Sunday. At noon. Sir?

T: Not yet. Wait for my word.

U1: Shall we continue with your membership preparations for the Canterbury Cricket Club?

T: Yes.

[End call]

The third call was from two days earlier.

THURSDAY OCT05, CALL INITIATED
4.22PM CAT/10.22AM EST.
TRANSCRIPT:

Target: Magombe.

Unidentified 2: It's me, Mariana.

T: Are we making progress?

U2: Yes, all the materials have been pre-positioned for the vote on Saturday. It's looking good. I think Gugu should feel confident.

T: Very good.

259

U2: How about the parallel voting tabulation?

T: We will be ready, Mariana. I will let you know when we have the real numbers.

U2: Excellent.

T: Have you spoken with your friend in Washington?

U2: Yes, Lucky. He will help us.

T: Has he agreed?

U2: Not yet, but I'm confident he will.

T: He'll have influence with the embassy?

U2: Yes. He's not part of the regular diplomatic corps. He's a special envoy. I've worked with him before. We can trust him.

T: His name is Rider?

U2: Ryker. Judd Ryker.

Shit. Sunday kept reading.

T: What else does he know?

U2: Only what he needs to.

T: Very good. Keep me informed.

[End call]

The final intercepted call was nearly a week old.

MONDAY OCT02, CALL INITIATED 11.54PM CAT/5.54PM EST. TRANSCRIPT:
Unidentified 1: Hello.

T: Is this the Canterbury Cricket Club?

U1: Is this Cannonball?

T: Yebo. Is this line clear?

U1: Yes.

T: Are you certain? We need to be careful.

U1: Yes, Cannonball. We are following security protocols.

T: Is the team here?

U1: The team has arrived. They are ready and awaiting your orders. The payment is complete. They only need the time and the target.

T: This Sunday. Noon.

U1: Yes, Cannonball. Sunday noon. And the target?

T: Chimurenga. General Simba Chimurenga.

U1: Confirmed, Cannonball. Chimurenga is the target.

[End call]

Shit, shit. He picked up the phone again.

Jessica was driving her white Honda minivan, both children strapped into car seats in the back, when her cell phone blinked. "Good morning," she answered.

"Ma'am. Sorry to call you again," Sunday said. "We've got another problem. A big problem."

31.

Harare, Zimbabwe
Saturday, 3:05 p.m. Eastern Standard Time
Judd pushed through the crowds outside the national stadium. When he finally spied the embassy car, he breathed a heavy sigh of relief. The driver opened the door and Judd dove inside, savoring the quiet and space of the rear of the vehicle.

"Are you all right, sir?"

"Yes, I'm fine. Back to the embassy."

"Are you quite sure, sir?"

"Yes, thank you. The embassy." Judd slumped back into the seat as the car accelerated. Relieved, he ran through the events of the past few minutes in his head and tried to make sense of them.

Ding. Text message from Sunday.

> New info. $275m today from
> Bangkok to Chimurenga.

Wow, thought Judd. He texted back.

How much?

USD 275,000,000

Bangkok?

Royal Deepwater

$ for what?

IDK. Working on it.

Thx. Keep me posted.

After a pause, Sunday asked:

Do you know Max O'Malley?

No. Who is he?

Royal Deepwater

What does that mean?

IDK yet. Still digging.

Judd turned his attention to the window and the passing scene. Rows of market stalls lined the road, displaying bright green avocados the size of footballs, mountains of small oranges, and stacks of brown bread loaves. The vehicle whisked past columns of women, each one carrying a baby on her back and balancing a huge bundle on her head. Judd noticed one woman sashaying down the side of the road with a colorful wrap around her waist, the middle of her wide backside displaying the smiling face of President Winston Tinotenda. Judd dialed a number.

"Mariana Leibowitz," the other end replied.

"It's Judd," he said.

"Yes, darling. Of course. What do you have for me?"

"I've just been to Tinotenda's campaign rally at the national stadium."

"It was scary, right?"

"It was huge."

"That's because the party buses them in from the countryside and gives them a free meal."

"They were all wearing Tino T-shirts," Judd said.

"Yes, of course. They give them those, too. Sometimes they even pay cash. I wouldn't be surprised if they drugged the boys before they got to the rally. It's all for show, Judd darling. Don't be fooled."

"I've seen my share of African elections, but this was still a sight. What are you hearing about the voting?"

"Not good. The entire southern belt is short of ballot papers and some voting stations haven't even opened yet. We're getting reports from many of our strongholds, like Mutare, Chitungwiza, and Gweru, that groups of party youth militia are openly threatening people if they vote for the opposition. We have video from Masvingo showing Tino's thugs in green jumpsuits escorting people into the voting booths. *Into the booths.* Can you believe it?"

"After what I just witnessed, yes, I can."

"The police aren't doing a thing. How can people possibly vote with someone holding a gun to their head? Can you imagine an election like this?"

"Didn't you expect organized intimidation?"

"Yes, but it's still a horrible thing to watch unfold. The worst abuses are taking place in the far north. The army has deployed all around Kanyemba. They've barred international observers and no one can get in or get out. Kanyemba is on complete lockdown," she said.

"What's going on up there?"

"No one is saying. I can't find out anything."

"So what are you going to do, Mariana?"

"We'll document all of the abuses and
present them to the observer teams. Not
much more we can do."

"You know that won't work," Judd said.
"The observers will report any incidents as
isolated problems. Unless you can prove it
affected the final outcome, it won't matter,
Mariana."

"I am well aware, darling."

"So then . . . ?"

"Gugu Mutonga can still win. She's that
popular."

"Assuming you get enough votes despite
Tino's thugs and the missing ballots, what
are you doing to keep the counting fair?"

"Oh, Judd," said Mariana. "That is an
excellent question. That is, in fact, *the* question. I'm so glad you asked."

"And?"

"We have a guardian angel."

"A what?"

"A guardian angel. Watching over the voting."

"Who's that?"

"I'm sorry, I cannot say."

"You just said you were glad I asked. Now
you won't tell me who it is?"

"I'm glad you asked because it means you understand what's happening in Zimbabwe today."

"But you won't say who?"

"I'll tell you when you need to know, darling."

"Is it an embassy? Is one of the foreign embassies helping you?"

"Fuck no, Judd." Mariana forced a laugh. "You should have learned that by now. We can't count on any of them. They are all too worried about relations to get involved with any one candidate. They're all neutral."

"Yes, yes. I know."

"And do you know who's the worst?"

"I think I can guess."

"Right. The Yankee fucking Doodle dandies. Sometimes it's embarrassing to be an American in Africa. And that Tallyberger is a joke. A sick joke."

"Okay, Mariana. If you survive the voting and you somehow make it through the counting, how do you stop Tinotenda and the army from just refusing to step down?"

"That would be a coup."

"Yes, it would."

"Well, that's where you come in, Judd. Why do you think I called you in the first place?"

"I'm still not sure."

"We've fixed a coup together once before. We succeeded marvelously in Mali. Why can't we do it again in Zimbabwe?"

"You dragged me into this because you are predicting a coup?"

"In a way, yes."

"It's a completely different situation."

"Well, you're here now. That's why Landon Parker sent you. To help me."

"I'm not sure Parker sees it that way."

"Of course he doesn't, darling. That's one of Landon's charms. Even when he's doing the right thing, he's not sure why. But, deep down, you also know that's why you're here. You have to accept it. You are here to help me ensure Gugu Mutonga beats Winston Tinotenda."

She's right. I am.

After an awkward pause, Judd asked, "What do you need?"

"I'll need you soon enough. The question now is, what can *I* do for *you*?"

"Actually . . ." Judd decided it was worth a shot. "You ever heard of Royal Deepwater Venture Capital?"

"Nope."

"How about Max O'Malley?"

"Max O'Malley?" she giggled. "What kind of Washington lobbyist would I be if I didn't know him?"

"So, you've heard of him?"

"Heard of him? I've been to *parties* with him, darling."

"Parties?"

"Max O'Malley is the definition of being plugged in. He goes way back with some very important people. He hit the big time during the Reagan arms buildup."

"He's a defense contractor?"

"I don't know what he's into these days, but that's how he got started."

"And why are you at parties with him?"

"He's a bundler."

"What's a bundler?"

"Oh, Judd, you're adorable. I forgot you are still new to Washington. A bundler is a fund-raiser. The guy is a money machine for politicians."

"Which politicians?"

"He's big-time. In the last election, Max O'Malley was one of the largest campaign fund-raisers for the President."

Oh, shit.

"Judd, darling, why are you asking? What's he got to do with Zimbabwe?"

"I'll tell you when you need to know."

32.

Sunday stared with disbelief at the page in front of him, dominated by thick black lines. This wasn't how it was supposed to be.

In hindsight, Sunday was perfect for the Directorate of Intelligence, the analytical branch of the Central Intelligence Agency. The geeks. His parents had fled Nigeria in the late 1960s, just around the time of the Biafran civil war, which killed close to three million people. Although Sunday's family was Hausa-speaking and originally from the north of the country, his father had been working in the southeast. He had seen trouble brewing and cleverly decided, for reasons never made clear to Sunday, that it was time to go. But rather than return to the north and the safety of his home village, Sunday's father took a fishing boat to Cameroon, then made his way via Chad,

Tunisia, and Paris to East London. Sunday's dad worked three jobs to earn enough money to bribe a customs officer to smuggle his young wife out of the country and into Britain. Once they were reunited, they followed a distant cousin to suburban Los Angeles, where one spring Sunday morning their first son was born and named for that day.

Like many new immigrants, they embraced their adopted country with relish. An American flag hung outside the family home. Sunday's mother fed her growing son macaroni and cheese while his father grilled hamburgers in the backyard while sharing lawn care tips with the neighbors.

But as much as Sunday's family became full-throated Americans, their pride in Nigeria never wavered. Every Thursday evening they ate okra and pumpkin soup, goat stew, and Hausa *koko,* a porridge made from millet. If they had special visitors from the homeland, which was more often than not, they would roast a whole lamb rubbed with spices in a pit in the backyard.

Most of all, Sunday's family closely followed political events back home: coups in 1975, 1983, 1985, 1994. The rise and fall of Shagari, Buhari, Babangida, Abiola, Abacha, Obasanjo, Yar'Adua. The dinner table debates were the main reason Sunday chose political science as his college major.

The taboo topic — the Biafran war and why his father fled — drove Sunday to focus his Ph.D. on political violence. After falling under the wing of Professor BJ van Hollen, Sunday studied the tactics used in Rwanda during the 1994 genocide, trying to understand the motivations of ambitious men and the methods of orchestrating a massacre. How could politicians get neighbors to turn on each other? How did evil men convince ordinary citizens to commit mass murder? What could we learn from these events to prevent them in the future? How to better understand these great moral failures to ensure it *never happens again*?

Sunday was always sharp and followed his father's rigorous work ethic. He knew his own heritage would be a benefit at any American university hungry for a young African star, which he learned could be leveraged into a successful academic career. Princeton, Yale, the University of Chicago — all came calling. But Sunday was swayed by his mentor.

BJ van Hollen had from the very first days urged his best students to consider public service. The campaign had begun with well-timed placements of short summer internships at the State Department and the Department of Defense. Sunday excelled at those opportunities, impressing his supervisors with his long days and incisive analysis of complex political trends. These attributes had also drawn the attention of the U.S. Intelligence Community.

One morning over breakfast, as Sunday was in final preparations for submitting his thesis, van Hollen gave him the pitch: *Join the CIA.*

Sunday presented his final two options to his parents: take a tenure-track job at the University of Chicago or become a junior CIA analyst. A prestigious professorship at one of America's elite centers of learning, writing books, security of tenure, even celebrity. Or toiling in anonymity for your country.

It wasn't even a close call.

Sunday also followed his mentor's advice and shied away from working on Africa early in his career. The last thing he wanted was to be pigeonholed in the continent. Or worse, expose himself to accusations of clientitis.

What he really loved about the job was the open access. To understand what was happening, to solve the world's many puzzles, he had entrée to more information than anyone on the outside. The bargain in his mind was giving up fame and status for the closest thing that existed on the planet to *total information awareness.*

That thought dug into his gut as he stared at the page before him.

Office of Acquisition, Department of Defense
Memo Ref: ███████████/August 1982
SECRET: Operation ███████: Alternative Uranium Sources
Operation ██████████ launched with
████████████████████████████████████
███████████ contractors exploring uranium mines in the following locations:
Shinkolobwe, Zaire
████████████████████████
Kanyemba, Zimbabwe
██████████████
Progress limited due to ████████
████████████████████████████████.
Kanyemba, Zimbabwe operations aborted following compromise of local security arrangements and ████████████
█████████.
Operation ██████████ closed.

Sunday dialed a familiar number.
"Ma'am. It's me again. I've been digging

in the archives looking for anything on Kanyemba. At first I could only find exploratory contracts. Nothing solid. But now I think I've found something. Buried deep in the vault. I've discovered a memo from the early 1980s about a DOD operation at the Kanyemba mine. I'm not sure exactly what it is, but all the key details have been blacked out, even at my security level. Practically the whole memo is redacted. Yes, redacted."

After a long pause, Jessica replied, "I will deal with this."

33.

Ambassador Arnold Tallyberger stood at a safe distance observing. He was strategically positioned in the parking lot of the school that was normally closed on a Saturday but today was a hive of activity.

A long, orderly line of voters had formed: younger men in T-shirts and flip-flops, while most of the older men wore ties and leather shoes. The women were similarly divided by attire. The middle-aged and the elderly showed off their church best and shielded themselves with sun umbrellas. The younger women wore casual dresses, many with babies safely cocooned on their backs in colorful print wraps. The line wasn't moving, but Zimbabweans had grown accustomed to waiting in long queues. It was what many of them did every day, waiting for the bank or a bus or a paycheck. Seizing

276

a captive audience, young boys walked the line selling gum, bags of fried mopane worms, and fluorescent orange Fanta soda. A uniformed policeman, swinging a night-stick, watched intently over the proceed-ings. Other men watched, too, from the shadows, unseen by most but with the full awareness of the crowd.

Tallyberger was trying to appear incon-spicuous today, so he'd replaced his usual pin-striped business suit with casual khaki. Not the tacky safari gear tourists wore, he thought, but the real stuff from South Africa. Hiking boots from a camping gear catalog in Maine and a hunting hat from Australia rounded out his outfit. He was trying to blend in.

The ambassador's attempt at discretion was undermined by the entourage standing directly behind him: two staff assistants, a political officer, his driver, two journalists, and four burly State Department security guards. Out of respect, the local voters pretended not to notice.

If anyone looked at Tallyberger's face, it would have been easy to detect his sense of satisfaction. Hands on hips, lower lip pro-truding, nodding.

But the true target of his approval that afternoon was not the voting. He wasn't even really absorbing the scene before him. Arnold Tallyberger, the U.S. ambassador to the Republic of Zimbabwe and at that moment the chief of the American Embassy Election Observer Mission in Zimbabwe, was daydreaming about London.

Tallyberger had given eight tours, twenty-four years of his life, to the U.S. Foreign Service. He'd stamped passports in Pakistan, Peru, and Papua New Guinea. He'd managed embassy budgets in Finland, Jordan, and Sri Lanka. He'd even survived the ugly incident in Haiti. He shuddered at the thought of that unpleasantness, but, like the Foreign Service, he'd decided what happened was better left quiet, safely out of sight. His rewards for loyalty were the ambassadorships to, first, Mongolia and then Zimbabwe. He was grateful to his patrons within the bureaucracy for his rise to the top. But he harbored a secret disappointment that when his moments of professional glory — being named chief of mission — finally arrived, it was in the isolated capitals of Ulan Bator and Harare. These cities were fine, of course. Lovely places, he thought. Friendly people. And the United States of America had important national interests everywhere, he'd convinced himself. But Mongolia and Zimbabwe weren't hubs for anything. No one ever dropped by on their way somewhere more important. For any trip Ulan Bator and Harare were, literally, the end of the line. But Tallyberger had one last diplomatic tour in him before retirement — the crown jewel, so to speak.

Arnold always loved British adventure novels: Rudyard Kipling, Robert Louis Stevenson, Arthur Conan Doyle. Now he could barely contain himself thinking that he, too, would soon be living in London and enjoying the high life. The black-tie parties, the afternoon strolls in Regent's Park, the chance to meet royalty. He'd paid his dues in the backwaters of the world. Now, at the pinnacle of his career, he was ready for *real diplomacy.*

If he was pleased finally to be posted to the United Kingdom, his wife, Bernice, was jubilant. Ever since she had had a tea set as a child, she'd dreamed of high teas at a posh Bloomsbury hotel. A pot of Earl Grey, raisin scones, strawberries with clotted cream, dainty crustless sandwiches of watercress and cucumber. *Civilization.* Not only would she soon be at the Dorchester or the Savoy whenever she desired, but she would *preside over high tea* as the wife of the U.S. deputy chief of mission. Arnold knew Bernice would love that.

It was too bad, Tallyberger mused, that he would have to be satisfied with playing number two in Britain. Like all the plum ambassadorships, Embassy London always went to a political appointee rather than a career Foreign Service officer. One of the unfortunate realities of the American diplomatic system, he thought. But no time to grumble, he reminded himself. Chin up! Arnold Tallyberger was going to London!

"How do you judge it so far?" asked one of the journalists.

"Excuse me?" asked Tallyberger, snapping back to the present.

"The voting, Mr. Ambassador. How do you judge the voting so far?"

"Ah, yes," he said, taking an exaggerated scan of the line of Zimbabweans waiting patiently for their turn at the ballot box. "Very orderly. Very calm."

"Is that all, Mr. Ambassador?"

Tallyberger turned to the entourage to see all eyes were on him. His political officer, a young woman in her late twenties with wide librarian-style glasses and a clipboard, nodded encouragingly at her boss.

"Are you ready?" the ambassador asked the journalist.

"Yes, sir," he said displaying his pen.

"Fine. The United States is today participating as an international observer. I am proud to be leading the American Embassy Election Observer Mission in Zimbabwe. We are cautiously optimistic the election today will be conducted in a free and fair manner. We are hopeful the will of the Zimbabwean people and their desire for democratic government will be reflected in today's historic vote. From what I have seen so far, I am strongly encouraged. I have witnessed only calm and orderly voting."

"When will the AEEOMZ be issuing a final verdict on the conduct of the elections?"

"Tomorrow."

"Have you spoken with any of the other observer team chiefs?"

"Not yet. But I shall soon call the ambassador from Great Britain."

Great Britain, he thought again.

34.

Georgetown, Washington, D.C.
Saturday, 10:36 a.m. Eastern Standard Time
"Safe!" yelled Jessica, jumping out of her forest green fold-up camping chair.

"Out!" called the umpire.

"Safe by half a step," she said a little quieter. Other parents shot looks of disapproval. "Little League umpires," she muttered under her breath, returning the stares with an awkward smile.

Jessica checked her phone again. Still no messages. *He's probably busy,* she thought.

"Good hit, Toby," she called out to her son, walking back to the dugout with his head hung low. He glanced up at her, expressionless. *No read.* "You'll get him next time!"

As the players, skinny six-year-old boys in baggy baseball uniforms, changed sides, she got up to stretch her legs. "Noah, honey, stay here. Mommy will be right back." She air-dropped a peanut butter granola bar in her son's lap and strolled down the first-base line toward right field. Out of earshot, but maintaining a clear sightline on her younger son.

The sun was already high in the sky, but the Washington autumn air had not yet warmed up. The parking lot behind the field was full of minivans and giant SUVs, packs of small children pouring out in brightly colored uniforms, dragging baseball, soccer, and lacrosse gear. In the distance, over the trees, she could just make out the top of the Washington Monument.

She checked her phone one more time. Nothing.

It's late afternoon already in Harare, she thought. "Fuck it," she said aloud, and pressed a button on her phone.

"Hi, Jess," Judd answered. *No read.*

"I'm sure you are busy. I just wanted to check in."

"Actually, now's a good time. I've got a short break between meetings. How are the boys?"

Jessica glanced up. Noah was happily munching on his breakfast bar. Toby was dancing in center field, straining to pay attention to the game. "They're good. We're at Toby's T-ball game."

"What's the score?"

"They don't keep score in T-ball. How are you?"

"Busy. How about you, sweets?"

"I'm busy, too. How's Zimbabwe?"

"Give me a minute," Judd said. Jessica could hear a door click closed and then her husband returned in a quieter voice. "Jess, I don't really know."

"What do you mean you don't know?"

"The voting is under way and everyone is acting like it's all going smoothly. On the surface everything appears fine. But I'm watching a slow-motion train wreck, and no one else sees it."

"What about the ambassador?"

"Checked out."

"What about your team? You have your superheroes yet?"

Judd knew his wife would eventually ask this very question, so he was ready for a quick mental inventory. Bull, Sunday, and Serena — he could definitely count on them. Mariana Leibowitz and Landon Parker were maybes. Isabella Espinosa? Brock Branson? Too soon to say.

"Yeah. I've got a few folks here I can trust," he replied. "I've got a core team to start with."

"That's good. You'll need them," she said.

"But we are being smothered by . . . how do I put this? By diplomatic impartiality."

"What does *that* mean?"

"Instead of backing one candidate, the embassy is pretending like we have no preferences. We've neutered ourselves. We are just waiting for the outcome everyone already knows. Tinotenda's put everything in place to ensure his reelection and I can't get anyone to see it. Or to change course. I'm shouting into the wind. And once the election results are announced tomorrow, we'll have no real options left."

"Don't get frustrated. You have to force the issue, Judd. Isn't that why you rushed there in the first place?"

"Yes," he answered. "I was worried I was getting here so late that I'd miss the window of opportunity. That I'd be too late."

"Minute Zero."

"Exactly. So, I thought I might miss Minute Zero in Zimbabwe. But now I'm starting to think it may never happen. Maybe nothing is going to happen."

"Then you have to *make* it happen. You have to create Minute Zero."

At that moment Judd knew immediately she was right.

"But how?" he asked.

She was ready. "If everyone is locked into

a position, you have to change things up. Introduce a new factor, a piece of information — something to break everything loose."

"I know everything here is connected, but I can't yet see how. I'm in the dark. I don't have the big picture."

"You can do this, Judd. It's just another puzzle you have to solve. You've done it before."

"A puzzle I have to solve to save S/CRU. To save my experiment."

"Forget about that," she said. "Don't think like a bureaucrat. Clear your head and focus on your outcome. Focus on Zimbabwe. If something bad is about to happen, then you have to stop it. Whatever happens to your job, you'll be able to hold your head high. That's your measure of success, not saving your office."

"I know I'm being played. Someone is pulling my strings. Not just Landon Parker."

"Who?" Jessica asked.

"I, um . . ." Judd thought about this for a moment. "I don't know."

"There's no Wizard of Oz, Judd. That's just in your mind."

"There's something else, Jess."

"Okay . . ."

"Blowback."

"What?"

"Political blowback. I'm onto something and worried about where it may lead. I think the trail here might go all the way back to Washington. To high-level Washington."

"Corruption?"

"I don't know."

"Well, *shit,* Judd. You better cover yourself. And fast. You have to bring someone else inside as insurance. You know anyone at the Department of Justice?"

Through the phone, Jessica could hear a loud knock, then a woman's voice apologizing, "Sorry to interrupt. The car is waiting for us."

"Yes, thank you, Isabella. I'm coming," Jessica heard her husband reply. Then back to her: "Thanks, Jess. I think I just might know someone."

35.

Undisclosed Location
Saturday, 10:50 a.m. Eastern Standard Time
Down in the parched valley, the heat radiated up from the ground, creating hazy ripples in the air. Tsetse flies and mosquitoes swarmed in dark clouds. Oblivious to the rising temperature or the biting insects, the Northrop Grumman RQ-4 Global Hawk taxied to clear the springbok antelope and zebras that had roamed onto the gravel runway. The beasts snorted at the all-white intruder and galloped away into the bush.

Once the first pass was complete, the Global Hawk spun 180 degrees and immediately accelerated. After a few seconds it veered upward toward the sun.

Exactly 9,981 miles away, in an airconditioned trailer at the edge of Creech Air Force Base in southern Nevada, a young drone pilot gripped his joystick. An open can of Mountain Dew and a half-eaten packet of teriyaki beef jerky lay on the desk next to him. He gnawed on a long piece of jerky as he tested the Global Hawk's rudder capabilities. The pilot flew the stealth surveillance drone in a tight figure-eight pattern and watched on the screen as the plane responded to his commands. Satisfied, he turned his attention to a second screen and flipped a switch, revealing a sepia version of the first screen. He scanned the images, confirmed all systems were working, gulped down the jerky, and touched a button on his earpiece.

"This is Leo Base One," he said into a headset. "We are live with Vapor Four. Geothermal scanner is also hot. Repeat, Vapor Four is geothermal hot."

"Roger Leo Base One" was the robotic reply. "Vapor Four is live and geothermal hot."

"Confirming target Kanyemba, Zimbabwe. GPS coordinates now being sent."

"GPS coordinates received, Leo Base One. Target confirmed."

"Are we a go?"

"Affirmative, Leo Base One."

"Roger that. Vapor Four is en route. ETA to target is eighty-six minutes."

"Roger that, Leo Base One."

The pilot flipped his headset mic up over

his head and turned to his colleague sitting nearby. "You better let AFRICOM know their special bird is wheels-up and hot."

A few seconds later the message was received by United States Africa Command headquarters at Kelley Barracks in Stuttgart, Germany. Less than one minute after that, Colonel David Durham, sitting in the medical unit at the U.S. embassy in Harare, felt his cell phone vibrate in his pocket. He set down the ice pack he was holding to his cheek, revealing a dozen stitches in a line under his eye. He fished out his phone and glanced at his message:

Bird up. U owe me a big one dude.

Bull pressed the cold pack back against his cheek, winced at the pain, and then allowed himself a little smile.

36.

Harare, Zimbabwe
Saturday, 4:55 p.m. Central Africa Time
The blast of frigid air-conditioning hit Judd smack in the face as he entered the hotel lobby. Wearing a gray pin-striped suit and retro G-man glasses, he looked like a professor dressing up as a banker. He was closely trailed by Isabella Espinosa, in the no-nonsense black suit of a legal prosecutor, and Bull Durham, in his formal Army service uniform. The silver eagle insignia of a U.S Army colonel, a Special Forces patch, and the dark green beret hinted at his military potency. Across Bull's bruised cheek, a row of butterfly bandages, like the laces on a football, gave the additional impression of a man calm on the outside but coiled underneath for extreme violence.

The three Americans marched into the hotel between two six-foot-high brass lions guarding the front. They were stopped suddenly by an African porter in a red colonial uniform.

"Welcome to the Meikles Hotel. Are you checking in?" the man asked with a dramatic bow at the waist.

"No. We are meeting someone," Judd replied. Over the porter's shoulder, he scanned the lobby for a man who matched the profile photo Brock Branson had shared back at the embassy.

One side of the lobby was crowded with middle-aged Europeans in matching sky-blue T-shirts. *UN peacekeeper blue.* On the fronts of their shirts was printed in black: **COMMONWEALTH ELECTION OBSERVER TEAM.** On the back was a large red capital *C.*

"Targets," Bull scoffed, elbowing Judd in the ribs.

At the other end of the lobby, Judd cataloged Korean tourists, South African businessmen, and American game hunters carrying long rifle cases and talking too loudly. A musical troupe, wearing beads and zebra skins, drummed in one corner. No sign of General Simba Chimurenga.

"Perhaps you'll be more comfortable waiting in the Explorer's Club, *baas,*" offered the porter, directing them to a lounge off the lobby.

The three Americans walked past a stuffed cheetah guarding the bar entrance. They settled into a quiet table at the back. Bull excused himself and took a scouting position by the door. Isabella also got up from the table and said she was going to check with the hotel staff.

Alone, Judd absorbed the unapologetic nineteenth-century imperial ambiance. The walls of the Explorer's Club were adorned with the stuffed heads of a cape buffalo, a crocodile, a warthog. A large kudu head stared blankly at Judd, its twisting horns pointing to the darkwood-paneled ceiling. Hung between the wildlife trophies were grainy black-and-white photos of European men posing over dead animals, holding up the horns in one hand and gripping a rifle in the other.

A waiter arrived and Judd ordered three gin and tonics.

After a few minutes, Isabella returned to the table. "Not here yet. But the front desk says we'll definitely know when the general arrives."

"Good," he said, just as the waiter delivered the cocktails. "So, Isabella. Why the Justice Department?"

She eyed him. "Why not?"

"I'm curious how anyone becomes a war

criminal hunter. How does that happen?"

"After law school, I tried the junior associate thing at a big Los Angeles corporate firm. Wasn't for me. Just seemed like a waste of all that studying."

"So you gave up the money for public service?"

"Yep," she said, taking a sip.

"What about your parents? Weren't they disappointed?"

"My mom wanted me to be a civil rights lawyer. That wasn't my thing, either. But she's happy with my career. She's now one of those annoying first-generation immigrants who won't stop talking about her successful daughter. What about you? How did you wind up at the State Department?"

Judd was preparing an evasive answer when loud noises from the lobby interrupted. Bull gave Judd a thumbs-up and then turned to watch the hotel entrance fill with armed soldiers. Judd heard shouting in a foreign language he assumed was the local Shona dialect. Bull stepped back from the bar door just as an entourage burst through the entrance, led by a face Judd recognized from the embassy photo.

General Chimurenga was sporting a freshly pressed military jacket with gold tassels on the shoulders and a rack of medals across his broad chest. His flat-top hat was pulled low, his eyes barely visible below the brim. He appeared fit and muscular, but the hint of a second chin suggested a weakness for heavy food. On his face, he wore an impatient scowl.

"Where's Branson?" he demanded.

"I'm sorry, General, but Brock Branson couldn't make it," offered Judd, accepting the general's crushing handshake.

"Typical Branson. He insisted on a meeting, but now *he's too busy.* You are aware today is our election, yes?"

"Of course, General."

"And I am managing election security for the entire country?"

"Yes, General. I know you are a very busy man."

"You see those foreigners from the Commonwealth in the lobby? They are my guests today. I'm responsible for their safety. How would it look if some troublemakers hurt those people while I am in a bar here talking with you?"

"General, I appreciate you making time on this important day. We only need ten minutes."

"You have five. What do you need?"

"I'm Judd —"

"Yes, Ryker," interrupted Chimurenga.

"You are the crisis manager from the State Department. And Colonel Durham is from the Pentagon. And Miss Espinosa is from your Justice Department."

"So you know who we are," said Judd.

"This is my country, Dr. Ryker. I know everyone who is coming and going. That is my job."

"Then you also must know why we are here."

"Yes. That is why I agreed to take this meeting. We have the same objective: to prevent any scoundrels from causing violence in my peaceful country. There are bandits, you must know, who use the cover of the election to make mischief. We cannot allow that. I am happy the American government, which so often misunderstands Zimbabwe, shares this view and has sent you to assist us in this important moment."

I can play along, thought Judd. "Indeed, General. We are concerned about election violence. How are events proceeding today?"

"Ahhh, very well. Our diligent preparations are paying off. Things are calm."

"What about the reports of attacks on Gugu Mutonga's supporters?"

"Shame. They are true. I am sorry to admit it, but some of our president's supporters are very patriotic. They are simple peasants who do not understand politics and how it is played. They can become fervent. Sometimes too fervent. Even violent. This is part of our education campaign. We must instruct the people to express their differences at the ballot box and not with a gun or a panga. I think the peaceful voting today suggests we are succeeding."

"I'm also here to express the American government's deep concern about the results of the election being honored by all parties."

"I have heard the speeches from Ambassador Tallyberger."

"I have been sent here especially by the Secretary of State to make this clear."

"And I am here —" began Bull Durham.

"What happened to your face?" asked Chimurenga, touching his own cheek.

"Accident," Bull said.

"Oh, sorry, Colonel. I am so sorry."

"Not your fault, General. Shall I continue?"

Chimurenga nodded.

"I am here representing the Secretary of Defense," Bull Durham said, standing tall.

"The Secretary of Defense sent you? Ahhh, the Pentagon. I've been there many times. We used to cooperate, to work together. But those days have passed."

"I don't know what you're referring to, General," Durham replied.

"History runs in circles, Colonel. We were partners once, and we will be partners again."

"I am here to share the Secretary of Defense's message that we expect the winner of the election will be allowed to take office."

"Of course, my friends. We all expect the same thing. However, we also expect the American government to accept the will of the people."

Bull and Judd both nodded.

"Ambassador Tallyberger has also given my government assurances the United States is prepared to be a stabilizer and, once you see how free and fair our elections are, you will make a statement quickly. That will help to erase any doubts and to deter troublemakers."

Bull and Judd looked at each other.

"And we expect," Chimurenga added, with the hint of a snarl, "sanctions — the illegal sanctions you have placed on my country — will be removed once the election is complete and the results are announced."

"That will depend, General," responded

Judd. *Let's see how he handles a curveball.* "There is the sensitive matter of Motowetsurohuro. We have questions about the killings in Kanyemba."

"Ahhh that. A terrible story. That Motowetsurohuro breaks the heart of President Tinotenda. We have investigated those stories thoroughly, and no bodies were ever found. I think that one is more legend than truth. We have told this to the United Nations." Chimurenga turned to Isabella. "I sincerely hope your Attorney General did not send you all this way to our beautiful country to investigate a fairy tale?"

Swing and a miss.

"No, sir," replied Isabella.

"Special Agent Espinosa is here to track suspicious financial transactions," Judd said.

"Ahhh, very good. You are welcome. There is indeed bad money coming into Zimbabwe. We have long suspected that international criminals are infecting our country by providing money to political parties. Illegal money. I trust you will be investigating the Democracy Union of Zimbabwe. They are funded by agitators. We have chased the scoundrels away, but they send their poisonous money back to Zimbabwe to cause trouble. I hope you will help us to stop that."

"Are you suggesting Gugu Mutonga is being backed by criminals?" Judd asked.

"She is an intelligent woman. One of Zimbabwe's best lawyers. I have great respect for her. But she does not know the snakes with whom she sleeps."

Strike two.

Isabella looked to Judd. *Where are you going with this?*

"Actually, General, we have identified one suspicious wire transfer." *How about an inside fastball?* Judd leaned in closer and lowered his voice. "Earlier today a very large amount was paid into a bank here in Zimbabwe from a well-known criminal cartel in Asia."

"That is suspicious," said Chimurenga. "Do you know the recipient?"

"Not yet. The sender was in Thailand — that much we do know. But such a large amount on an election day is raising red flags in Washington."

"I see." *No reaction.*

"When there is a suspicious transaction of two hundred and seventy-five million dollars, it draws the attention of my government."

Chimurenga's poker face broke. He turned to look at Colonel Durham, who just nodded slowly.

"How much did you say, Dr. Ryker?"

"Two hundred and seventy-five million."

"Are you quite sure? That's a lot of money for a poor country."

"Yes. We have it from a very reliable source. That precise amount arrived in the country this morning from an account in Bangkok."

"Well, that is worrisome. I will call the central bank. I will have my people look into it right away."

"Thank you, General. Anything you hear back, you can pass to Mr. Branson."

"If you will allow me, Dr. Ryker." The general stood up. "Now I must go. I have urgent business to attend to."

"Yes, General."

"Enjoy the rest of your stay in Zimbabwe. I trust you won't be disappointed if we do not have a crisis during your visit. I'm sorry you've come here and wasted your time."

37.

Harare, Zimbabwe
Saturday, 5:22 p.m. Central Africa Time
"His Excellency, Father of the Nation and Warrior of the People, President Winston H. R. Tinotenda, will see you now," said the butler.

Retired General Solomon Zagwe, formerly the President of Ethiopia and once the leader of a fearsome million-man army, bowed his head and entered the salon alone.

"My dear Solomon. Come in, my brother," said Tinotenda, gesturing to a chair beside him. Like all the other seats in the room, it was six inches shorter than his throne, a deliberate furniture alteration that had grown over the years as the president's slouch worsened.

"Thank you, Mr. President, for seeing me today."

"Of course! For you, my dear Solomon, of course!" replied the president, shooing away the staff with a flick of his wrist.

Once the two old men were alone, the visitor looked up at his protector. "I know this is a very busy day for you, Winston."

"Election today? Ha!" Another dismissive flick. "So many elections . . . The work for today was complete long ago. There was nothing for me to do other than to speak to the people and then go home to my *kumusha* to vote. It was rather boring." The president coughed gently, then wiped his mouth with the back of his hand.

"I understand your speech at the national stadium today was a great success," Zagwe offered.

"I have given so many speeches . . ." Tinotenda trailed off, his attention distracted by a bird landing on the windowsill.

Tino's head jolted as if he had suddenly awoken. He looked again at his visitor as if for the first time. "Solomon! So good of you to come see me! We have been through much together, haven't we?"

"Yes, Winston."

"Poland?"

"Saudi Arabia. You remember Jeddah?"

"Yes, of course. Jeddah. Horrid place. Den of troublemakers. You were so young. So hungry. Just a boy. But they made you a man."

"Yes, they did."

"And they gave you a start in business — your first mining investment if I am not mistaken."

"Yes, Winston. I met many powerful people in Saudi Arabia."

"Yes, yes, Solomon. Your first mining investment. You and the prince and the American. It was right here in Zimbabwe. Somewhere in the north. Kan . . . Kanya . . . Kanyambo, is it?"

"Kanyemba."

"Ah, yes, Kanyemba! Of course. Horrid place. Den of troublemakers." The president coughed again, then looked frantically over his shoulder. "Where is the steward? Where is my tea?"

"You sent him away, Winston. Shall I call him back?"

"No. He cannot be trusted."

"The tea boy?"

"None of them."

"Who, Winston? Who cannot be trusted?"

"The Saudis. The British. *The Americans*," he sneered. "They are all traitors and sellouts." The president's face suddenly contorted with confusion. "Solomon, my dear. What has happened to your face?"

Zagwe touched the bandage on his nose, broken by the punch from the American woman. "Oh, this? It is nothing. A small car accident."

"Car accidents can be very dangerous in Zimbabwe."

"Yes, Winston."

"Chenjeri Mutomboro, Dumiso Dube, and Herbert Chingawa — all dead."

"Yes, I know, Winston."

"They were two of my generals and a high court judge. All dead in car accidents."

"Yes, Winston."

"They were accidents. Nothing was ever proven."

"No, Winston."

"No proof!" he shouted.

"Of course not, Mr. President."

"Is that why you are here, Solomon? To inquire about the dead?"

"I am here to check on you, Winston. I'm here to visit my friend."

"But you chose today to visit me, did you not? Election day. I don't believe in co-incidences. What do you need, my old friend?"

"I only came to see how the election is going. To ask how great a victory will you achieve today?"

" *'Après moi le déluge!'* " cried the president, who stood up with a loud groan.

Zagwe reached out to help his friend to his feet.

"I can do it!" Tino insisted, pulling away. "They will regret when I'm gone. But I have no plans to go! You hear that? No plans!"

"Yes, Winston. No one wants you to go."

" 'Après moi le déluge,' " he repeated, slumping back down into his chair with a thud.

"I came to check on you and the election results."

"Ha! Don't lie to me, Solomon," he said, patting Zagwe's hand. "You have come to me today to ask for protection."

Zagwe bowed his head again. "Yes, Mr. President."

"You fear I will lose?"

"No, of course not. You cannot lose. But there are people still chasing me. Those who want to reopen ancient history. To bring the lies of my enemies from Ethiopia here to me. To your beautiful country. I already dealt with one such mosquito."

"Yes, Solomon. I know about Victoria Falls."

"I am sorry about that. I don't want to create problems, Winston. You have been so generous to me. I don't want to bring you any trouble."

"Tourists!" spat Tinotenda.

"It won't happen again. I can assure you."

"Was your accident today another mosquito?" asked Tinotenda, touching his own nose. "Another tourist?"

"No, I don't think so."

"Good. What can I do for you today?"

"You have been a good friend. You have allowed me to live with dignity here in your beautiful city. To continue to work for a living."

"Yes."

"And I have tried to show my gratitude. To stay quiet."

"Yes."

"And to provide you with resources when you need them."

"Yes."

"When you need money for the First Lady, whom can you trust? When you have another campaign, whom can you count on?"

"Yes, yes, Solomon. What is your point?"

"But, Winston," Solomon whispered, "I fear our enemies are getting closer. And we are getting older. What will happen to you when I am gone?"

"Ha!" laughed the president. "You surely did not come here today because you are worried about me."

"You are too wise."

"Why, then, are you here, Solomon?"

"I want to know what will happen to me when you are gone?"

"I have made arrangements."

"What kind of arrangements? Do I need to go back to Jeddah? I need to know, Winston."

"Solomon, my dear" — the president took Zagwe's hand and stroked it gently — "old friends do not abandon each other in their time of need."

38.

U.S. Embassy, Harare, Zimbabwe
Saturday, 5:35 p.m. Central Africa Time

"It says right here, UMBRELLA ROSE is shut down until further notice," repeated Ambassador Arnold Tallyberger, handing the classified cable to Judd. "The uranium mine surveillance program is off."

"Any idea what happened?" Judd asked Brock Branson, who was sitting at the back of the room.

"Nope," he said, shaking his head. "Sorry, amigo. Game off."

"New information must have changed the threat assessment," offered Tallyberger. "Happens all the time, Dr. Ryker."

"But so fast?" Judd realized how naïve his question sounded and immediately regretted asking.

"Washington probably changed their minds," scoffed Branson. "Who knows where the fuck the intel came from in the

309

first place. Once you start paying people for information in the world's shitholes, you get all kinds of weird bullshit. Most of it right out of *Alice in* fucking *Wonderland*."

Tallyberger stared at his shoes.

"So where does that leave us with the drone?" asked Judd.

"Drone?" scoffed Tallyberger. "There was never any drone for Zimbabwe. Who told you that?"

Judd looked to Branson, whose face was a total blank.

"I . . . uh . . . I just assumed, since Zimbabwe was on the list, that a drone would be deployed."

"I am sorry to disappoint you, Dr. Ryker, but it doesn't happen that way. I doubt Zimbabwe would ever make it far enough up the list to warrant a drone overflight. And if it did, I don't see how the local authorities would approve it. Certainly not in the middle of an election. They are very sensitive about sovereignty. Isn't that correct, Brock?"

"Yep. These Zimbos are fucking obsessed with sovereignty. They'd rather starve than give an inch to the imperialists."

Judd's phone buzzed in his pocket. The little screen, in a text from Serena, read simply:

Judd replied:

Who?

Organic juice bar and yoga
studio king of Florida

Ur telling me why?

U asked

I did?

Next US ambo to Egypt

Huh?
"Excuse me, gentlemen." Judd stepped
out of the room and dialed a phone number.
"Foreign Office," answered a woman on
the other end.
"Simon Kenny-Waddington, please."
"May I ask who is calling?"
"Judd Ryker, State Department."
"Ah, yes, very good," she said. "He's been
waiting for your call."

39.

General Simba Chimurenga rolled over in the bed to reach for a highball glass of Johnnie Walker Blue. He was still breathing heavily, so he paused before sipping. Once he caught his breath, he inhaled deeply, then tipped the glass back. The smoky cool liquid ran down his throat. For the second time that evening, he exhaled intensely and moaned from an ecstatic sensation. He licked his lips.

Simba turned his attention to the body lying next to him, a rolling wave of tight black skin glistening with sweat. A white bedsheet covered one leg, but her other leg was in full view. His gaze started at her toes and inched up over her calf, her thigh, her plump *magaro*.

He took another swallow of the Scotch and purred, "Mmmm . . . gooood."

"Yaah, that was good, baby," murmured the woman, rolling over to face him. She clutched his hand and stroked it gently. When he didn't seem to respond, she dug her claws into his skin and scratched the length of his forearm. "You are my lion," growled Harriet Tinotenda.

Simba stared down at her hungrily, but when her eyes met his gaze, he turned away and set the Scotch glass back on the side table.

"Tell me again," the first lady pleaded.

"I told you. It will be soon."

"When, Simba? I don't know if I can take another day."

"I said soon!" He pulled his arm away and poured more Scotch into the crystal glass. He made a mental note to buy another case the next time he passed through Dubai.

"I can't live with that man any longer. Tsaaah! He is so old. So soft. I deserve to be with a real man. I want to be with you. I want us to be together."

"So do I, baby."

"In public."

"So do I. But you have to be patient."

"I *have* been patient! I have kept our secret for years. But I don't want to hide any longer. I can't do it!"

"You won't have to."

"I want it all. And I don't want to apologize for it." She dug her nails into his chest. *"I want it all."*

"You will have it all, Harriet. I promise you."

"Once you are president, I have many ideas. For the schools. For women's health clinics. To make Zimbabwe great again."

"Yes, Harriet."

"Yaah. I want to build a hospital, too. A modern one. Named after my mother."

"She would be proud."

"And I want our first state visit to be to China. I want to go to Hong Kong again."

"Yes, Hong Kong. If that's what you wish."

"Or Paris."

"Yes, Paris."

"I will need all new clothes. The French paparazzi are the cruelest. Tsaaah! They have no scruples. I cannot possibly be photographed next to the French First Lady in old clothes."

"Yes, of course. Whatever you wish, Harriet. You can have it all."

She liked the sound of that. "That's what I want, Simba."

"I will give everything to you."

She nestled into the crook of his arm.

"Did you receive anything special today?"

he asked.

"Oh, yaah. Someone sent me the most beautiful diamond necklace," she said with mock confusion. "But he never left a note, so I do not know who he is. I cannot thank my gallant suitor properly." She pressed against his chest and wiggled her hips.

"I had it flown in especially from a jeweler in Asia," he said, ignoring her gestures. "But made from the stones of our homeland."

"Zimbabwe diamonds."

"*Our* diamonds."

"Yaah. *Our* diamonds," she repeated. She especially liked the sound of that. Harriet rolled over on her back and stared at the ceiling, dreaming of the possibilities of what was about to happen.

"But you must be patient," he scolded. "No one can know about us until the time is right."

"Yes, Simba."

"There will be political considerations."

"Yaah. I understand. I know about politics."

"I still have to clean up a few loose ends."

"Please hurry, my lion." She lowered her chin and glared into his eyes. This time he did not avert her stare. As their eyes locked, she ran her hand under the sheets, up his leg.

Simba Chimurenga snatched the Scotch and took another slug. Setting the glass back on the side table, he missed and it tumbled to the floor. Neither cared about the small pool of golden brown seeping into the carpet.

"Mmmm . . . gooood," groaned the general.

40.

Johannesburg, South Africa
Saturday, 8:13 p.m. Central Africa Time
Lucky Magombe hadn't moved from his seat in ten hours. His eyes watered from staring at the screens through his reading glasses. A steaming cup of tea, recently delivered by his assistant, rested on his desk. A plate of beef stew, bitter greens, and *sadza,* the cornmeal paste that is the national dish of Zimbabwe, sat cold and untouched.

Lucky couldn't eat. His focus was on the eight flat panels arrayed in front of him. At that moment two screens broadcast live television news. The national ZBC1, the government-owned channel, was broadcasting President Winston Tinotenda's speech from earlier that day at the national stadium on a loop. Tinotenda was hunched over the lectern, pounding his fist, and stirring up the crowd. The shot panned to show thousands of the president's supporters raising their fists in unison. Lucky couldn't bear to listen to another Tino rant, so the volume was off. The other TV screen, also silenced, was tuned to the South African Broadcasting Corporation. SABC was running highlights from the South Africa versus West Indies five-day test. Cricket. No news on Zimbabwe.

But Lucky's attention was really concentrated on the other monitors, the ones tracking Zimbabwe's election results in real time. A panel to his left revealed Lucky's hack into the electoral commission's own computers showing the voter roll and live count. He had broken into their system to see exactly what the president's henchmen could see.

It was his own small, private victory against the government that he had hacked their network by himself. He was slightly disappointed it hadn't been more difficult. Didn't the president have enough respect for the opposition to install a proper security system? Of course, Lucky reminded himself, the old man didn't know anything about computers. He probably had never even used one, Lucky guessed. But surely those around him would know better? Surely his national security advisor, Simba

318

Chimurenga, knew about cybersecurity?

An adjacent screen mirrored the official results, a parallel voting tabulation Lucky was compiling through crowdsourcing. The Zimbabwe National Youth Training Association, a nonprofit also secretly bankrolled by Lucky Magombe's personal foundation, had sent its trainees into the field with the latest — and, for Africa's dictators, the most dangerous — weapon in an election: mobile phones. At each of the country's 9,015 polling stations, votes were counted on-site as they came in and the periodic tallies posted on a chalkboard outside every few hours. Lucky's secret army of volunteers was discreetly watching and sending in text messages with the number of voters in line and the voting results as they were posted. Lucky's computers then aggregated all the data, allowing him to compare the official results with the actual results and turnout figures being reported by his parallel network. So far, the two different databases were reporting a 96.45 percent correlation. An acceptable margin of error. Tinotenda was not cheating, thought Lucky. *At least, not yet.*

A third monitor on his right displayed the same election data on a detailed map so Lucky could visualize who was winning each district. So far the results were as expected. Tinotenda was holding his base in the rural swathes of the northern two-thirds of the country. The top half of the map glowed a bright green to show the zones where the president was winning. This was where most Zimbabweans lived and also were places the government could most easily control. The southern third of the country, Matabeleland, was reporting a solid red. Gugu Mutonga was handily winning the south. This was little surprise, as this part of the country was never a power base for Tinotenda. They hated him, in fact. It was also an area his government, by no coincidence, chronically neglected and to which it repeatedly sent in the army at the slightest sign of trouble. Unfortunately for Lucky's electoral math, it was also sparsely populated.

The real battleground today was the cities, especially the burgeoning capital of Harare. The election would be won or lost on the swelling urban youth vote. Would they brave the police and the Green Mambas to come out in support of Gugu Mutonga? Lucky wondered as he focused on the map showing results in Harare. Gugu's advisors were convinced this was the crucial question. But they didn't know the answer.

Harare, smack in the middle of the country, glowed bright red on the monitor. Lucky zoomed in to see the results in more detail. Highfield was red. Dzivarasekwa red. Mufakose red. Mbare red. Rugare red. Epworth red. Glen Norah red. Warren Park red. Kambuzuma red. The cities were coming out to vote in droves. And Gugu was dominating.

For the first time that day, Lucky Magombe took a bite of food and relaxed his shoulders. And for the first time that day, Lucky allowed himself to smile. *And to hope.*

He picked up the phone, paused, then thought again and set it back down. He stroked his chin and tried to suppress any emotions. The math was swirling in his head. He knew he had to be cold and calculating. That was the only way. Hope was a folly for idealists and politicians. His path could only be through hard numbers.

Lucky opened a software program and uploaded the data for one more check. He ran statistical tests on the census figures, the voter rolls, and the election results rolling in. He didn't believe it at first, but the numbers couldn't lie. Statistical probability gave him the answer. It was screaming loud and clear. Even if he was the only person on the planet who knew it yet, *the election had been decided.*

Satisfied, Lucky picked up the phone again and dialed a familiar number.

In a posh waterfront hotel in Cape Town, 785 miles to the southwest, a middle-aged American woman in a lavender tracksuit was power walking on a treadmill and watching CNN to keep her mind fresh while she waited. Her phone lit up and vibrated from an incoming call. She hopped off and answered.

"Mariana Leibowitz."

The voice on the other end said simply, "It's over. Gugu has won."

41.

Harare, Zimbabwe
Saturday, 9:05 p.m. Central Africa Time
"Baba, you still awake?" asked Harriet.

President Tinotenda, in pale blue pajamas buttoned up to the top of his neck, was sitting up in a four-poster bed. "Yes, my *kiti*. Please come in."

"I know it is late for you, Baba," she said sheepishly.

He glanced through thick reading glasses at the antique English clock on his French Louis XVI replica side table. "It is only a few minutes after nine. I will stay up for the First Lady of the Republic." He patted the sheets, beckoning her to join him. She approached him, sitting on the far corner of the bed with her legs tucked tightly together.

"I will go back to my room soon and allow you to rest. I must change." She suddenly felt foolish sitting on his bed while still wearing a formal dress. "I must change.

I know you've had the most exhausting day, Baba."

"No, my dear. I found today invigorating. They are my people."

"You were very inspiring today. I am sure you rallied the people to vote for you again."

"They are like children. They need their father to scold them. To remind them who they are and who has brought them their freedom. They can become distracted by fancy lies. Like children."

"I am sure they will show their appreciation."

"We shall see, Harriet. That uppity little girl Gugu seems to be very popular among the traitors and sellouts. There are so many. Our youth are very susceptible to the tricks of the West."

"Gugu Mutonga," she hissed. "She is a *bete*. A cockroach."

"She is a lawyer, Harriet."

"Tsaaah! I am certain you will crush her once the people have spoken. Once the voting results are announced, everyone will know she is nothing more than a *bete*."

"We shall see. Is that what you wanted to talk with me about? The election?"

"Yaah, Baba." Harriet moved closer to her husband on the bed.

"What is on your mind, my love?"

"Do you have any early results?"

"I was just briefed by the commissioner before I came to bed. The boys are still counting. The final results won't be known until morning, but he assured me we will have a wide victory. The Revolution will be triumphant. I am confident."

"I am confident, too, Baba."

"So why do you ask?"

"I hear things which make me worry."

"You silly women and your gossip!" He laughed and shook his head.

"Tsaaah. They are just rumors. Lies spread by bandits to make trouble."

"I see."

"But I hear them, Baba."

"You are worried, my *kiti*?"

"I am sorry, Baba." She looked down in shame.

"Tell me." Tino gently patted her back for reassurance. She looked up at him with wide eyes.

"What would happen if you lose, Baba?"

"I just told you that won't happen."

"But if you did lose, what would happen to *me*?" she pouted.

"I won't allow that to happen. You mustn't worry yourself about things that will never come to pass."

She peered at him for a moment and then

dropped her eyes. "I know, Baba. But I can't help it. I am ashamed. I am worried about my future. I know you are strong. But after you win reelection, I am still worried about what will happen to me."

He rubbed her back harder. "I told you, my *kiti*. I have made arrangements for you. If it ever becomes necessary, there is a special account overseas. Simba Chimurenga has taken care of everything. You will be taken care of."

"Simba? He has my emergency bank account? Do you trust him?"

"He's the only one I can trust."

"What about me? Don't you trust your wife?"

"Of course, my dear. But I need Simba to protect my most important treasures," he said. Winston Tinotenda, suddenly more awake than he had been all day, pushed his hand lower on her back and squeezed.

She abruptly stood up and turned her back to him.

"I am hungry, my *kiti*."

She looked over her shoulder at her husband, his pajamas, his drooping face, his oversized eyes leering at her through thick Coke-bottle glasses. She weighed her options, considered the multiple ways this evening could evolve, the consequences of each, the costs and risks of her next move.

After a moment she turned her head away from him. Then she unzipped her dress and allowed it to fall to the floor.

42.

CIA Headquarters, Langley, Virginia
Saturday, 4:40 p.m. Eastern Standard Time
"Now that UMBRELLA ROSE is down, I'm going to need you working on something else, starting Monday."

"Yes, sir," said Sunday into the telephone. "Zimbabwe is still hot, of course. Even if the uranium issue is not."

"Nah," dismissed his supervisor at Africa Issue, who was unaware his best analyst was a covert detailee to the ultrasecret Purple Cell. "There's no intel opportunity in Zimbabwe. Let's not waste any more time."

"Sir?"

"You can keep covering the election, but it's a dead end without the uranium angle."

"The politics are still quite interesting. I wouldn't mind staying on and seeing if something breaks."

"You're not hearing me, Sunday. There's no demand for that. No one upstairs gives two shits about that place."

"Yes, sir."

"Maybe if the old man Tinotenda dies and it's taken over by a jihadist. Maybe you'll get lucky and al-Qaeda will try to move into Victoria Falls. Then I'll let you work on Zim."

"Zimbabwe voted today. Election results due tomorrow."

"Is anything gonna change? The geezer and his cronies will win again, right?"

"Not clear, sir."

"Same old, same old."

"There's a nontrivial chance something could break."

"There's a nontrivial chance we'll all be dead tomorrow."

"I assess the probability of a fatal attack on CIA headquarters is lower than a political change in Zimbabwe, sir."

"Well, don't waste too much time on that," he laughed, which irked Sunday even more. "Unless UMBRELLA ROSE is turned back on by Monday morning, I'm pulling you to work Somali pirates."

"Isn't Glen on that already, sir?"

"I need to throw bodies at Somalia. The Office of the Director of National Intelligence is worried about Iranian supplies to radicals running through the Gulf of Aden.

Could be a connection with Somali jihadists and their criminal pirate rings. We'll be shifting bodies over for blanket coverage."

"Yes, sir."

"Unless Zimbabwe blows up today, you might as well start reading in. The intel volume has been turned up. Not like the usual dribbles you're used to in Africa Issue. You'll be drinking from the fire hose. Would do you good to get a head start."

"Yes, sir, Somalia."

Sunday's computer screen chirped with a special message:

Your bird.

"I'll get right on Somalia, sir."

"I knew you'd get it, Sunday. You're a pirate hunter now. Think like one."

He resisted the urge to growl and instead mumbled, "Yes, sir." Sunday threw down the phone and quickly clicked on his new message.

First pics from Vapor Four over Kanyemba.

He double-clicked on the images to give him full-screen views. They were a sequence of aerial photos of a green-covered hill. In the center he could see a small brown square, which he presumed to be the mine shaft entrance. Otherwise, the pictures showed nothing but an overgrown tree-topped ridge. Even the old track that must have connected the mine to the main road was invisible, having been reclaimed by Mother Nature. *This is nothing,* thought Sunday.

Chirp. Another message.

Bird, money shots.

Click.

Vapor Four, Geothermal.

Double-click.

The same pictures as the first message appeared, but instead of normal photographs these were multicolored X-rays of the earth. Sunday needed a few moments to reorient himself to these new images. He opened both versions of the photographs side by side to compare. The ridge and the mine shaft entrance provided reference points. On the geothermal version he could see, under the ground, that the mine shaft ran down and then horizontally along the ridge, an underground tunnel with caves or excavated side rooms. He zoomed in further to try to identify the contents. He was searching for any sign of recent activity, any hint of what had been going on inside the Kanyemba mine.

Then he saw the unmistakable outlines. He could see, clearly, what he hoped he would never find. *La ilaha illallah. There is no God but Allah.*

43.

At Josiah Tongogara Primary School in the posh low-density Gun Hill neighborhood, the deputy headmaster was padlocking the gate after a long and grueling day. It had been a ringing success. The ballot boxes were stacked neatly in his office and all of the voting cards were counted, the results posted on the schoolyard chalkboard. The papers were all signed and sent to the central election commission office for safe-keeping. Election day had been tense, but with the help of the police it passed without incident. He was sure the local party chief would notice his loyal work that day and recommend his promotion to full head-master when the old *ambuya* who ran the school finally retired. Exhausted but satis-fied, he turned to walk down Samora Ma-chel Avenue to catch a taxi home. He was

333

debating whether to tell his wife about the extra cash he'd earned that day or to spend it instead on one of his girlfriends. He was so deep in thought, he didn't notice the battered black Nissan sedan pass him and turn into Gun Hill.

Isabella Espinosa inched the old car down the nearly empty street. She was still two blocks away from her destination but turned off the car's engine and waited in silence. Although Brock Branson had found her a nondescript car for tonight, he was worried that she might be followed, so he'd provided explicit instructions.

Isabella drove south, all the way down Chiremba Road to the balancing rocks at Epworth, executed several U-turns, looped back toward the city center, and then veered northwest toward Gun Hill.

She was pretty sure she wasn't being followed. Brock had given her surveillance detection route 101 and assured her the Zimbabwean intelligence services were none too subtle. But she wasn't taking any chances. Now that she was close to her target, she didn't want to blow it again.

After a few minutes of silence and no perceptible movement, she started up the Nissan and drove past General Solomon Zagwe's villa. The security lights were on at the front gate but she couldn't see any guards. All the lights inside the main house appeared to be off. Once she passed safely out of sight, she shut off the car's lights and U-turned again. Isabella rolled the car underneath a tree that gave her a sight line across Zagwe's main gate. Still no movement.

Brock had discouraged Isabella from venturing out into the city alone, especially to stake out a cold-blooded mass murderer who knew he was being hunted. But she had a strong hunch that if Zagwe was going to make a move, it would be tonight. If the general was going to flee the country for a new safe haven — Venezuela? North Korea? Saudi Arabia? Did it matter? — she'd need to stop him before he got over the border or out of Zimbabwean airspace.

Branson, valiantly risking his own career, had offered to go with her, but Isabella refused. The surveillance debacle earlier that day with Colonel Durham had only reinforced her initial instinct to do it on her own. This was something she had to do by herself.

If Isabella Espinosa had learned anything from growing up in East Los Angeles and fighting every step of the way through UC Irvine and then UCLA Law, it was to be wary of offers of assistance. They always came with unforeseen entanglements. She knew she always had to be self-reliant. It had taken all her strength to swallow her pride and ask Judd Ryker to join him on this trip.

Now here she was, again needing help. Brock was concerned about Isabella's safety. Perhaps too concerned? So far the CIA and the rest of the U.S. government didn't seem to care much about her mission for justice in a decades-old crime on the Horn of Africa. She'd realized long ago no one cared about dead Ethiopians. Why was Brock Branson being so helpful? What was in it for him? Or did the way he looked at her suggest another, perhaps less principled motive?

Even if it wasn't in her nature to rely on others, she'd decided that if the CIA chief of station was willing to go out on a limb to help her accomplish her mission, she would smile and accept. The perpetrator of the Red Fear, the man who'd killed all those innocent people, was more important than her ego. Isabella even gently flirted with Branson while telling him no, she'd go alone tonight.

"All right, sister. I get it. You wanna play Lone Ranger."

"Thank you," she had said, tucking her hair behind her ear.

"But if you get any clear signs of flight, you have to call me first. Got that, Special Agent Espinosa? If that scumbag tries to make a break for it, let me do my job."

"Which is what, exactly?"

"Don't you worry about that. I know a guy or two. If he runs to the airport or to the border at Beitbridge, we'll stop him."

"And then what?"

"And then that's your department. You'll get your fucking DOJ game on, right, sister?"

"Extradition could take years."

"I wouldn't know," Brock had said.

"You ever hear of a CIA rendition for a war crimes case?"

"The CIA doesn't do renditions, Special Agent Espinosa."

"Of course not."

Sitting alone in the car in the dark, the question returned: What *would* she do if Zagwe fled? Chase him? Try to apprehend him? Then what? She pushed the thought out of her mind and raised her binoculars to scan the front gate of the villa. Still nothing.

Isabella checked her watch. Nearly midnight. Would Zagwe wait for the election results before making his move? Or was he so confident in Tino's victory he hadn't even made contingency plans? Was her entire trip for nothing? Was she chasing a ghost?

Suddenly the security lights went dark. Isabella lifted the binoculars. She saw something. Movement at the gate. Or maybe just a shadow? Yes, a shadow raced left, then right. She spun the dial to try to refocus the binoculars. Was that a man running? Was it a dog? The trees blowing? Was her mind just playing tricks? She squinted in the dark, her heart galloping, but still unsure. Her breathing quickened. Then . . . nothing.

Deep exhale. Just as she was preparing to slump back in her seat, Isabella's tunnel of vision through the binoculars suddenly flashed bright white. A millisecond later, her ears rung with a KAAA-BOOM! Isabella ducked her head as the car was splattered by falling debris. The windshield cracked into a spiderweb.

Isabella raised her head above the dashboard to see flames rising over the villa walls. No one inside could possibly have survived that blast, she thought. Had Zagwe been killed? Had she just witnessed the perpetrator fleeing? Who was it? Who would have wanted Zagwe dead? Her mind was

racing. Then, like a second explosion in her
mind, she realized: I'm an American government official sitting in an unmarked CIA
car fifty yards from a political assassination.
Get the hell out of here.

44.

U.S. Embassy, Harare, Zimbabwe
Saturday, 11:56 p.m. Central Africa Time
Ambassador Tallyberger had provided Judd a modest office in the secure section of the embassy. Just outside his door was a small reception area with several couches and a television where staff gathered to watch CNN. Tonight the screen was showing angry men protesting in Cairo's Tahrir Square. The sound was off, but Judd recognized the reporter who was talking fast and wearing a khaki flak jacket and a nervous expression. At the bottom of the screen scrolled BREAKING NEWS: $50K CASH FOUND IN CONGRESSMAN'S FROZEN TURKEY.

"Anything, Bull?" asked Judd.

"Nah. No news." Bull twisted his neck to make eye contact with Judd. His cheek was a circular purple bruise around the bandage covering his stitches.

"Anything at all on Zimbabwe?"

"Not yet," said Bull, turning back to the TV.

"I'm going to make a call and then we can go back to the hotel for some shut-eye."

"Whatever you say, chief."

"We'll probably catch Isabella back there. Where'd she go again?"

"She didn't say."

Judd shrugged it off and stepped into the office. The walls were bare, a simple gray government-issue phone on the desk. A computer, unplugged, lay on its side on the floor.

Judd stared up at the ceiling, noting a small brown water stain in the corner. Did it look like a cloud? Or a map of Russia? *Man, am I jet-lagged,* he thought, shaking his head to clear the cobwebs.

Foreign policy wasn't supposed to be like this. He knew it wasn't about cocktail parties and state dinners. Yet, sitting in that drab, windowless room in a far corner of a remote U.S. embassy, it couldn't have felt less romantic. Or less adventurous.

Worse, Judd fought the creeping sense that he had lost any idea of what was really happening. Or even what the hell he was doing in Zimbabwe. He had flown eight thousand miles to rush here supposedly to fix things,

341

but instead he was losing control. Or, more like it, he was realizing he had never had any control in the first place. What was he thinking, coming to Zimbabwe at the last minute? What could he realistically do? What was Landon Parker's real agenda?

Judd's mentor, BJ van Hollen, had offered advice just before he died: "They talk about the fog of war, but there's a fog of diplomacy, too. The real world isn't like the academic world. You won't be solving a math problem. And policy making isn't like in the movies. You aren't going to be the hero who saves the day by throwing caution to the wind and rescuing the girl."

"I know, BJ" was Judd's dismissive reply. But BJ wasn't finished.

"Policy is messy and uncertain. It's not like you're a drill sergeant or an orchestra conductor, either."

"So what's the analogy, Prof?"

BJ rubbed his chin in mock deliberation. "It's like . . . whitewater rafting. Pick your direction and try your darnedest to avoid big rocks."

"Rafting? When have you ever gone white-water rafting?"

"You aren't ever in control. The best you can do is to keep going forward. And just hold on."

Just hold on. That stuck in Judd's mind.

"That's usually the best you can expect," van Hollen continued, increasingly satisfied with himself. "When you get to the end, if you are lucky enough to reach your goal — if you get there and you are still alive — sure, you can pretend your skills and wise decisions got you there. But deep down you will know you were just along for the ride." BJ lowered his eyes and his voice for the dramatic finish. "And fucking lucky."

Judd smiled to himself as he remembered that day. "Fucking lucky" were the very last words BJ had said to Judd.

Judd wished for BJ's counsel now. How long had it been since he'd passed? A year already? Time was moving too fast. Judd shook his head again. *Focus.*

Time for a mental inventory. His first day in Zimbabwe had come to a close, but what had he accomplished? If anything, Zimbabwe had fallen further down the U.S. foreign policy agenda with the closing of UMBRELLA ROSE. *How exactly had the uranium threat risen from zero to urgent and back to zero in less than forty-eight hours?*

If the uranium scare was what had brought him to Zimbabwe, then what about the election? The voting was complete and there'd been no major outbreak of violence. The election commissioner was due to release the official results tomorrow, likely at noon. Twelve hours away.

Judd could see, even after being in the country for only a day, that President Tinotenda and his cronies were well entrenched. He could also see that Gugu Mutonga was genuinely popular and the country hungered for change. Yet there didn't seem to be anyone who believed Mutonga could actually win. Apart from a few idealists like Mariana Leibowitz, there wasn't any international support. *Hell,* Judd thought, *I can barely get anyone in Washington even to pay attention. How am I supposed to engineer a fair election? Or regime change? Is that my goal? Is that what the Secretary wants? What, really, does the White House want? Does Washington even know what it wants?*

He could already see Tallyberger and Rogerson were set to accept whatever the Zimbabweans announced tomorrow. As far as he could tell, Tinotenda had everything in place to win reelection. His people were in the villages, General Chimurenga had blanketed the country with his security forces, and the vote-counting was taking place in a black box. In Chimurenga's black box. The general wouldn't have taken the risk of a truly independent count, would he?

Judd sighed. *Maybe Rogerson is right. Maybe we should prevent chaos where we can. But the United States can't be the world's policeman.*

What about his own selfish motives? Landon Parker's instructions had not been to try to rescue Zimbabwe, exactly, but to save S/CRU. Judd was supposed to prevent a crisis from ever blowing up in order to keep Zimbabwe off the Secretary of State's desk . . . as a way to protect his own job. Was that what he had become? Another bureaucrat more concerned about his own small patch of turf than the bigger picture? He parked the thought in a corner of his brain. For another day.

Focus. Keep Zimbabwe from exploding. But even if he succeeded, would that work? How would Judd ever prove he had caused the absence of a problem? If an emergency was avoided, who would get the credit? Rogerson? Tallyberger? Parker? A familiar doubt crept back into his thoughts: *Am I being set up to fail again?*

Then another thought returned to his brain: *Suck it up.* That's what Jessica had said. That's what she would say now if she were here. Don't focus on what you don't

345

know or can't control. Determine your goals and who you can trust. Use your team of superheroes. *My Justice League.* If no one is paying attention and you've got no tools, use what you have. You have no other choice.

Judd checked his watch. He remembered he had lectured the Egypt team back at State about how their window of opportunity began once polls closed and ended when results were announced. For Zimbabwe, he realized, the window was right now. *Suck it up.*

Judd picked up the phone and dialed a 202 cell phone. After one ring, it clicked.

"Mariana Leibowitz."

"Mariana, it's Judd."

"Where are you calling from? The number is scrambled."

"I'm in the U.S. embassy in Harare."

"Well, la-dee-dah for you, Judd. Where is the embassy statement about the elections? I haven't seen anything official yet."

"The ambassador —"

"Tallyberger? That idiot wouldn't know a fair election if it bit him in the ass. Did you see his press interview today?"

"No."

"He said the United States was strongly

346

encouraged. That voting was calm and orderly!"

Before Judd could reply, Mariana shouted into the phone, *"Calm and fucking orderly, Judd!"*

"I know the embassy —"

"It's not like Tinotenda is sending out the army to force people to vote at gunpoint. It's more subtle than that. You know Tinotenda's going to try to steal this election right out from under your nose. You know that, right? How does the embassy not understand that?"

"I get it, Mariana."

"What's the point in even having an embassy if they don't know what the fuck is going on? You're supposed to be with the good guys on this one, remember, Judd?"

"I *am* with the good guys. *I* called *you,* remember?"

"Christ almighty!"

"I called you because we need something to shake things up. Something to rattle Tino's cage."

"Like what?"

"I don't know yet. What do you know that might be helpful?"

"How about I know Gugu Mutonga won this fucking election? Even if the U.S.

embassy doesn't see it right before their eyes."

"How do you know she won already?"

"I know because I have the data."

"You do?" Judd asked. *Data.* The wheels started to turn.

"Of course I do. You didn't think I was going to throw my candidate to the wolves and just hope the American government would save her, did you? You didn't think I'd take a real-life superhero like Gugu Mutonga and then trust her future, her life, to someone like Arnold fucking Tallyberger, did you?"

"I wouldn't think so."

"Of course not. I'm a professional."

"Is the election data the guardian angel you mentioned before?"

"In a way, yes."

"Well, Mariana, that's exactly what we need. Send it to me."

"Not yet."

"Why not?"

"It's not iron-clad yet. We need all the numbers to come in to prove she won. It has to be incontrovertible. Soon."

"So when it's ready, you'll send it me?"

"Depends."

"On what?"

"Depends on what you plan to do with it.

I've got one wild card and I'm not wasting it if you aren't going to play it."

"I'll play it."

Judd waited for a reply, but nothing came.

"You still there, Mariana?"

"You'll play it?"

"Yes."

"How do I know you will?"

"What are your options? You going to give the data to the South Africans? The British? The Chinese? You really don't have any choice but me."

"Hardball from Dr. Judd Ryker. That's what I like to see!"

"Don't patronize me, Mariana."

"Judd, I need your assurance you'll fight to the end with me on this."

"I will."

"How do I know?"

"How about I throw a golden nugget your way? As a down payment on your election data."

"I'm listening."

"Remember I asked you about Max O'Malley?"

"Yes, the President's bundler. I remember."

"Well, it looks like he might be in business with some very senior Zimbabwean government officials."

"O'Malley? Really? That slippery prick. How do you know?"

"I can't say."

"What kind of business?"

"I can't say. Actually, I don't know yet."

"Wow, Judd. That is quite a nugget. And potentially radioactive. You better be careful with that."

"I am only telling *you.*"

"Are you certain it's true?"

"Yes."

"Then you better be damn careful, Judd."

"I really can't say any more. I've already shared too much. But now you owe me the election data."

"The thing I don't get —"

A loud KA-BOOM! went off in the distance. A second later, Bull Durham flung open the door. "You hear that? Definitely an explosion. Three to five miles away." Judd nodded, his eyes wide-open.

"Mariana, I've got to get off. Send me the data as soon as you can," he said, and hung up before she could respond.

■ ■ ■ ■

Part Three:
Sunday

■ ■ ■ ■

45.

U.S. Embassy, Harare, Zimbabwe
Sunday, 10.20 a.m. Central Africa Time
It had already been a long and anxious morning.

Judd and the rest of the team stayed all night at the embassy to watch the television reports about a blast "with likely but unconfirmed casualties" in Harare. They learned that a massive bomb had gone off at the home occupied by General Solomon Zagwe, former President of Ethiopia and perpetrator of the Red Fear, a campaign of wanton violence against innocent civilians that had killed at least five hundred thousand people. Zagwe was presumed dead, but the government of Zimbabwe had yet to make any official statement. U.S. ambassador Arnold Tallyberger had tried to reach the foreign minister on his cell phone, but there was no answer.

The BBC, the SABC, Al Jazeera, and

CNN all aired the same stock footage of Zagwe leading a battalion of tanks through a mud village, along with still photos of the Harare villa on fire. The Al Jazeera report also showed a short clip of their local stringer claiming he had tried to get close to the location of the explosion but the police had sealed off the entire neighborhood of Gun Hill. The reporter recounted that the policeman had insisted he was under strict orders to keep all civilians out until the fire was under control.

No real information.

Sitting next to Judd at the embassy, staring blankly at the TV, was Isabella Espinosa. She had arrived back at the embassy not long after midnight and looked terrible. Plums under her eyes, tousled hair, same clothes as yesterday. "Couldn't sleep" was all she would say. Now she glared at the television reports, watching her case, three years of her life, go up in flames.

Colonel David "Bull" Durham lay on a couch in the corner, nursing a tall mug of weak embassy coffee. He had slept there, too, and was drifting in and out of sleep.

As unsettling as it was, the mysterious bombing wasn't the source of Judd's anxiety that morning. He was worried about the election. The electoral commission was due to announce the official tallies at noon, just ninety minutes away. But there had been no confirmation it was happening. No sign whatsoever. The government wasn't talking about the explosion, and it wasn't talking, period. Tallyberger, who pretended not to be annoyed that these visitors were crowding up his embassy, agreed the Zimbabweans were being unusually tight-lipped. But he cautioned Judd not to jump to any conclusions.

"This is their election, not ours, Dr. Ryker. They will do it on their schedule, not ours."

Judd didn't respond.

"I've got a political officer camped out at the Information Ministry's hall," Tallyberger said. "That's the main podium where they make all their big announcements. He'll let us know when the commissioner arrives to release the election results. So far he says it's all reporters and foreign embassy staff talking to each other. Let's be patient."

Just then Brock Branson entered the room looking fresh and well rested. His beard was newly trimmed. "G'morning, comrades!" he said too loudly, and slapped Judd on the back. "What's news?"

"Zagwe's house blew up. No election results," Judd replied, unsmiling.

"Yeah, I heard. I tried to call Simba Chimurenga to find out what the fuck's happening, but he's not answering his phone."

Isabella glanced up at Brock. Judd thought she was going to cry.

"How you doin', sister?"

She nodded and steeled herself.

"Hang in there. I'll try to find out what I can about your target. Maybe he went out for smokes or something. Maybe Zagwe's not dead."

She shook her head and returned her gaze to the television. Brock pulled on Judd's sleeve and motioned with his head toward the door. "A word, Dr. Ryker." Durham sat up to eye the two men depart down the hallway.

Inside the station chief's office, Judd took a seat and Brock closed the door.

"I'm worried about her, too," said Judd.

"Espinosa?" asked Brock, jerking his thumb toward the hallway. "Nah. She'll be fine. She's tough."

"She looks awful. Like she's in shock."

"It happens when your target is unexpectedly eliminated. It's happened to me plenty. She'll get over it and get her game on again in no time. Just like us, amigo."

"I'm not so sure," Judd said.

356

"I didn't ask you in here to talk about Isabella. I need to talk to you about your *other* friend."

"Who?"

"Your friend in South Africa who's deeply involved in this election and is about to get into a heap of trouble. If you're really their friend, you need to tell them to cease and fucking desist. And I mean A-fucking-SAP."

"Mariana?" asked Judd. "What's she done?"

"Who the fuck is that?"

"Mariana Leibowitz. The K Street lobbyist helping Gugu Mutonga. I know she's deep into this election but I didn't think she was doing anything illegal. I'd be surprised."

"Not her."

"Then who are you talking about?"

Brock stroked his beard and lowered his chin. "Are you feeling 'Lucky'?"

"Lucky? I don't understand," Judd said.

"Magombe. Lucky Magombe. That's who I'm talking about."

"I don't know any Lucky Magombe."

"Don't lie to me, Ryker. I can't help you if you're bullshitting me."

"I'm telling you, I don't know him."

"Stockbroker. Out of Joburg."

"Nope."

"Fled Zimbabwe twelve years ago."

Judd shook his head.

"Seems to know *you*."

Judd shook his head more vigorously, running his hands through his hair.

Brock tilted his head to one side slightly and scanned Judd's face. After a few seconds he smiled. "Okay. If you say so, comrade."

"What's he done?"

"You State Department boys really don't know what the fuck's going on, do you?"

"Not a thing. Why doesn't the CIA enlighten us?"

"That's what we're here for. Lucky Magombe is the Gugu Mutonga campaign."

"What does that mean?"

"He's behind the whole operation. He's the one bankrolling her. The T-shirts, the posters, the radio spots, the cars, the computers — everything that goes into her campaign. He's the one who put Gugu Mutonga on the stage. He's been funneling cash from South Africa into accounts controlled by her party. He's also probably the one paying your friend Leibowitz."

"Well, what's wrong with that? Maybe we should be helping him."

"That's not the problem."

"Then what is?"

"I'm not supposed to share this with you,

but I'm going to, since I know this land mine could blow up your whole goddamn project here."

"Land mine?" Judd asked, leaning in.

"I can't show you the report, of course, but" — Brock lowered his voice — "we've got SIGINT indicating Lucky Magombe is plotting to assassinate senior officials in the Zimbabwean government."

"He is?" Judd's eyes widened.

"Yep."

"When?"

"Today. Noon."

"Who?"

"Sorry, can't say."

"Why?"

"Don't know yet. Maybe he's pissed off his candidate isn't going to win? Who knows? But we do know that if we have the SIGINT, then so, too, do the others. And even if they don't know about it yet, we are obligated under duty-to-warn protocol to share this information with the Zimbabwean authorities."

"You can't do that."

"We aren't doing anything yet. But this can't be buried forever."

"So what do you want *me* to do about it?"

"I want you to tell Lucky Magombe to

cease and desist. Shut this clusterfuck down before it goes any further."

"I don't know him. I already told you that."

"The SIGINT has him mentioning your name."

"It does?"

"Are you Judd Ryker?"

"Yes, but I don't understand."

"Well, you're in the record, amigo. If a foreign official is assassinated and there's a connection to a State Department envoy . . . well, you know it's not gonna be pretty."

"What should I do?"

"Tell your non-friend to cut the shit out. Personally, I don't care who he kills. But he should at least stop talking about it on the fucking telephone."

"I could pass a message through Mariana," Judd offered.

"Now you're thinking, amigo."

"What exactly should I say?"

"Good. Now, listen carefully . . ."

46.

Harare, Zimbabwe
Sunday, 10:35 a.m. Central Africa Time
"His Excellency, Father of the Nation and Warrior of the People, President Winston H. R. Tinotenda, will see you now," said the butler.

"My dear Simba."

"Thank you, Your Excellency. I am not interrupting your morning tea?"

"Please come in. It is a glorious morning for Zimbabwe. Would you like some tea?"

"It is indeed a beautiful morning, but I have no time for tea. I'm afraid I come bearing some troubling news."

"Oh, dear," said the president, who coughed and then shooed away the butler with a flick of his wrist.

"I hoped you would be coming to tell me of another landslide victory. I have great plans for my next term. For you, Simba, in my next term."

"*Sekuru,* I am coming to you straight from the election commissioner's office."

"Who is the commissioner? Whittington?"

"No, Your Excellency, you dismissed Chief Justice Whittington years ago. The current commissioner is Judge Makwere."

"Ahh, that's right. Makwere. That old fool. My wife's uncle. He owes his career to me. He owes his life to me. I made him chief justice?"

"No, *Sekuru,* you made him election commissioner."

"Of course, of course."

"*Sekuru,* I just came from Makwere's office and he had some disturbing news. He refused to come here to brief you himself. He is afraid."

"Afraid? Who is afraid to give me bad news?"

"*Sekuru,* you know the answer to that. That is why I am here."

"That is why I can trust you with my most important assignments, Simba. What is this bad news?"

Simba Chimurenga, despite his ample self-confidence, took a small step back as he delivered the message. "According to the current vote tally, Your Excellency . . . Gugu Mutonga has more votes."

Tino dropped his chin and shook his

head. "I have lost?"

"No, Your Excellency, you have not lost. Not yet. The count is not yet complete. Not yet official. I have ordered Makwere to check his figures and recount if necessary."

Tino shook his head and slumped deeper into his chair.

"Makwere's recount will, I am certain, show you have won reelection, Your Excellency. If he makes a mistake again, I will be sure any errors are corrected."

"I lost . . ." the president muttered to himself.

"*Sekuru,* do not talk that way. If you are ready to retire, we will arrange for you to do so after you are reelected by the people. You will rest when you are ready, not when the traitors and turncoats have cheated you. You will retire when you are ready. When *we* decide you are ready. Not like this."

"I am tired of fighting. Perhaps it is more honorable to step down now?"

"Is it honorable for the puppets to be manipulated by the British and the Americans? To trick our people — *your people* — with their propaganda? No! Your legacy is too important to allow the enemies of the revolution to succeed. No! We cannot allow them to win!"

"I don't know, Simba."

"I will take care of the voting, *Sekuru*. You will only have to accept victory later today. I will arrange everything. You only need to arrive and claim your triumph."

The president coughed against the back of his hand and turned to the window. "Where are my herons?"

"Your Excellency, leave it to me. I will take care of everything. It cannot be any other way. We cannot give up now when the barbarians are at the gate. They are clever, but we must be steadfast. We must be ruthless."

"I don't see my herons," Tino muttered.

"If someone is stealing from us, do we turn the other cheek? No. If someone is stealing from us, do we allow that? No. They will be crushed."

The president coughed weakly.

"How did we deal with Chirundu and Gokwe and Kanyemba? We crushed them, did we not?"

"We did," said Tino, still looking away.

"I must give you some more bad news, Your Excellency," said Simba impatiently.

"What could be worse?"

"General Zagwe is dead." Tinotenda turned to meet Chimurenga's face.

"Solomon? Dead? Why didn't anyone tell me?"

"Who could tell you other than me?"

"How?"

"A fire at his villa around midnight destroyed the house and killed everyone inside."

"A fire? How did that happen? Who could have done that?"

"The investigation is not yet complete. I have sealed off the area."

"But I promised to protect him."

"I am sorry, *Sekuru.*"

"You were in charge of his security, Simba. You were supposed to protect him for me. Who could have killed him? How could you have failed?"

"I did not fail."

"What?"

"Zagwe was stealing."

"What are you saying?" The old man's eyes narrowed.

"I am certain he was stealing from you and from me."

"What are you saying, Simba?" Tino's hands clenched into fists.

"If you receive two hundred and seventy-five million dollars and only tell your partners you have one hundred and fifty million, then are you not stealing? Do you not agree, Your Excellency?"

"What are you saying, Simba?"

"I already told you. If someone is stealing from us, they will be crushed."

"Solomon was under my protection."

"Sekuru" — Chimurenga took a step closer to the old man and looked down at him — *"you* are now under my protection."

47.

Molweni Hotel, Cape Town, South Africa
Sunday, 11:05 a.m. Central Africa Time
Mariana Leibowitz couldn't believe what she was hearing. They were so close and now it was all going to hell.

"Missing?"

"Yes, ma'am, he's missing."

"How does the goddamn election commissioner go missing an hour before he's due to announce the results of the biggest election in the country's history? How the fuck does that happen?"

"I don't know, ma'am. Maybe he has the fear."

"The fear? You mean he fled? Where would he flee?"

"I don't know, ma'am."

"Maybe they killed him?"

"Yes, ma'am. Maybe."

The young Zimbabwean campaign staffer, embarrassed by the American woman's brash manner and foul language, was grateful when Mariana's phone rang.

"About goddamn time I heard from you, Judd!" she shouted, picking up after one ring. "Where is the embassy? Where is the fucking embassy? I haven't heard shit from them!"

"Good morning, Mariana."

"Don't give me that, Judd. Where is the United States government when we need them? I told you Gugu Mutonga won this thing!"

"I'm waiting on your data."

"I told you! We're working on all the numbers, but it's clear she won by a landslide. A fucking landslide, Judd."

"Congratulations, Mariana."

"I'm not celebrating. This thing is far from over. You know Makwere is missing, right? He's goddamn missing!"

"Who's Makwere?"

"Oh, good Lord, Judd. He's the goddamn election commissioner! He's supposed to announce the official results in less than an hour and no one knows where he is."

"So where is he?"

"If he was smart, he's fled to Botswana or Dubai or somewhere far away. But he was never too clever, so he's probably dead. I wouldn't be surprised if we find out later today he's been killed in a car accident."

"Car accident?"

"Zimbabwe's top politicians are always having car accidents. Didn't you read your briefing book?"

"So what's our next move, Mariana?"

"That's where you come in."

"I'm listening," Judd said.

"We have no idea what's going to happen with the official announcement. Clearly, the government is panicking. If they haven't figured out yet that Tinotenda has lost, they will soon. I'm going to need the U.S. embassy to release the *real* results. Can you make that happen?"

Judd didn't answer.

"Judd," she continued, with mild panic rising in her voice, "you *are* going to make this happen, right?"

"Yes. I think so."

"Isn't that why you called me? To get the election data?"

"No, actually, I called for a completely different reason."

"What could that possibly be?"

"I know about Lucky Magombe."

"Yes, fine, Judd. I should have told you he's the one paying me. I didn't tell you. But I didn't see it as relevant. I don't see any problem."

"That's not the issue. How well do you know Lucky?"

"He's a client. A self-made millionaire. Smart as a whip. Data freak, like you. Patriotic, too. He's just trying to fix his country so he can go home. That's why he's backing Gugu Mutonga. That's why he's paying me."

"Do you know all his activities?"

"Of course not. How could I?"

"Well, it's a problem."

"I don't believe he's into anything illegal. Why would he? What's he done?"

"I can't say. But trust me, it's serious."

"So why are you telling me?"

"I need you to tell him to cool it. To call it off. He's only going to make matters worse. It'll destroy everything we are doing. It'll destroy Gugu, too."

"Tell him to call *what* off, Judd?"

"Just tell him to stop playing cricket. I can't say any more. Lucky will understand."

"What?"

"*Cricket.* He'll understand. You have to trust me on this one. And you have to do it right now."

"Okay, okay. I'll pass the message."

"And for God's sake, Mariana, tell him to stay off the telephone."

"The phone? Is he bugged?"

370

"It's a deal, right?" Judd asked.

"Are *we* bugged right now? Who is listening to us, Judd?"

"Tell me it's a deal, Mariana."

"Yes. Okay. Deal. You work on the embassy and I'll get you the election data."

"And you'll tell Lucky."

"I'll tell Lucky," Mariana repeated. "Is there anything else?"

"I need you to reach out to Landon Parker again."

"Me? You work for him."

"I know, but this message is better coming from an outsider. It's better coming from you, Mariana."

"Which is . . . ?"

"You remember I asked you about Max O'Malley?"

"Sure. The President's bundler."

"And you asked me what he's got to do with Zimbabwe?"

"Yes . . . Don't tell me he's involved with this cricket business?"

"No. It's quite the opposite."

"I'm listening."

"He's funding the other side."

"What do you mean?"

"Max O'Malley is the secret business partner for" — Judd swallowed hard — "Simba Chimurenga."

48.

Leesburg, Virginia
Sunday, 5:16 a.m. Eastern Standard Time
William Alfred Rogerson lay awake in his four-poster bed staring at the Georgian-era cornice on his ceiling. The sun had not yet risen, so he couldn't see the trees outside his window or the barn beyond them that housed his prize show horse, a chestnut gelding named Roosevelt.

Instead, he lay there, listening for predawn birdsong and trying to block out the frustrations of the office. The chirping of a phone broke his bedroom's serenity. *Khartoum?* That was the first thought that ran through his mind. *Or maybe Kinshasa? Or Stuttgart?* Rogerson groaned as he rolled over in bed to reach for the handset. He squinted with one eye. A video call from Embassy Harare. He groaned again and answered.

"What's the emergency?"

"Sorry, Bill," said the pale face on the

screen. "I didn't want to wake you, but we've got a problem."

"What is it, Arnie?" asked Rogerson as he plucked his reading glasses off the side table and slid them onto the end of his nose.

"Ryker."

"Goddamn Landon Parker!" blurted Rogerson. "I told him sending Ryker was a stupid idea. But you know the seventh floor. They always know best. What's Ryker done this time?"

"Completely off the reservation on the election statement."

"You woke me before sunrise on a Sunday morning for an election statement?"

"I'm sorry, Bill. The official election results are due to be announced at noon local time. That's forty minutes from now. I'm trying to get the U.S. statement ready to release as soon as they announce the results. I don't want a moment of uncertainty. I want to nail this thing down as quickly as we can. We can't have confusion here about where the United States stands. It could create problems if we wait too long."

"Fine, Arnie. So what's the problem?"

"Ryker won't clear it."

"What do you mean he won't clear it? He doesn't have to goddamn clear it."

"Ryker has some of the bureaus back in D.C. worried about crossing Landon Parker. They're holding things up until we get agreement on the text."

Proxy war punk, thought Rogerson. He steeled himself and exhaled deeply. It was too early to get pissed off about Ryker. "Can we live with his changes to the statement? It's not policy. It's just a report of your observer mission, right?"

"That's the problem. It's not a few tweaks. Ryker's insisting we go in a *completely different* direction. He wasn't even part of the observer team, but he's refusing to cave. I keep telling him this is what headquarters wants. *This is what* you *want.* But he's stonewalling. I can send it over now. If you clear it, I'll get the others to go along."

"Don't send it. We can do this right now. Read it to me."

"Yes, Bill. One second. I've got it right here . . ." Rogerson glanced at the clock. *Five eighteen in the morning. For* Zimbabwe?

"Okay, ready, Bill. 'On behalf of the United States of America, I want to congratulate the people of Zimbabwe for their peaceful vote. The election has been an historic opportunity for the people of Zimbabwe to come together to build a better future. Across the country, ordinary

374

Zimbabweans turned out by the thousands to exercise their fundamental democratic rights. We are inspired by the population's desire to make their voices heard through the ballot box. We applaud the patience of those who waited hours to vote and commend all parties for waiting for the official tally. The American Embassy Election Observer Mission in Zimbabwe was satisfied with the conduct of the elections. We strongly urge all parties and their supporters to respect the determination of the election commission and to settle any disputes through the courts rather than the streets. The United States stands with Zimbabwe and will continue to be a strong friend and ally of the Zimbabwean people.' "

"Poetry, Arnie."

"I'm glad you still like it, Bill."

"Still?"

"It's the statement you and I wrote together after the elections in Benin back in '96. Nearly word for word."

"Holds up, Arnie."

"Yes, it does."

"So what's Ryker's problem?"

"Ryker insists there are major problems with the election. That AEEOMZ got it wrong. That *I* got it wrong."

"What went wrong?"

"If you ask him, everything. The conditions for a free and fair vote, the polling stations, the vote tallies."

"Did you tell him it's Africa? That no vote is perfect? That he's being naïve?"

"Of course. He's holding his ground. I told him a delay in the U.S. statement would have consequences. It would create uncertainty and could even spark violence. But he doesn't care."

"If persuasion won't work, what about the facts? You've got the observer mission reports on your side. What's his evidence?"

"He doesn't have any. He says it's coming."

"Coming? The United States is supposed to sit on its hands and unnecessarily invite chaos in a foreign country while we wait for him? Ryker wants to withhold the U.S. endorsement on a hunch?"

"He's not just asking for a delay. It's much worse than that. He's proposing alternative language condemning the official result. I'll read it to you."

"No, don't. I don't want to hear it. Ryker is trying to single-handedly change our policy."

"Right."

"That's not his job."

"That's what I told him, Bill."

"I won't allow it."

"He's using his direct line to Landon Parker as leverage."

"Not for long. I'll sort this out," said Rogerson.

"One more thing, Bill."

"What is it, Arnie?" he growled.

"Ryker and this woman Espinosa from DOJ are asking questions."

"About what?"

"An incident twenty years ago. An army operation in the north. Supposedly there were civilian deaths. I'm hearing from my staff they are digging deep and asking some tough questions around town about what happened."

"Twenty years ago?"

"Yep."

"He was sent to deal with the election and now he's sticking his nose into ancient history?"

"That's what I told him."

"Ryker is supposed to be fixing crises, not creating new ones, goddammit."

"Uh-huh," Tallyberger grunted.

"Are there bodies in the streets? Are there bodies, Arnie?" Rogerson asked.

"No, sir."

"Well, then, it's not a crisis. Is it?"

"No, it's not. What do you want me to do

about it, Bill?"

"I told you, I'll sort this out. I'll sort Ryker out once and for all."

49.

Mufakose, Suburb of Harare, Zimbabwe
Sunday, 11:24 a.m. Central Africa Time
"The Green Mambas are stealing our votes!" shouted Tinashe, bursting through the door.

Tsitsi looked up from the stove where she was stirring a black pot full of *sadza.* With one hand on her hip, the other wielding a wooden spoon like a baton, she tsked. "Tssss, Tinashe!"

"The Green Mambas. Tino is using those boys to steal our votes. Sekai says they have ways to make our votes disappear."

"Sekai? Tssss! Where was he? Drinking *chibuku* at the shebeen again?"

Tinashe didn't answer.

"This fool is drinking beer on a Sunday morning?" She was shaking her head. *"On the Lord's Day?* And you are listening to him? What does that make *you?"*

"Sekai's brother is in the army. He says

379

the big men have special powers. He says they have magic!"

"Why do you believe such foolishness?"

"The big men use the Green Mambas to make our votes disappear."

"The street boys they pay to beat up old women? Those Green Mambas?"

"*Ehe.* They are dangerous."

"Tssss!"

"The big men give them *muti* to make them numb."

"Tinashe, you are too clever for this."

"When they take the *muti,* they have no fear. They can kill without feeling."

"Tssss! They are street boys who don't even have shoes. What magic can they have? Why do you believe such rubbish?"

"Why hasn't Gugu been declared the winner? Sekai says —"

"*Sekai?!?* Why do you listen to anything that fool says?"

She turned her back on him and stirred her pot.

"You are right. Forget Sekai. But, Tsitsi, do you believe our votes will be counted? Do you believe Gugu will be allowed to beat the old man?"

Tsitsi felt a rush of tension rise from her toes up through her body and into her neck. She didn't answer.

"Sekai says the people are gathering in town. At two o'clock. If there is no announcement of the election, the people will demand it."

Tsitsi turned and, for the first time that day, really looked at Tinashe's face, recognizing the fear.

"We must go," he said, his eyes wide. "We must stand up for Gugu."

She set down the spoon and turned off the stove. She brushed the front of her apron, then nodded. "Let's go."

50.

Bangkok, Thailand
Sunday, 4:45 p.m. Indochina Time (5:45 a.m.
  Eastern Standard Time + 11 Hours)

Max O'Malley swished the golden Scotch in his mouth, feeling the leathery liquid burn his tongue. He swallowed hard, smacked his lips, and exhaled a loud "Ahhhhh." He collapsed in his leather desk chair and spun around to take in the view. The city simmered silently below, the weekend traffic already coagulating Bangkok's arteries.

So many opportunities out there, he thought. *Ripe pickings.*

The sun was still high in the sky, but the skyscrapers cast elongated shadows. Definitely not too early for good Scotch, he assured himself. He reached again for the bottle.

As he poured a second drink, O'Malley wondered if all this hassle was worth it.

After all the years, all the close calls, all the money, did he really need more? He had spent more than four decades putting together complicated business deals in complicated places. That's why the margins were so fat. O'Malley had learned early on that a little knowledge, like the right kind of chemicals to determine copper ore content or the latest spectrometry technology, could be highly profitable in the right place at the right time. Once he threw in knowing the right people, the profits could be disgusting. *Dirty fuck-you money.* The kind that could buy you a jet or your own island. Or a president. At that thought, he smiled and took another gulp.

O'Malley had gotten his start through sheer luck. He knew that. The dormitory lottery at Notre Dame put him in a ten- by twelve-foot room with a spotty teenager from Newport News, Virginia, named Randolph Whitaker. What luck that the Whitakers were a fourth-generation U.S. Navy family and Randy's mother was connected deep into the Washington political fundraising circuit. That combination of fortune had projected little Randy meteorically through the ranks of the Pentagon hierarchy, eventually making him the youngest-ever Undersecretary of Defense for Acquisition.

The Pentagon's checkbook. *The little prick,* thought O'Malley, tipping back his glass.

Even if no one could have predicted all those years ago his college roommate's eventual success, O'Malley regularly congratulated himself for recognizing a rising star early and getting close. Even better, he'd leveraged his friendship with Randy to break into defense contracting, just as the Reagan Cold War buildup was gaining steam. *Shooting fish in a barrel.* A small heavy-equipment procurement contract was parlayed into ever larger deals and, more importantly, new relationships around the world.

Technology + contacts + discretion = fat profits. That was Royal Deepwater Venture Capital's business model. It was the formula that had made Max O'Malley rich and powerful. *Dirty fuck-you money.*

In the early days of Royal Deepwater, Randy approached Max to put together a top secret deal for the U.S. government, some kind of experimental uranium exploration in a godforsaken corner of Africa that required extreme discretion and arm's-length deniability. O'Malley jumped on the opportunity. The Kanyemba mining project had barely started when the local security forces got out of hand and the whole thing was shut down. It was always petty local politics that complicated the really big deals. He had seen it first in Zimbabwe. And then in Bolivia and Sri Lanka and Ethiopia.

His team was pulled out of Kanyemba, and the very next day thick-necked men arrived at his office in northern Virginia to seize each and every document related to the deal. The whole project was wiped clean from company records. That's when he opened offices in Panama, Dubai, and Bangkok. O'Malley thought at the time that that was the end of the Kanyemba investment, that it was a total write-off, and he moved on.

Even when the mining deals would go bad, Max O'Malley always extracted a commodity more valuable: new contacts. Back then he hadn't realized that failed ventures in Ethiopia and Zimbabwe would one day prove even more lucrative. After diamonds were discovered in the same country that had granted refuge to Solomon Zagwe, O'Malley fell into another combination of fortune.

Technology + contacts + discretion = fat profits. The formula was paying hefty dividends again. O'Malley also knew he needed protection from unforeseen consequences. The political wind could blow one way and then the other. He never wanted to find himself defenseless, too far out on a limb. He had seen it in too many places, and not just in the developing world, but in the most dangerous place of all: Washington, D.C.

Fortunately, buying influence in Washington wasn't too difficult. Host a cocktail party for well-connected friends, write a few small checks to campaigns and a few large checks to political action committees, and you were in. The prize was not the "People's Defender" certificate hanging on his wall or even the celebrity photos. Sure, they stoked his ego and even occasionally proved helpful in sealing a business deal. But their real value was insurance. If things ever went bad, someone would answer his phone calls.

At that thought, Max O'Malley's phone rang. His caller ID showed a 202 area code, but the rest of the number showed as 000-0000. A scrambled call from Washington.

He picked up the phone and grunted into the handset.

"Diamond smuggling?" shouted Landon Parker on the other end. "Really, Max? *Diamonds?* What the fuck are you thinking?"

"Calm down. You don't know what you are talking about."

"I know a bank account linked to your business is transferring large sums from Asia to accounts controlled by the military in Zimbabwe. How do you explain that?"

"The State Department doesn't always have the whole picture. You should know that by now, Landon."

"Does the *Washington Post* have the whole picture, Max? I didn't get this from intel. I know about your diamond business because a civilian plugged deep into the *Post* told me. A motherfucking civilian, Max! Now, how the fuck do you explain that?"

"You know I have many business interests," replied O'Malley. "You know I can't possibly control every entity in the value chain."

"Cease and desist, Max. You got that? *Cease and fucking desist.*"

"I haven't done anything to cease, Landon."

"Do you really want everything out in the open, Max? Do you really want reporters digging into the history of Royal Deepwater? In Zimbabwe, for Christ's sake? Of all places, you had to go back to *Zimbabwe*? Do any of us want that?"

"I never did anything wrong. The mistakes were all the Pentagon's. I don't have anything to hide. Uranium exploration isn't illegal."

"That's not the point. How do you think

the White House will react? Political donations are public records, Max. They
screened you. You think they'll just allow
this to come out? You think they'll take this
lying down?"

"That's not my problem."

"What about the Secretary of State? Do
you think she's going to allow this?"

"That's not the right question, Landon.
The right question is, how does the Secretary plan to run for the highest office
without my money? Do you know how
much the next presidential campaign is going to cost, Landon?"

"You are threatening the wrong guy, Max.
We don't need you. There are plenty of rich
assholes in Washington."

"But the Secretary has *already* needed me.
You've *already* accepted this asshole's
money. Check the PAC records."

After a brief pause, Landon Parker yelled,
"Fuck you!" and shattered his phone against
the wall.

51.

Harare, Zimbabwe
Sunday, 12:12 p.m. Central Africa Time

A buzz rippled through the crowd as a fat man wearing a tight pin-striped suit waddled from a side door up to the podium. A floral bouquet of microphones adorned the top of the stand. The Ministry of Information's banquet hall had been turned into a makeshift press room for the election announcement.

The man tapped the microphones roughly before removing his sunglasses and eyeing the room of journalists and diplomats. He then extracted a white handkerchief from his pocket and wiped his forehead. All eyes in the room focused on him. Judd Ryker, standing at the far back, craned his neck to get a better view.

"Ladies and gentlemen," the fat man began, a slight quiver in his voice. "Thank you for your patience. The election commissioner has not yet arrived. Therefore we do not have results to report."

"Where is Commissioner Makwere?" asked a reporter in the front row.

"I'm not taking questions."

"Do you know where he is?"

"No, I'm not taking questions," he replied.

"No, you don't know where he is? How does the ministry not know the location of the commissioner?"

"No, no . . ." he repeated, waving his hands and turning to leave. "That is not what I said. No questions."

"Is there any truth to the rumor that Commissioner Makwere is missing?" shouted a journalist at the back.

The spokesman averted his eyes and wobbled toward the exit, unleashing a barrage of new questions from the audience.

"Is Makwere missing?"

"Is Makwere still the commissioner?"

"Has he fled the country?"

"Is Makwere alive?"

"Can you confirm the election commissioner is still alive?"

At that last question, the man reached the door, ducked inside, and slammed it shut. On cue, the journalists and diplomats all dialed their phones in an outburst of chatter.

A few seconds later, on the other side of town, in a windowless conference room, phones vibrated in the pockets of Arnold Tallyberger and Brock Branson.

Judd's mind raced. *What's happening? Is this Minute Zero? How can I know?*

Judd plucked his phone out and was about to dial when a sudden movement at the front of the room sent another ripple through the crowd. With no warning, General Simba Chimurenga marched in through the side door. The crowd gasped and then hushed. Chimurenga strode up to the microphones and, without hesitation, began speaking.

"Ladies and gentlemen. I know you are here for the election results. I will come to that in a moment. But I first must address an urgent threat facing the Republic of Zimbabwe. As many of you have seen on the television, Zimbabwe was attacked early this morning. A terrorist explosion in our own Gun Hill neighborhood resulted in the deaths of several of Zimbabwe's patriots. This was a direct attack on our great nation. I do not have any further details to share at this time, but as the president's national security advisor, I assure you we will find the culprits and bring them to justice.

"I am urging the public now to assist the authorities by providing any information you may have about the bombers. What I can share with you now is we are on the lookout for a black Nissan sedan seen in the area at the time of the attack. We have reports of a foreign woman driving the Nissan. *A white woman,*" he snarled.

"If anyone has further information about the car, this woman, or her coconspirators, please alert the authorities. Cash rewards will be available for anyone who provides information leading to the capture of these terrorists."

Chimurenga paused to assess the audience. As he scanned the back of the room, he caught Judd's eye. Judd wasn't certain, but he thought Chimurenga's eyes narrowed.

"I'm afraid I have another important announcement. Our security forces charged with protecting the people have uncovered an assassination plot against senior members of the government. This is a grave threat to the nation and to Zimbabwe's precious democracy. In the midst of our election, this is a direct assault on the people. But I am here to tell you, the public and our friends around the world, we will not be shaken. Zimbabwe is strong," he said as he pounded his fist on the lectern.

"I cannot go into any detail for security reasons, but we have new information linking this conspiracy to members of the Democracy Union of Zimbabwe. I am shocked and appalled, as I'm sure all Zimbabweans are, that one of our own political parties is engaged in violent and treasonous activity to destabilize the state. We do not yet know with certainty if the attack in Gun Hill and the new plot are connected, but we believe they are. The army and police are conducting sweeps as I speak, rooting out our enemies. I urge the public to assist the security forces in this task. Rest assured, we will not allow these traitors and sellouts to succeed.

"As a result of the disturbing developments today and the threat to sovereignty of the nation, and on the orders of His Excellency the President of the Republic, I am hereby announcing a state of emergency." The crowd erupted.

"Ladies and gentlemen, please!" he shouted. "Until security is reestablished and the stooges and traitors are rooted out, we are expanding the powers of the security forces to protect the people. I urge all citizens to cooperate with the army and the police and for our friends abroad to understand the special circumstances which required us to take this action today."

Chimurenga raised his hands. "We are all in this together. God Bless the Republic of Zimbabwe."

"Will you take questions, General?" asked a journalist in the front row.

"I have nothing to hide. What is your question?"

"Where is President Tinotenda?"

"I have spoken with His Excellency, President Winston Tinotenda, a few minutes ago and I can assure you he is safe and he is strong. He will address the nation soon."

"When?"

"Today. The president will address the nation this afternoon," Chimurenga announced.

"You said the DUZ is responsible for the attacks. Is Gugu Mutonga under arrest?" asked another journalist.

"I said we have information linking the DUZ to a conspiracy against the government and the bombing in Gun Hill. We are seeking Ms. Mutonga for questioning."

"Is Gugu Mutonga a suspect?"

"We are seeking her cooperation. If her party is involved in a plot against the state, then it is a very serious crime. As head of the party, we will want to know what she knows."

"So she is not in custody?"

"Not yet. I urge her to turn herself in and to share with the authorities any information she may have that might help with the investigation."

"How long will the state of emergency last?"

"As long as necessary to restore order. One last question."

Judd raised his hand.

"Yes, you at the back. Our American visitor. What is your question, Dr. Ryker?"

"General, we were all gathered here for the election results. Can we still expect them today?"

"The unexpected events of today will unfortunately postpone the election results. We regret the delay. But let me be very clear. We will not allow terrorists and traitors to disrupt our democracy. I assure you the election commissioner is working on the final tallies. When he has completed his work, we will make the official announcement."

Chimurenga gripped the lectern with both hands and hunched over. "Until that time, I urge the media and our friends around the world to refrain from spreading false rumors which only serve to destabilize the nation. Those who wish to destroy our democracy cannot be allowed to succeed. The enemies of Zimbabwe have declared war on the nation." Chimurenga slammed a fist down on the podium. "Zimbabwe will defeat them!"

He raised his fist and stared into the camera. "Forward with progress!" he yelled, punching the air. "Forward with democracy! Forward with Zimbabwe!"

And then he turned and walked out.

52.

The U.S. Assistant Secretary of State for African Affairs, William Rogerson, called the meeting to order with a non-apology.

"Sorry to call this meeting so early on a Sunday morning. None of us want to be here. The events in Zimbabwe over the past twelve hours, combined with" — he glanced up at the screen showing Ambassador Tallyberger and Judd Ryker sitting in a poorly lit conference room on the other side of the globe — "gridlock in this building, made this emergency meeting unavoidable."

Rogerson, in a freshly pressed light gray suit, sat at the head of the conference table like a king holding court. Tall paper coffee cups dotted the table, which was surrounded by bleary Foreign Service officers in weekend casual dress. No one was smiling.

Judd had raced back to the embassy from the press conference after receiving a text from his assistant, Serena, about an emergency Zimbabwe policy meeting. No one had alerted him, but Serena was keeping a close watch through a network she'd built up over fourteen years working at the Department of State. Serena had also quietly engineered the delay of the elections statement, discreetly calling in favors to stall clearance by horse-trading favors with friends in the crime and democracy bureaus. She couldn't get senior policy makers to change their minds. But she could use their assistants to slow the whole process down.

Judd hadn't specifically asked her to do it, of course. But they had developed a rhythm and she knew this was her next move.

"Okay, people," Rogerson began. "Let's start with Embassy Harare. Ambassador, can you brief us on where we are?"

"Thank you, sir," responded Tallyberger, leaning in toward the camera. His face consumed most of the screen, jolting those in Washington to sit back in their chairs. "The election was completed yesterday and our observer mission team concluded its report. There were some problems, of course."

"We've all seen our share of African elec-

398

tions," offered Rogerson. Nods all around the table.

"Yes, sir. Some problems, of course," Tallyberger continued. "But we did not witness any violence and we observed only limited misconduct by the security forces. Nothing too worrying. Overall we have judged the elections to be at least minimally satisfactory. Our main concern is now over delays in releasing the results. A long delay could create a window for instability."

"Which is why we are here this morning, correct, Ambassador?" Rogerson asked.

"Correct, Mr. Assistant Secretary. The election results have been postponed because of new security issues raised by the government. The authorities have declared a state of emergency in response to an explosion at the home of an Ethiopian exile and reports of a foiled plot against senior officials. We cannot confirm the details of either event, but the government is clearly on edge. They've asked for our patience and understanding with the election results."

"Who exactly is the Ethiopian, Ambassador?"

"General Solomon Zagwe. He was once President of Ethiopia but fled the country after a revolt. Tinotenda gave him refuge and he's been here ever since."

"Red Fear Zagwe," said Rogerson. "I didn't realize he was still alive."

"He isn't, sir. We believe he was killed last night in the explosion," Tallyberger said.

"I see. What about this plot? Is it a coup attempt?"

"I don't believe so. Zimbabwe has never had a coup in its entire history. Right now the only details we have are from General Chimurenga's statement about an hour ago. He claims to have uncovered an assassination plot linked to the main opposition party, but we can't confirm any of this."

"Do our intelligence services know anything about this?"

"The chief of station here is looking into it," Tallyberger replied. "But he doesn't have anything yet."

"Thank you, Ambassador. What is your recommended course of action for the United States?" Rogerson asked.

"The recommendation from Embassy Harare is to pursue a three-track strategy —"

"Excuse me, Ambassador," interrupted Rogerson. "I think you mean two tracks."

"Yes, did I say three? I meant two. The recommendation from Embassy Harare is to pursue a two-track strategy to stabilize the situation. One" — Tallyberger held up one finger — "we issue our election statement erasing doubts about the legitimacy of the vote. Two" — he held up a second finger — "we offer American assistance to investigate the bombing and the plot. These two steps would help to squelch the growing uncertainty and reduce the chances of a meltdown on the streets."

"Very good, Ambassador. What specifically would you recommend as a next step for each of your recommended two tracks?"

Judd tried to keep a straight face but, watching through a video screen, he couldn't read the body language of his colleagues. This was obviously a rehearsed setup, he thought. *Everyone sees that, right?*

"Mr. Assistant Secretary," replied Tallyberger. "Embassy Harare recommends that, one" — the finger again — "we release the statement calling on all parties to respect the election commission's determination and urge them to settle any disputes through the courts rather than on the streets. That statement was drafted earlier this morning and is currently stuck in the State clearance process.

"And two" — two fingers up — "we offer to fly in an FBI forensics team to assess the bomb site and an intelligence assessment of the alleged conspiracy. I'm confident our intelligence services could, if directed, help determine the truth here. These two acts would be high-value good faith gestures and accomplish our stabilization objective."

"Thank you, Ambassador. Before I share my own views, let's hear from around the building."

"Political-Military Affairs concurs."

"International Narcotics and Law Enforcement concurs."

"Democracy, Human Rights, and Labor, too . . ."

And around the table rang approvals. With each one, Judd winced, realizing Rogerson had precooked the meeting. This was no debate. It was all political theater. Despite Serena's delaying tactics, Judd had walked right into a classic State Department ambush.

Finally, everyone had spoken except Judd. "Very well, colleagues," announced Rogerson. "I see everyone wants to get back to their families —"

"I have a question," interrupted Judd.

"S/CRU isn't on the clearance list, I'm afraid, Dr. Ryker."

"I understand the desire to mitigate uncertainty," he said, ignoring Rogerson's slight, "but are we sure any of the information we have is accurate? Are we sure the election results aren't *fraudulent?* Without any independent verification, how can we be sure the alleged plot isn't also a deception? How do we know we aren't getting played here?"

"Does S/CRU have any new information to share with the other bureaus that might contradict what we have just heard? And remind me, Dr. Ryker: You arrived in Zimbabwe when?"

"Yesterday."

"Right, yesterday. And your new information since yesterday is . . . ?"

"I don't have anything yet. But if we move forward immediately with our approval, we close off our options to influence events. And if we are wrong, then we'll have helped Tinotenda subvert the election and consolidate power."

"Ambassador Tallyberger, you are our man in Harare. You've been sent there by the President of the United States to be our eyes and ears on the ground. You've been there for the past three years. What's your assessment, Ambassador?"

Tallyberger rubbed his mustache as he stared into the camera. "Without any countervailing evidence, I think Dr. Ryker's scenario is . . . unlikely."

"And the costs of delay?"

"Given the low-probability, the costs of delay outweigh the benefits."

"I agree," said Rogerson quickly. "I don't think we have time to consider low-probability outcomes, Dr. Ryker. The prudent approach is the two-pronged strategy outlined by Ambassador Tallyberger. I've also spoken with Landon Parker this morning and he assured me we'll have seventh-floor concurrence. Meeting adjourned."

Tallyberger pushed the button, turning off the video feed.

"I'm sorry, Dr. Ryker," he said without emotion.

"No apologies necessary, Ambassador."

"A vigorous policy debate is always healthy. But sometimes you lose. That's the game."

"Game?"

"Yes, this is all a game. Foreign policy. The Foreign Service. That's what we do. Sometimes you win and sometimes you lose. Sometimes you are lucky and sometimes you aren't lucky."

Lucky? thought Judd. *Lucky Magombe.*

53.

Georgetown, Washington, D.C.
Sunday, 7:12 a.m. Eastern Standard Time
Jessica Ryker's tank top was soaked through with sweat. She stepped off the treadmill and slapped a towel over her shoulder. As she wiped her neck and forehead, she checked on her two boys in the next room, sitting happily catatonic in front of the television.

"Boys?" They didn't answer. "Mommy is jumping in the shower." No reply.

Jessica walked upstairs to the bathroom, peeling off the damp gym clothes and leaving a trail in the hallway. In the bathroom she caught herself naked in the mirror. The muscles on her thighs and calves rippled under her mocha-colored skin. She let her long black hair down from the ponytail and shook it out. She turned her head side to side, examining her own face in detail. She was in her late thirties, but her skin was still tight and her high cheekbones gave her a youthful permanence. *From my mother,* she thought.

Jessica lifted her chin and with one finger traced a scar along the underside of her jawbone. As her runner's high receded, the suppressed anger of the past returned. *For my mother,* she thought.

She turned on the hot water and inhaled the steam. Jessica had received a text message in the middle of the night confirming General Solomon Zagwe's untimely death. Someone had gotten to him.

As she showered, Jessica could feel the salty residue washing away, leaving her clean and fresh. The bitterness of the past that she had held tight was being replaced by the cool aromas of her lemon and sandalwood shampoo. She closed her eyes and pushed out any unpleasant emotions, clearing her head for the mental inventory of what she needed to do today. Jessica Ryker knew she had unfinished business.

On the other side of the bathroom door, on top of the pile of wet acrylic lying in the hallway, her cell phone played a dance song and illuminated. A pudgy hand reached down and grabbed the phone, a familiar photograph flashing on the screen. A sticky finger pressed the answer button.

"Daddy?" said the voice.

"Noah?" asked a surprised Judd.

"Uh-huh. Hello, Daddy!" he gurgled.

"Where's Mommy?"

"I don't know."

"Is everything all right, Noah?"

"Uh-huh."

"What are you doing?"

"Watching TV."

"With Toby?"

"Uh-huh."

"Very nice. Are you having fun, Noah?"

"Daddy, are you on the airplane again?"

"Yes, Noah. I'm in Africa."

"Africa," repeated the three-year-old.

"Do you remember I showed it to you on the map?"

"Uh-huh."

"I miss you, Noah."

"Uh-huh."

"Do you miss me?"

"Uh-huh."

"I'll be home soon. Just a few days."

"You see birdies?"

"Birdies? Yes, there are lots of birds in Africa. They have some big, beautiful birds here in Zimbabwe. Right where I am now."

"Mommy won't let you kill the birdies," Noah whined.

"What?"

"Mommy said no one can kill the birdies. She won't let them."

"Okay. I'm sure Mom is right. No one is killing any birds here. Don't you worry, Noah," said Judd. "Can you find Mommy for me?"

"Purple umbrella."

"What, Noah?"

"Umbrella. Mommy talked to the man about selling the purple umbrella."

"What man, Noah? Selling what umbrella?"

"I don't know."

Jessica opened the door, holding a towel around her chest. "Who are you talking to?"

The boy stared up innocently at his mother, a donut squished in one fist, her cell phone gripped in the other. He dropped the phone on the floor, jammed the donut into his mouth, and stumbled away. Jessica glanced down, a photograph of her husband's face illuminated on the screen. She snatched it. "Judd?"

"Jess?"

"Did Noah call you on my phone?"

"No, I called you and he answered. What's going on over there?"

"Nothing. I was in the shower."

"He was telling me you aren't going to let anyone kill the birds. Are you sure everything is all right?"

"Yes, yes," she laughed. "It's from some cartoon the boys were watching."

"And a purple umbrella?"

"Purple *umbrella*?" Damn! She'd been careless. But she laughed again. "It probably belongs to a green giraffe he kept telling me about yesterday. The giraffe was eating pickles, too. See what you're missing when you travel?"

Judd sighed. "I know."

"*You* called *me*. Is everything okay?" she asked.

"I didn't want you to worry."

"I'm not worried. Has something happened?"

"Yes. But I'm fine. I'm fine," he said. "If you turn on CNN, you'll see there's been an explosion. But I called because I didn't want you to worry."

"An explosion? I wasn't worried until now," she said. "Do you have to leave? What's the embassy telling you?"

"They've confirmed that a bomb went off, but they don't believe it was political. They're telling us it's probably just a business dispute. Nothing to do with the embassy and no threat to foreign nationals."

"What do *you* think?"

"I'm sure the embassy knows what they're

talking about, Jess."

"Pretty suspicious to have a bombing right in the middle of an election, don't you think?"

"Could be a coincidence."

"Do you believe in coincidences, Judd?"

Good question.

"Judd, do you believe in coincidences?" she asked again.

"I have to focus on the election right now," he said. "That's why I'm here."

"And what about it, Judd? Who's going to win?"

"No results yet. That's what I'm working on," Judd stared down at his computer screen. **UNITED STATES' CONCERNS ABOUT THE INTEGRITY OF THE ELECTION IN ZIMBABWE** was written across the top. Below the title, the screen displayed a table showing reported election results compared side by side with the parallel voting tabulation he'd received from Mariana.

"Remember you told me to force the issue? That's what I'm doing, Jess. I'm seizing Minute Zero."

"Good for you."

"I'm taking your advice, sweets."

"You were worried about some kind of political blowback?"

"I think I've got that covered, too. Your

advice again."

"Good. I'm glad I was helpful."

"For the first time since I got to Zimbabwe, I think we've got a real chance to make a difference here," he said.

Jessica's phone buzzed and flashed **DANIEL DOLLAR**. Her shorthand code for DDO, the deputy director of operations. Her boss. She pushed **DIVERT TO VOICEMAIL**.

"Sweets, I'm glad things are looking up," she said. "The kids are starting to shout. I've got to go, I'm sorry."

"That's fine, Jess. Just know I'm safe. Don't worry."

"I won't. I only wish I could help you."

"You've helped plenty already. I'll call you again soon. I love you."

"Love you, too." She blew him a kiss and ended the call.

Once they were disconnected, Judd stared at his phone, unsure of his next move.

Jessica, however, knew exactly what to do. She immediately dialed a different number.

"Yes, ma'am?" Sunday answered.

"We haven't got much time. I need you to copy the best of the shots from our bird over Kanyemba and send them to Judd in Harare. We need the ones that are very clear, the indisputable ones."

"Yes, ma'am."

"Now. Do it right now. Don't take any other calls. Don't do anything else. Don't even talk to anyone until you are done. Just send the pictures."

"I'm on it."

"Thank you, Sunday."

"I'm being pulled off Zimbabwe, ma'am. Starting tomorrow."

"I know. Somali pirates get all the glory. More of a reason to hurry."

"Yes, ma'am."

Click.

Jessica was satisfied the pieces were falling into place. And she thought she'd pulled off the misdirection with Judd on the phone. She knew the manipulation of her husband would come back to haunt her. She would have to deal with that problem soon enough. For now, she had to stay focused on her task. After years of waiting, this was her moment. She couldn't allow sentiment to cloud her judgment. Or deter her. She finished dressing and descended the stairs to make her children breakfast.

Eight thousand miles away, Judd's computer chirped with an urgent message from Sunday. He double-clicked and opened the attached photos. Sunday's only notation was: Kanyemba mine. Taken over the past 24 hours. Scroll in sequence.

At first he wasn't sure what he was looking at. But then he realized Sunday had sent the photos in order of increasing amplification. When he got to the final picture — a close-up geothermal image of an underground room within the Kanyemba mine — and he could see what was inside, the moment he realized what was hidden in that hole in the ground, his stomach convulsed. His mind spun and he felt dizzy. He turned and vomited violently into the trash can.

As Judd coughed and spit the sour acids from deep in his stomach, he suddenly realized the sickening image on his screen was in fact . . . a magnificent gift.

54.

Harare, Zimbabwe
Sunday, 2:38 p.m. Central Africa Time
People cleared the streets when they heard the sirens coming. The president's convoy began with two dozen policemen on motorcycles, blocking traffic and chasing slow pedestrians from the oncoming assault. Next came six military trucks, each bristling with soldiers in sunglasses, their AK-47s pointing menacingly in all directions. They shouted obscenities at the bystanders and cleared whatever traffic remained. The third wave was a train of three identical black Mercedes limousines with tinted windows. One of those — no one could ever be sure which — carried President Winston Tinotenda. The final wave was an ambulance and communications vehicle surrounded by another cloud of policemen.

Tinotenda had initially been resistant to the idea that he needed such protection to

414

move around his own capital. He worried that it isolated him from his people and displayed arrogance. But as his paranoia grew, so, too, did his security entourage. General Simba Chimurenga had proposed the mass show of force combined with extra vehicles as a deterrent to potential assassins. Who those assassins might be was a question no one ever asked. But over the years, both the president and the public had grown accustomed to this regular tornado of security blowing through the city whenever the president was on the move.

On this day, Tinotenda, sitting in the backseat of the second limousine, squinted through thick reading glasses at the text in front of him. It was a victory speech one of his public relations lackeys had prepared that he'd been due to give nearly forty minutes ago. The speech was to follow the announcement of the final results of another overwhelming election landslide. He now intended to explain the need for the state of emergency and the new security measures he was taking to protect the nation.

Tino had considered a reconciliatory speech. He'd even toyed with the idea of using the occasion of another massive victory to reach out to his opponents, perhaps even offer Gugu Mutonga a cabinet position, something small and powerless. Maybe even create a new ministry. No budget or staff, of course, but it would come with a government house and a generous expense account. The point would be an unmistakable peace offering. Maybe that would shut her up. Maybe it would smooth the way for whatever came after his eventual death. He saw that the people didn't believe he would ever die, that the father of the nation would live forever. But after eighty-eight years he also knew his time on earth was limited.

But no, the First Lady had convinced him otherwise. Reaching out to *that woman* would make him seem weak and indecisive. It would only embolden their enemies, Harriet insisted. She counseled lowering the hammer. Using their defeat at the ballot box to crush them once and for all. Tinotenda was unsure, but Chimurenga agreed with Harriet. So the president was reading a text full of revolutionary vitriol. It was red meat for the party faithful. It attacked the opposition as traitors and sellouts.

Tino slouched back in the seat, oblivious to the sirens and the chaos outside his limousine. No, he thought, that was not the right path. He would soften the speech, he decided, if only to show he was no monster. President Tinotenda reached into the breast pocket of his jacket to find his fountain pen. After fumbling for a few seconds, his unsteady fingers grasped it. He eyed the black and gold Mont Blanc Special Edition closely, remembering fondly it was a gift from the Malaysian prime minister. Yes, he would make a peace offering. He would rewrite the speech, even if his people had to wait.

As he touched the paper with his pen, the president suddenly sensed a whoosh of air in his eardrums. His vision went bright white, a loud explosion cracked through his skull, and then everything went solid black.

55.

Twickenham, London
Sunday, 1:40 p.m. Greenwich Mean Time

". . . Not in this land alone,"

bellowed eighty thousand rugby fans in unison.

"But be God's mercies known,
From shore to shore!
Lord make the nations see,
That men should brothers be,
And form one family,
The wide world over."

Simon Kenny-Waddington, sporting a sparkling white England jersey with a bright red rose emblem on his left breast, took a deep breath for the final stanza.

"From every latent foe,
From the assassin's blow,

God save the Queen!
O'er her thine arm extend,
For Britain's sake defend,
Our mother, prince, and friend,
God save the Queen!"

Simon suddenly remembered the call he really should make before the game began.

"Pardon me," he said as he slipped past a line of men in identical shirts.

"Where you off to, my boy?" asked one of his friends.

"Shan't be a minute," he said. "I'll be back in my seat before kickoff."

"The office?"

"Simon, you must be joking!" scolded another.

"The Empire never sleeps," he replied with a shrug, and ducked out of the aisle and into a tunnel.

With a finger in one ear and the phone pressed hard against the other, he shouted in the phone, "Judd, my boy!"

"Yes, Simon, it's me. What's that noise?"

"Samoa."

"What?"

"Samoa!"

"You're in the Pacific?"

"No, rugby, my boy! We're playing Samoa! You're hearing the roar of Twickenham!"

"Samoa?"

"They're bloody good! They gave the All Blacks a rough go!"

"I can barely hear you, Simon," said Judd, trying not to yell himself.

"I'll be quick. It's almost kickoff. I'm calling because I discovered something that may be of interest."

"Yes?"

The roar of the crowd grew louder as the English team took the field. "Can you hear me, Judd?"

"Yes!" Judd shouted back into the phone.

"I think I figured out why your man Tino loves his boy Simba so much!"

"Yes! Go ahead!"

"Kanyemba."

"Kanyemba, right! What's the connection?"

"Simba was the commander."

"The commander?"

"Our man confirmed this today."

"Motowetsurohuro," muttered Judd.

"What?" shouted Simon, pressing the phone tighter to his ear.

"The massacre. You're saying Simba Chimurenga was the commander during the massacre at Kanyemba twenty years ago."

"That's why I'm calling you!"

"So that's why Chimurenga rose so

quickly through the ranks?"

"Seems so, yes!"

"That's why Chimurenga is trying to cover up the massacre now?"

"I think you're onto something, my boy!"

"That's why the two of them have remained so close?"

"I think so, yes!"

"That's why they have protected each other!"

"Yes —"

But Judd didn't hear that affirmation from Simon. The only thing he heard was the soft thud of another explosion off in the distance.

56.

Harare, Zimbabwe
Sunday, 2:44 p.m. Central Africa Time

When Tsitsi heard the explosion, her first instinct was to run toward the sound. Tinashe tried to pull her away, but she resisted. "Tssss! We must see!"

A cacophony of crying and frantic shouting filled the air. The crowd rushed past them. Sirens wailed in the distance. An old woman holding her forehead, blood running through her fingers, stumbled past in a haze. Up in the sky, a thin cloud of smoke was rising, guiding them to the bomb site.

As they neared the wreckage, an acrid smell of burning rubber invaded Tsitsi's nostrils. She covered her face with a handkerchief, one she'd brought for tear gas.

"My God . . ." she said to herself, staring down at twisted metal and the unmistakable sight of a severed human arm.

"The president's car?" Tinashe asked.

Tsitsi nodded.

"The president?"

Tsitsi shrugged.

They both turned back to the wreckage, when Tsitsi noticed a black and gold pen lying on the road between her feet. She bent down and picked it up, gently rolling it in her fingers. Amid the soot and smoke and debris, it was remarkably shiny, she thought.

"Where are the police, Tsitsi?" asked Tinashe, grabbing her other hand and squeezing tightly. They scanned the scene, no police, no army could be seen, just people running in every direction. The crack crack crack of gunfire went off in the distance.

"Chaos," she said, tossing the pen away with a dismissive flick of her wrist. "It's chaos."

57.

Harare, Zimbabwe
Sunday, 3:02 p.m. Central Africa Time

"Is the Presidential Mansion on lockdown?" demanded General Simba Chimurenga.

"Yes, General," said the soldier, saluting stiffly. "We are Emergency Code Red activated. All the roads leading up to the mansion have been closed. The gates have all been locked down. Tanks and Hippos have all been moved into defensive positions. The Presidential Guard has been fully deployed to all critical locations. Nothing is getting in here, sir."

"Commander, have they been issued with emergency orders?"

"Yes, General. All Presidential Guards have live ammunition and been granted emergency shoot-to-kill permissions."

"Good. What about the First Lady?"

"Sir?"

"Harriet Tinotenda! The First Lady!" he

growled. "Where is she, soldier?"

"In the bunker, sir."

"I want your best men protecting her. Redeploy immediately."

"Yes, General. Right away. Is there a threat against the First Lady?"

"Commander, we don't know yet. We must be on our highest alert. The nation is under attack as we speak and we are the last line of defense. I want the First Lady protected at all costs. Do you understand, soldier?"

"Yes, sir!" he barked, saluting again.

"Good. I'm going to check on the First Lady now and assure her she has nothing to worry about."

"Yes, sir."

"That is all. Go, Commander!"

"Sir?" asked the soldier quizzically.

"Make it quick, Commander. I have a nation to save."

"The president, sir?"

Chimurenga paused, then glanced down, averting his eyes. "The president is in critical condition. He sustained massive injuries from the terrorist blast that destroyed his car."

"Is President Tinotenda alive, General?"

"I don't have confirmation one way or the other. Once I know, the nation will be informed. For now, we must fight to protect Zimbabwe."

"Who is in charge, sir?"

"I am, Commander. Now go!"

The soldier paused for a brief moment and looked into Simba Chimurenga's eyes. "Yes, sir!"

Chimurenga descended a secret flight of stairs and walked down a long hallway lit only by bare industrial bulbs. The only sounds he could hear were the hollow click-clack of his own footsteps on the concrete floor. And a steady drip . . . drip . . . drip echo of water drops.

After fifty meters, he reached a steel door. He rapped on the door three times and a small sliding window opened. Two angry yellow eyes appeared.

"Open the door, soldier!" hissed Chimurenga.

"I'm under strict orders not to open the door for anyone, sir."

"Do you know who I am, soldier?"

"Yes, sir. But my commander —"

"*I* am your commander. Now open the door!"

"Open the door, you fool!" said a husky woman's voice inside the room. The window slid shut and the yellow eyes disappeared.

After a few seconds the hallway was filled

with the sound of scraping steel and a loud clang. Then the door banged open.

Inside, six soldiers in army-green uniforms and black berets drew their handguns and stood in a semicircle aiming at the general. Behind them was an ornate living room. French sofas were arranged around a large television set. Off to one side sat a radio, boxes of canned food and bottled water, and a rack of brand-new AK-47s.

"General!" exclaimed a woman sitting on the sofa.

"Stand down, soldiers!" insisted Chimurenga, holding up his hands and showing both palms. "I'm unarmed." But they didn't move.

Yellow Eyes spoke first. "Ma'am, we are under strict orders not to allow anyone in here."

"This is General Chimurenga, you fool. He is here to protect us."

"We are Code Red. The presidency is under attack and our orders are to protect the First Lady."

"*I* issued those orders, soldier," said the general through clenched teeth. "Now stand down."

"Tsaaah! Stand down, fool!" hissed Harriet, pushing the soldier aside. Yellow Eyes nodded to his colleagues and they all lowered their guns.

"I'm sorry, General," he said, hanging his head.

"I understand, soldier. These are unusual times. You are doing your job. Now leave us."

"Sir?"

"Leave us alone. You are being redeployed. Check with your commander."

"Ma'am?" he asked, looking to the First Lady for instructions.

"Leave us!" she said, pointing to the door.

Once the soldiers departed, Harriet closed the door, threw her arms around Chimurenga's neck, and burst into tears.

"Oh, Simba! They haven't told me anything! What's happened? Is Winston dead?"

"He is gone."

"Ahhhhhhh!" she wailed and gripped his neck tighter.

"It will be all right, baby," he said, lightly patting her back as she sobbed. "Your lion is here to protect you . . ." After a few moments she caught her breath and backed away.

"Simba, what have we done?"

"There is no time for that, Harriet. We can now be together. Just like we planned."

"Yaah . . ." she whimpered.

"We will rebuild Zimbabwe together. We

428

will make it great once again. You and me. Together. We can visit Paris, Hong Kong, wherever you wish. We can have it all."

"Yaah . . ."

"You can have it all, Harriet."

"Yaah. I know that's what we wanted. But it's so terrible. Winston is dead."

"There is no time for second thoughts. We must now be strong."

"What about me? What will happen to me?"

"I am taking care of everything. We must follow the plan. I will assume the presidency. You will lay low. You will mourn the loss of your husband. And when the time is right, when enough time has passed, you will return as the First Lady. *My* First Lady."

"But what if something goes wrong?"

"What will go wrong?"

"But what if something does? Someone killed Solomon Zagwe. It could happen to you!"

"What happened to Zagwe will not happen to me. I assure you. That thief deserved a violent death."

"You killed him?"

"No one steals from us."

Harriet gulped on the news. But deep down she already knew.

"Anything can happen, Simba," she

pleaded. "You saw even the guards were confused. No one knows what will happen next. Life is so fragile. They could have killed you and it would have all been over, Simba!"

"The guard? I will have him and his whole family killed for his insults today. Don't you worry about that."

"I don't care about him. What will happen to *me*?"

"I told you. You will have everything."

"But what if something happens to *you*? What do I do then?"

Simba dropped his shoulders in surrender. "If something goes wrong, I have taken care of everything. You will go to Thailand. To Bangkok, to see a man. He will take care of you."

"Who? How will I know how to find him?"

"If it becomes necessary, I will give you instructions. But you need not worry, Harriet."

"You promise, Simba?" she said, relief washing over her face.

"I am your lion, remember?"

"Yes, Simba. You are my lion."

58.

U.S. Embassy, Harare, Zimbabwe
Sunday, 3:40 p.m. Central Africa Time
Ambassador Arnold Tallyberger ran his hands over his head and could feel his greasy scalp on his fingers. *I should be packing for London,* he thought, *not stuck in the middle of this banana republic mess.*

"What is happening out there?" he demanded, pointing out the window.

Brock Branson, the CIA station chief, didn't know. *"Après Tinotenda le déluge,"* he said under his breath. Brock pulled down one of the venetian blinds to scan beyond the embassy gates. The streets were filled with people running, and a haze of smoke, or more likely tear gas, drifted over the compound walls. "It's chaos, sir," he said.

"I can see it's chaos, goddammit. How do we not know what's happening?"

"Sir, with all due respect, we are a very small station. You know we have very few assets in Zimbabwe. We've got only a handful of eyes and ears on the street. I've got my guys at a few key locations, that's all."

"What do you know?"

"Mr. Ambassador" — Brock bristled at having to answer to Tallyberger, but kept his cool — "we know that at around 14:44 local time, just under an hour ago, the presidential limousine struck an IED. That's an improvised explosive device."

"I know what 'IED' stands for," Tallyberger sneered.

"My apologies, sir. Just being thorough. Shall I continue?"

Tallyberger responded with a flick of his wrist, as if beckoning a servant.

Brock bit his lip and inhaled though his nostrils. "The IED penetrated the security cage of the vehicle, causing massive injuries for all occupants."

"Is Tinotenda dead?"

"The Zimbabweans aren't confirming the president's condition one way or the other. I've got a man at the hospital on the lookout for any information."

"What's your opinion, Brock?"

"Based on the explosion profile and the damage I've seen from photos taken at the scene, I would say his chances of survival are . . . zero."

Tallyberger dropped his head and exhaled loudly.

"I doubt they've even recovered all of his body," added Branson.

"So if he's dead, who's in charge?"

"No one, sir."

Tallyberger lifted his head to make eye contact with Brock again. "No one?" he snarled. "How can that be?"

"Sir, their constitution states the line of succession starts with the vice president. But no one has seen him for months. It is widely known the vice president is in late-stage dementia and has been living in his rural home, essentially in hospice care by his daughter. That's just not an option."

"So who's next in line? What's the constitution —"

"The constitution isn't relevant, sir. That's my point."

"It's not? What are you talking about?"

"Tinotenda packed the constitutional court with his cronies, who have repeatedly dismissed the constitution whenever it has been inconvenient. Remember the Gokwe bank case? The Chimanimani diamond expropriation? The Chitungwiza by-election? In each case, the court ruled that executive discretion outweighed constitutional rule under exceptional circumstances."

"I don't remember those."

"Well, they set a precedent that the president could overrule the constitution if he declared a pressing national interest and some exceptional conditions. I'd say the assassination of the president is about as exceptional as you can get. That means the presidency can declare anything it wants."

"But who is the presidency if the president is dead?"

"He's not officially dead, sir. That's the point."

"So who is in charge?"

"That's what we don't know. I assume Simba Chimurenga will assert his authority. But it depends on what happens next. Whoever killed Tinotenda will probably go after Chimurenga, too, so he may be keeping his head low until he has the security forces lined up."

"We don't know who did it?"

"No, sir."

"We have no idea? The CIA has no idea who just assassinated the president of Zimbabwe? Right here under our noses?"

"It wasn't us, sir."

"Well, I should hope the hell not!"

"Yes, sir."

"Who could it have been, Brock?"

"I wouldn't want to guess at this stage, sir."

"The Iranians? The South Africans? Al-Qaeda? Who?"

"Unlikely any of those. If I was a betting man, and I'm not, I'd put my money on an internal dispute. Maybe the Matabele finally got fed up? Or one of Tinotenda's business partners. He had many of those."

"Could it have been the opposition?"

"The DUZ? Gugu Mutonga? Mr. Ambassador, I don't think that's a likely scenario."

"Maybe Mutonga found out Tino was going to declare victory and she had him killed? Why is that implausible? Isn't that why Chimurenga is looking for Mutonga? Because she was linked to an assassination plot?"

"Sir, I don't doubt Tino was intending to declare victory. We've got an analyst back at Langley working on this very question. But there's no evidence Gugu Mutonga or any of her allies had any intention or capability to assassinate senior government officials."

"I see," said Tallyberger. "I think . . . I should reach out to Chimurenga. Yes, I can assure him of American cooperation and support at this critical stage. We can help to stabilize the situation with an assertive American position. Can you get him on the phone for me?"

"I've been trying to contact Chimurenga for the past hour, but no luck. He's not answering his phone."

"Should we go find him?"

"I wouldn't recommend leaving the embassy compound right now, sir. The police have abandoned their posts, and the army is mostly AWOL. We've got reports of looting by army units. The whole command-and-control of the security forces has collapsed."

"It's chaos out there is what you are saying?"

"Yes, sir. Chaos. Total breakdown. State of nature."

"So we do what? Shelter in place?"

"Yes, sir. This won't last. Until order is restored, we stay here behind the compound walls."

Tallyberger nodded reluctantly. He didn't like being constrained by the CIA, even though he knew Branson was right. But what else to do? Then he remembered: *Pack for London.*

59.

Georgetown, Washington, D.C.
Sunday, 10:05 a.m. Eastern Standard Time
"It was the Pentagon," said Sunday.

"What are you saying?" Jessica asked into the phone as she spied through a crack in the curtains out her front window.

"Kanyemba was a covert Defense Department operation. They were using a private contractor to hunt for supergrade uranium, but then it all went wrong."

"No wonder . . ." she said as a black Chevy Suburban with blacked-out windows came to a screeching halt in front of her house. "Hold on, Sunday . . . Toby, sweetie! Take your brother up to the bedroom and put on *Dora the Explorer.* Mommy needs to finish her call and then talk with some men." Then back into the phone: "Sunday, you better hurry."

"The records have been wiped, but I think I've figured out what happened. Soon after independence in 1980, an American company, working with a Saudi investor and some local authorities, began exploring at Kanyemba for uranium. As far as I can tell, things were proceeding on track. But then, in July of 1982, the Zimbabwean security forces swept into the area to suppress a local dispute and the operation got out of hand. President Tinotenda sent in his protégé, Simba Chimurenga, who wiped out whole villages."

"Motowetsurohuro."

"Aaay. And the mine was forced to close."

"And why did the mine shut?" asked Jessica. The doors of the Suburban opened, and a security officer, with sunglasses and a wire in his ear, held open the rear door.

"That's where it gets interesting. The company claimed the mine was exhausted and shut down for commercial reasons. But that makes no sense, given they had just started early-stage excavation. The timing tells me that it closed because of the military operation. The Kanyemba mine was shut because of Motowetsurohuro. This fits with the new pictures from our bird."

A short man in a dark gray suit with a shiny bald head stepped out of the SUV and peered up at Jessica in the window. She released the curtain and turned back to the room.

"So they sealed Kanyemba to hide the bodies."

"Aaay. The images from the Global Hawk confirm several hundred bodies buried in the mine."

"So a DOD site became a mass grave. No wonder they tried to whitewash it. Why not just let the company take the fall?"

"Because the Kanyemba Mining Company is Max O'Malley."

"Who is?"

"A major political contributor. Plugged in at the highest levels."

"Judd's blowback," she whispered.

"And that's not all. Max O'Malley is back in business in Zimbabwe as we speak. This time he's not mining uranium."

"Diamonds," Jessica said. The visitor strode up the front steps, followed by another man carrying a briefcase.

"Diamonds," Sunday repeated. "And you want to guess O'Malley's new business partner?" The doorbell rang. "Simba Chimurenga."

Jessica opened the door. "A guest has just arrived, dear," she said loudly into the phone. "Please make sure you share your news with my husband. *Au revoir!*"

439

She hung up the phone and instantly dropped her cheery demeanor.

Her eyes met those of the bald man standing on her doorstep.

60.

"It's all going to shit!" Mariana Leibowitz screamed into the phone.

Judd Ryker, on the other end of the line, took a deep breath and tried to calm her. "I'm working on a strong statement. Ambassador Tallyberger —"

"Tallyberger? You think this is about the American embassy? Judd, we are way past that now!"

"I am rewriting —"

"Fuck that. Fuck. That. Gugu's gone into hiding."

"Hiding?"

"Tino's dead. Everyone knows that now. They are going to use the assassination as an excuse to clamp down. And before you ask, no, she's got nothing to do with Tino's death. I swear. But I'm sure they are going to try to pin it on Gugu. That's why she's

441

gone underground."

"Who is 'they'?"

"Chimurenga! Who the hell else could it be? You're supposed to be the one on top of all this. Fucking American government!" she shouted.

Simba Chimurenga. Sunday said so, now Mariana. It all keeps coming back to him, Judd thought. "I'll make sure the U.S. is on the right side. What else do you need?"

"What have I been saying all along? I need your help. Gugu's definitely going to need you. I have to reach her. I can't get through on the phone."

"Okay."

"Judd, I need to be able to count on you."

"You can."

"I hope so."

"But, Mariana, you've got to let me know what you know. We're in the dark."

"In the dark. Yes, Judd, we're all in the dark."

"What's that supposed to mean?"

"We never know everything we need to know. Not about our enemies. And not about our friends."

"Do we ever know everything we need to, Mariana?"

"Not in our business. Hell, I do my home-work on every client — on every contact —

and I still get caught by surprises."

"Like Lucky Magombe?"

"I spoke to him about your cricket warning. He said there was never going to be a match, so you needn't worry. Whatever the fuck any of that means."

"As long as it's over."

"Everyone has their secrets, Judd," she said, calming herself down. "Shit, I just found out my daughter has a baby she never told me about."

"You're a grandmother?"

"Fuck you. I'm telling you something personal."

"Sorry, Mariana."

"Sorry is right. I'm not looking for sympathy. I'm just making the point that we never know everything. Even your own family can surprise you."

"What does that mean?"

"Nothing, Judd. Nothing at all."

61.

"Hello, Jessica," the CIA's deputy director of operations said without emotion.

"Hello, sir."

He looked down at the device in her hand. "Your phone does work." Back to her eyes. "I was starting to worry you might have been thrown off a bridge or something."

"No, sir. I'm here. I'm working."

"So I've been told."

"I'm working hard on a special operation."

"Even if you don't believe it, you still work for me," he said.

"Yes, sir."

"Is there something you should be telling me, Jessica?"

"I don't know what you mean, sir."

"Who did you come to when you had the bright idea for Purple Cell?"

"You, sir."

444

"And why did you come to me, of all people?"

"Professor van Hollen suggested it. He said you'd understand the concept. That you like fresh ideas. That you might take a risk on something new."

"Right, BJ van Hollen. That old kook is why you have a job in the first place. He swore you were the brightest recruit he had ever known. He's why you were fast-tracked through training. He's why you rose so fast through the Agency."

"Yes, sir."

"BJ van Hollen is the reason I ever agreed to Purple Cell in the first place."

"Yes, sir."

"And it was BJ van Hollen who swore to me I could trust you."

"Uh-huh."

"So it was for BJ that I stuck my neck out when no one else believed a young new case officer could launch a new kind of off-grid operational cell."

"Yes, sir."

"I trusted BJ and I trusted you with Purple Cell."

"Yes, sir."

"Then, Jessica, why are you fucking with me?"

"Sir?" she asked, as innocently as she

could muster.

The deputy director lowered his chin and peered at Jessica below his brow. "The President of Zimbabwe was killed in an explosion forty-five minutes ago. And you are running a rogue CIA operation in that same location. Need I say more?"

"We didn't kill President Tinotenda. We're trying to figure it all out ourselves."

"What about the Ethiopian. What's his name?"

"Zagwe," said the man standing behind him. "General Solomon Zagwe. Killed last night in another unexplained explosion."

"Yes, I know," Jessica said.

"So we have two senior politicians killed by explosions within fifteen hours of each other and you are running an unauthorized operation, all in the same city. I don't buy it," said the deputy director. "So, you tell me, what the hell is going on, Jessica?"

"It's my operation. I take full responsibility."

"For what exactly?"

"If there's an investigation. If Congress starts asking questions."

"Congress won't want you!" he laughed. "You don't even exist as far as they're concerned."

"Then why are you here, sir?"

"I want to hear it from you."

"Hear what, sir?"

"If you want to play it that way . . ." The deputy director demanded, "Read the charges."

The man standing behind him opened the briefcase, extracted a stack of papers, and began reciting, "Failure to adhere to operational chain of command, failure to clear operations in a timely manner, failure to follow a direct order to abort operations, failure to adhere to duty-to-warn obligations, willful negligence, insubordination —"

"Enough," interrupted the deputy director. "This is currently an internal Agency matter. The more serious charges about the unauthorized assassination of General Solomon Zagwe are still under investigation. The lawyers are looking into it. Jessica, tell me you didn't kill that bastard."

"No, sir. It was not me."

"No one in Purple Cell?"

"No, sir. No one in Purple Cell killed that bastard."

"Well, someone in the building isn't convinced. I hope you have covered your ass on this one."

"Am I under arrest?"

"Arrest? No."

"Am I fired?"

"Did you have prior knowledge of an assassination plot against a senior official of the government of Zimbabwe?"

"That was a false report. It was just idle phone chatter."

"And you knowingly sat on it! Why didn't your people follow duty-to-warn protocols?"

"That had nothing to do with Zagwe or Tinotenda."

"It doesn't matter. One of your people broke intelligence protocol and now two men are dead."

"Sunday didn't do anything wrong."

"Why did one of your people provide false information to senior White House officials?"

"Sir?"

"Why did your team falsify information to get Zimbabwe included in Operation UMBRELLA ROSE?"

"He was following my orders. He doesn't know anything about it."

"Anything about what?"

"The operation."

"What operation, Jessica?"

"If there is any fallout, sir, it should land on me, not my team."

"Why did you need Zimbabwe in UMBRELLA ROSE? Why did you keep the

Global Hawk flying after UMBRELLA ROSE was shut down? Why did you have people asking questions in Ethiopia? What the hell are you looking for?"

"How do you know about all of that, sir?"

"I know everything, Jessica. I just want to hear it from you."

"It's all part of the operation."

"What operation is that?"

"Purple Cell was on a mission to detect and neutralize a potential WMD threat against the United States, sir. We thought we had a line on a possible second super-grade uranium site."

"Don't give me that bullshit! I didn't give you that order. What the fuck were you investigating?"

"Uranium."

"Uranium? I'm supposed to believe that?"

"And possible war crimes linked to the mine. We were gathering evidence."

"On whose orders?"

"No orders, sir."

"Then what the hell are you really up to, Jessica Ryker?"

"I thought you knew everything, sir."

"Fucking van Hollen," he laughed to himself. "BJ fucked me from the grave." He shook his head.

"I'm prepared to hand in my notice," Jessica said.

"What?"

"My resignation. Monday morning. If that's what I have to do to protect my team. If that's what's best for the Agency, sir."

"I can't have you running rogue operations. I just can't have it."

"Yes, sir. I understand."

"I don't want your fucking apology."

"I'm not offering one, sir."

"What?"

"I'm not apologizing, sir. I'm offering to resign. If that's what's best."

The deputy director rubbed his hands and turned to his aide, who revealed no emotion. "Fucking van Hollen . . ." he muttered to himself. Then he turned back to Jessica. "No."

She suppressed a smirk.

"But as of today," he snapped, "Purple Cell is suspended until further notice."

"Yes, sir."

"We're going to need a full damage assessment."

"Yes, sir."

"You're going to have clean up this fucking mess."

"Yes, sir."

"Until Purple Cell is reactivated, I'm going to have to find someplace else in the

Agency to put you, Jessica Ryker."

"Thank you, sir."

"But if I find out you did kill Solomon Zagwe . . ." He shook his head as he trailed off. "Jessica, there is one thing I really don't understand."

She looked up at him, suddenly feeling sorry for her boss.

"I've been racking my brain and I just don't get it."

"Yes, sir?"

"You're one of our best. You're calculating, deliberate, decisive —"

She shifted her weight. She didn't like where this was going.

"— cold-blooded, even. It's what makes you so effective," he said.

"Sir?"

"So what I don't get is . . . what I really want to try to understand is . . . why?"

"Why what, sir?"

"See, that's precisely what I mean. Cold-blooded. I want to know why you give a shit about some forgotten Ethiopian general hiding out in a forgotten corner of Africa. I want to know why you risked your entire career over some two-bit retired thug."

A loud "Mommy!" came from upstairs. Jessica turned her head. "Sir, I've got to go."

"Why did you insert Purple Cell into

Zimbabwe on your own accord?"

"I'm not cold-blooded, sir."

"What does *that* mean? I've just saved your career for the second time. You owe me an explanation. Jessica Ryker, why did you care so much about this?"

Jessica turned and just walked away.

62.

The little girl with mocha skin and a bright white smile marched down the pathway cut into the side of the hill. On her head she wore short braids and balanced a bronze calabash full of water. Her mother, three steps behind, wore long braids and carried an even larger calabash. Several strands of thick wooden and glass beads hung around her neck, creating a rhythmic click-clack, click-clack as they walked. The tempo of the beads comforted the little girl, a constant reminder of her mother's presence.

As they hauled water back to the family compound from the nearest well several kilometers from the village, they followed a familiar goat path between the coffee trees, the green shrubs with bright red berries grown on those hillsides for centuries. When the girl got too far ahead, out of sight, she would stop underneath one of the umbrella-like acacia trees that dotted the landscape and provided an oasis of shade.

As she did every day, the mother watched closely over her only daughter. Her steps were careful but deliberate.

"Faster," she urged. "You cannot be late for school today."

"Yes, Mama," the girl replied, and resumed their hike.

Although the mother had never herself been to school, she knew, even when this girl was a tiny baby, she was a clever one. She knew her little girl was destined for something greater than the hard life of a remote village in the Ethiopian highlands.

Once the girl turned five years old, the woman and her husband made a major decision: This one would go to school. The family would have to grow and sell extra teff, the grain used to make injera bread, to pay for her uniform and the unofficial fees the teacher would demand in exchange for allowing a girl to attend. In addition to the financial burden, the whole family would also need to wake earlier than the rest of the village to collect water. It was the only way she could be back home in time for her daughter to wash, dress, and still make the forty-minute trek to school.

That had been a year ago. Now the early chores had become their normal daily ritual.

None of the other six-year-old girls in the village were going to school, and most never would. The few boys who attended school teased her for being the only girl, for being out of place, for trying to be something they said she could never be.

But her mother instructed her daughter to ignore their taunts and to focus on learning. The girl followed these orders. Her mother also counseled that the best response to silly boys was to prove to them she belonged there, that a girl could even be the head of the class. She did this, too.

On this particular day, as they came around a bend in the path approaching the village, the girl's head was already filling with letters and numbers. Her father came running to meet them, terror on his face. "The Red Fear is here! The soldiers are coming!"

"What are you saying?" her mother asked, gently placing down the calabash. "Who is coming?"

"The army! To this place! Now!"

"Why here?"

"I don't know. We must run. Now!"

"Why us?"

"I don't —" he started to answer, but was

455

interrupted by the hollow whump whump whump of artillery shells in the distance, and then, nearer, the sharp crack crack crack of small-arms fire.

"Mama?" the little girl cried.

"The Red Fear is coming. It is Zagwe!" shouted her father, grabbing his daughter's hand.

The crack crack crack grew closer. They turned to run just as a bullet shattered the calabash on the girl's head, drenching her with the cool water.

"Nooooo!" wailed her mother, throwing herself on top of the girl.

Suddenly, advancing soldiers poured over the hill and into the village. The first wave, in green uniforms and hard hats, slung long guns at their hips and fired wildly as they charged. The girl's father raised his hands in surrender, but before he could speak, before he could plead for mercy, his body was raked by bullets, *crack crack crack,* and he crumpled lifelessly to the ground.

Her mother, now wrapped like a blanket over the girl, suddenly went limp, too. The little girl felt warm blood mix with the cool water.

At that moment, as the little girl hid underneath her mother's dead body, when her entire world was coming to an end, when she should have been screaming and crying but instead sat perfectly still, calculating, deliberate, decisive, one name stuck in her head, a name she would carry with her to her next life in America — the very last word her father had ever spoken: *Zagwe.*

63.

U.S. Embassy, Harare, Zimbabwe
Sunday, 4:47 p.m. Central Africa Time

"You need to see this!" yelled Colonel David Durham from his perch on the couch.

"What is it, Bull?" asked Judd, emerging from his office-cave into the foyer with the television.

"Chimurenga. They were showing music videos on state TV, but now it broke to a live press conference with Chimurenga. I think this is it."

"Turn up the volume," ordered Ambassador Tallyberger, who was running in, followed by Isabella Espinosa and a crowd of embassy staff.

"Ladies and gentlemen, the great people of Zimbabwe . . ." began Simba Chimurenga. The general was standing behind a podium in formal military uniform with a wall of soldiers at attention behind him. *A show of force,* thought Judd.

"Is this a coup?" asked one of the staff, who was quickly shushed by the ambassador.

". . . I have important and sad news to share with you today. His Excellency, Father of the Nation and Warrior of the People, President Winston H. R. Tinotenda, has passed."

Chimurenga then paused as the room erupted with gasps and camera flashes. The television picture jerked back and forth as the camera was jostled.

"Be calm!" insisted Chimurenga, holding up both palms. The camera steadied and the room quieted. "Our great leader was murdered today by terrorists. Our great nation is under attack. But we have identified the culprits and we will bring them to justice. I assure you of that. The security forces are now fully mobilized and rounding up suspects. We have sufficient evidence pointing to senior members of the Democracy Union of Zimbabwe. The DUZ was once a legitimate political party and enjoyed the benefits and freedoms of our democracy. But it has become poisoned by violence. The DUZ is responsible for the assassination of our president and the explosion in our capital last night. Our prime suspect in these murders and attacks on the nation is

Gugu Mutonga."

"No!" shouted Isabella.

"Ms. Mutonga is not yet in custody. It is only a matter of time," declared Chimurenga, pounding his fist on the lectern. "We have sealed the borders and have erected roadblocks around the capital. We call on all peace-loving members of the public to assist the security forces in apprehending her and her coconspirators."

"This is bullshit," hissed Durham.

"Their president was just murdered," snapped Tallyberger.

"I want to assure the people of Zimbabwe and our friends abroad," Chimurenga continued, "Zimbabwe will survive this unprovoked attack and we will emerge stronger. I want to convey to the nation and to the world our assurances the government is still in control. We are still in charge. *I am in charge.*"

"It *is* a coup!" Isabella shouted at the TV.

"We are still operating under the state of emergency I announced earlier today. According to Section 128 of the Constitution of the Republic, the president may initiate special decrees in a time of extraordinary circumstances. Early this morning" — Chimurenga held up a sheet of paper — "the president signed Special Presidential

Decree 128.7, which appoints the national security advisor as interim head of state if the president becomes incapacitated during a state of emergency. Based on this authority, I have assumed executive authority."

"It *is* a coup," Judd said, making eye contact with Durham.

"The election results which were due to be announced later today would have given President Tinotenda another five-year term. However, following the unfortunate events over the past twenty-four hours, we will, as soon as possible, hold new elections. The elections held yesterday are hereby declared null and void.

"I urge all Zimbabwean patriots to remain vigilant in defense of the nation. If anyone has information about the whereabouts of Gugu Mutonga or any subversive activities, you are obligated to share that information with the security forces. Thank you. And God bless the Republic of Zimbabwe."

The screen went dark.

"Everyone out! Back to work!" ordered the ambassador. "I need Bill Rogerson on the phone right now!" he demanded as the embassy staff filed out of the room. "And where the hell is Brock Branson?"

"Ambassador," Judd began. "We need to —"

"We aren't doing anything until I hear from Bill Rogerson. We need to reconvene the Zimbabwe task force before we do anything rash. I'm not running some rogue operation here, Ryker."

Before Judd could reply, Brock Branson appeared in the doorway, out of breath.

"Sir. We've got a situation outside the embassy gates."

"What is it now?" asked Tallyberger, color draining from his face.

"A crowd is forming, several hundred people."

"Have the marine guard put us on lockdown!"

"They've already sealed the perimeter. That's not the issue."

"Well, what is it?" Tallyberger's eyes widened.

"It's not just any crowd, sir. Gugu Mutonga is at the gate."

64.

Landon Parker jumped out the taxicab and paid the driver by flicking a twenty-dollar bill over the headrest. A uniformed policeman immediately stopped him.

"I'm sorry, sir, this road is closed. No pedestrians."

"Good morning, officer," he said, and flashed his State Department ID. The officer apologized and waved him through.

Parker walked the remaining block before encountering plainclothes diplomatic security officers at the bottom of the circular driveway. After he showed his ID again, he strode up toward the Georgian Colonial mansion, with its tall white columns and redbrick façade. The porch was already decorated with pumpkins and an autumn wreath hung on the front door. He rang the doorbell.

"Landon!"

"Hello, Madam Secretary."

"We couldn't wait for you. I'm sorry, we started brunch already. I was starting to worry you wouldn't make it!"

"I apologize, ma'am. Got hung up with something at the office."

"Well, you're here now," she said. "That's what counts."

"Yes, ma'am."

"Senator McCall is regaling us with stories about his recent trip to Indonesia and New Zealand."

"Yes, ma'am."

"I hope you weren't delayed by anything too important. No new crisis, I hope?"

"No, ma'am."

"Russia again?"

"Just a small problem in Thailand."

"Thailand? What's going on there?"

"Nothing you need to worry about, Madam Secretary. I made the problem go away. I promise you that."

"Wonderful. I hope you're hungry."

"Yes, ma'am," said Landon Parker, accepting a tall crystal flute of champagne from the Secretary of State and stepping into her foyer. "I'm still hungry."

65.

"We have to let her in!" Isabella insisted.

"She is a sitting duck out there, sir," said Branson. "If we know she's here, then so does Chimurenga. There's an army post less than one kilometer away. If we are going to act, we need to do so *right now.*"

"If we let her in — if we give her refuge — we are taking sides in an internal political matter," Tallyberger said, shaking his head.

"What's your option? Let them arrest her?" Judd asked.

"And probably kill her," Isabella said.

"I estimate you've got two minutes, sir," said Branson.

"I need Washington on the line. Where the hell is Bill Rogerson?" screamed the ambassador.

"Trying to reach him, sir," a voice shouted

465

from another room.

"The crowd is getting bigger," said Bull, peering out the window.

"Ambassador, if you don't open the gate and let Gugu Mutonga into the embassy, then you are sealing her fate," Judd said. "That's not neutral, either. If you allow her in, that should give everyone time to calm down. Some breathing space. The embassy can be a stabilizing force and not allow this thing to spiral out of control. We can shut the window of chaos."

"I'm not inserting the United States government into this fight without explicit instructions from headquarters. We aren't doing anything until I hear from Washington."

"Ambassador, a word, please," said Judd, indicating the door to the ambassador's private office. Once inside, he closed the door.

"Mr. Ambassador, you've got an opportunity to do the right thing here. For Zimbabwe and for the United States."

"Ryker, don't you come here and, after one day in my country, start telling me how to run my post!"

"You can do the right thing and show some balls, Arnold."

"Get out of my office!"

"I didn't want to have to do this, but there's no more time. Ambassador, this is how it's going to play out. One: You're going to order the gates opened and allow Gugu Mutonga and her people onto the embassy compound. Two: You're going to grant Gugu Mutonga immediate asylum and full diplomatic protection. Three" — Judd jabbed his finger toward Tallyberger — "you and I are going to draft a statement together outlining how the United States is going to support a peaceful, democratic transition. I've already done most of the work. You'll just need to read it."

"Who the hell do you think you are, Ryker?" Tallyberger's face went from pallid white to blood red. "Why on earth would I do any of that?"

"Because it's the right thing to do."

"That's not your call, Ryker! You are way the hell out of your lane!"

"And," Judd said calmly, "because I know all about what happened in Haiti."

The ambassador's face returned to ashen.

"I already have an inquiry from the British Foreign Office — I spoke to them just a few hours ago, in fact — and they were asking some pointed questions about your suitability to be deputy chief of mission in London. They haven't yet agreed to you."

"There's no agrément for a DCM. You don't know what you're talking about, Ryker."

"I know there's no formal agrément. But if our friends in London knew about Haiti, I'm sure they would find a way to let the Secretary of State know your presence in the United Kingdom was . . . undesirable."

"Undesirable? Why is the British Foreign Office calling you about my posting? What the hell do you have to do with any of this?"

"It's a good question," said Judd, nodding and trying to restrain any sign of smugness. "It's a very, very good question, Ambassador."

"You blackmailing me, Ryker?" Tallyberger narrowed his eyes.

"No, Mr. Ambassador. This is most definitely not blackmail. This is *diplomacy.*"

66.

U.S. Embassy, Harare, Zimbabwe
Sunday, 8:00 p.m. Central Africa Time
"Ladies and gentlemen, please!" Ambassador Arnold Tallyberger implored the crowd. But no one was listening.

The ambassador was standing under the fluorescent lights of the modest stage in the embassy pressroom. The State Department seal, a bald eagle gripping arrows in the talons of one foot and an olive branch in the talons of the other, was pasted, slightly crooked, on the front of the podium. Also on the stage, off to one side, a large flat-panel television announced WELCOME TO THE U.S. EMBASSY, HARARE. American and Zimbabwean flags hung together on the back wall.

Half a dozen embassy aides with dark circles under their eyes crowded onto the same stage around the ambassador and the TV screen. Their suits were badly rumpled.

Several burly security guards, with short-cropped hair and coiled wires in their ears, formed an imposing perimeter around the stage.

The room was mayhem. Word had spread quickly, likely aided by Brock Branson's discreet network, that the Americans had a major announcement at a press conference called for eight o'clock. Reporters, staff from other embassies, and a curious turnout of Zimbabwean government officials rushed the embassy gates. A lucky few made it into the pressroom, where they squeezed into all the available chairs and stood packed along the back. Several hundred more people who had not been allowed inside swarmed outside in a growing throng.

Bull Durham had suggested the embassy broadcast the press conference on a projection screen at the front gate, but Tallyberger objected on security grounds. Instead, Bull and Isabella helped the marine guards rig up several speakers, so the crowd outside could at least hear the audio.

But now, the only thing anyone could hear, both inside and out, was the pleading of the ambassador.

"Ladies and gentlemen, please!"

Judd, standing off to the side of the stage, was huddled over a laptop, loading slides he had been assembling. He clicked a button and the screen next to the podium flashed **UNITED STATES' CONCERNS ABOUT THE INTEGRITY OF THE ELECTION IN ZIMBABWE.**

"Ladies and gentlemen, if I may, thank you very much," said Tallyberger, finally gaining their attention. He fiddled with his tie, trying to hide his discomfort with what he was about to do. He cleared his throat. "Welcome to the Embassy of the United States of America. I am Ambassador Arnold Tallyberger. I am here today to share with you some new information. Thank you for joining us on such short notice. I am pleased to see so many friends and colleagues here this evening." He searched the room for familiar faces. "We have taken the unusual step of calling this press conference this evening, but I am sure you will all agree, these are unusual times in Zimbabwe."

Another murmur went through the crowd. Tallyberger coughed into his hand, taking the pause to check his notes again, words that had been carefully negotiated with Judd over the past few hours.

"The United States is a friend of Zimbabwe and a friend of the Zimbabwean people. I want first to share our deep condolences for the loss of your president today in a terrible act of terrorism. The international community stands with Zimbabwe at this critical time and condemns any violence intended to spread fear, desperation, or chaos. President Tinotenda's wisdom and leadership will be missed."

Tallyberger, closely following the instructions in his notes, paused here and bowed his head.

After a moment he continued, "It is precisely for these extraordinary reasons we are taking the extraordinary step of calling you here today. As many of you may know, the election commissioner Justice Makwere is missing. Our hearts go out to his family and we hope he will be found safe and be able to return to his duties. We understand from the government that the election results are therefore being delayed. However, democracy cannot wait for one man. Fortunately, this evening we are able to share with you an independent assessment of yesterday's election results."

Judd clicked on the mouse and the screen changed to ZIMBABWE ELECTION RESULTS.

The ambassador continued, "As a complement to the brave and tireless efforts of Zimbabwe's election commission, a parallel voting collection system was deployed by a nongovernmental organization working closely with the Zimbabwe National Youth Training Association. Based on these data, which the U.S. Department of State has analyzed and certified, we are able to announce, with a hundred percent confidence, the victor in yesterday's elections."

Tallyberger gripped the lectern with both hands and took a deep breath. Then he turned to Judd and gave him a nod. "Dr. Ryker?"

Judd pressed the button on the laptop, showing the next slide:

Tinotenda 32%
Mutonga 68%

The crowd exploded with shouting, a mix of jubilation and anger. The security guards tightened the perimeter around the stage as part of the crowd surged forward.

"Please! Please!" shouted Tallyberger. "Before you ask, yes, we are prepared to share the full results publicly so there can be no doubts." Tallyberger held up a thick binder. "We are fully confident that when the election commission's official results are revealed, they will confirm this conclusion. However, it is in no one's interest to further delay the election results, especially in this time of great uncertainty.

"Based on these results and in the interest of promoting stability in Zimbabwe, the United States is also providing security for President-elect Mutonga until she is sworn in as the next President of the Republic of Zimbabwe. Until the inauguration tomorrow at high noon, she will remain under the protection of the embassy at an undisclosed location."

Judd resisted the urge to look up at the ceiling, toward Tallyberger's office, where he knew Gugu was watching the proceedings on a closed-circuit monitor.

"We have not taken this step lightly. But following the events of the past several days, and the clear desire of the people of Zimbabwe to exercise their democratic rights, this became unavoidable. When a friend is in need, you help them through tough times. That is what the United States is doing today: helping a friend through a difficult period. We are confident that in the coming days, with the hard work of the Zimbabwean people, the nation will persevere and emerge even stronger.

"Before I close this event, we have one final announcement. I am turning the podium over to Special Prosecutor Isabella Espinosa from the U.S. Department of Justice. Ms. Espinosa?"

Tallyberger backed away and Isabella emerged from behind a security guard. She approached the microphone, angled it down, and cleared her throat.

67.

Outskirts of Harare, Zimbabwe
Sunday, 8:08 p.m. Central Africa Time
A police car, the first in a line of more than a dozen security vehicles, flashed its lights and pulled over the white Mercedes CL600 luxury coupe. The vehicles formed a ring around the Mercedes and beamed lights into the driver's seat, revealing a hefty African man talking on a cell phone.

"Driver! Exit the vehicle with your hands up!" a policeman shouted through a bullhorn. Several officers took up positions, aiming rifles at the Mercedes.

The driver ignored the order and continued speaking into the phone.

"Driver! Exit now or we will shoot!" yelled the bullhorn.

Calmly, the man set down his phone and reached for something on the passenger seat, prompting the sharpshooters to cock their weapons.

"Hands! Hands!" screamed the bullhorn.

The man delicately placed a flat-top army-green cap on his head and then clicked open the door.

"*Muchinono! Muchinono!* Slowly! Slowly!"

The man carefully exited the vehicle with his hands raised. As he stood up straight, his impressive size and his military uniform revealed an imposing figure.

"*Do you know who I am?*" bellowed General Simba Chimurenga.

"Yes, sir. I'm sorry, sir. We are under orders to take you into custody."

"What orders?"

"From our commander, sir."

"*I* am your commander," the general said.

"No, sir. I'm sorry, sir. My direct orders are to take you into custody."

"You realize, small boy, you are risking your life. Your life and the lives of everyone in your family. Your entire village will be mine."

"I'm sorry, sir," the policeman said, clasping on handcuffs and frog-marching the general toward one of the cars.

"All of you," Simba sneered at the other officers. "I will eat all of your children."

"No, sir. I don't think so," the policeman said as he pushed Chimurenga's head down and into the back of the vehicle.

Chimurenga dropped into the seat and realized another man was sitting beside him: another big man, an American.

"Hello, General," said Colonel David Durham.

"*You?* What are *you* doing here? You Americans have *nothing* to do with this."

"I'm afraid we do now, General."

"This is a domestic political matter. We are a sovereign nation. You have no business here!"

"I'm here to ensure you are taken safely into custody —"

"The arrogance!"

"— and delivered to the court."

"The court? What court?"

"If I wasn't here, they probably would have killed you, General. The tide is turning. It's over."

"Over? The hypocrisy! Where is Brock Branson?"

"Once you are at the court —"

"Where is Branson? You tell Branson I will reveal everything I know. *Everything!*"

"Excuse me, General. Once you are at the court —"

"I will burn him! I will burn everyone!"

"It's over, General."

68.

"Ladies and gentlemen," Isabella Espinosa began. "Thank you, Ambassador. I'm with a special unit of the U.S. Department of Justice investigating international war crimes. We have spent years amassing evidence about atrocities in Cambodia, Ethiopia, Sudan, the former Soviet Union, and other countries. Our team's purpose is to hold accountable those perpetrators of mass civilian killings. Our goal is to enable the victims of these crimes to seek justice, to assist countries in healing from these terrible episodes in their history, and to deter future aggression against innocent people.

"Zimbabwe was not originally on our list of countries under investigation," she continued. "However, we have unearthed, so to speak, new evidence we believe should come to light. Dr. Ryker, if you will?"

Judd projected the next slide on the large TV for the embassy audience. The screen flashed with an overhead shot of trees. "These photos were taken yesterday in the Kanyemba district in northern Zimbabwe. In the center, you can see these lines." Isabella pointed to faint brown lines running along the ridge. "And this" — she pointed to a black square — "is the opening of the Kanyemba mine shaft which was sealed in 1982. Next."

The screen changed to a multicolored photo, a swirl of red, yellow, blue, and green. "This is the same photo using geothermal readings. I'm going to ask Dr. Ryker to show increasing magnification of the photos."

As Judd clicked through the slides, the images zoomed in on an area showing a dark underground room with hundreds of tiny gray dots.

"Ladies and gentlemen, we've sent these images to our experts back in Washington, D.C., who have used similar technology to search World War II sites in Germany and Poland. They have confirmed our worst fears. The Kanyemba mine is a mass grave site. We believe this is the missing proof of the Great Rabbit Fire."

"Motowetsurohuro!" shouted someone in

the crowd. A gasp went through the crowd.

"We are still gathering evidence, but we now have army records and testimony from more than two dozen witnesses, all pointing to a special unit of the Zimbabwe National Army as the perpetrator of this massacre."

The crowd wailed. Isabella pressed ahead. "We will be turning all this evidence over to the new attorney general of Zimbabwe once one has been appointed by the new government. The U.S. Department of Justice and the Federal Bureau of Investigation will remain engaged on this case for as long as necessary. The United States stands ready to assist the new government in any way possible to bring this case to court and to closure.

"Ladies and gentlemen, I have one final piece of information to share at this time. From the evidence we have gathered, we now believe we can identify the prime suspect for the massacre at Kanyemba, the disposal of the bodies in the mine, and the subsequent cover-up. The person responsible for Motowetsurohuro is" — she paused in front of a room of wide eyes — "General Simba Chimurenga."

69.

The elderly monk set down a chipped enamel cup of steaming hot tea and excused himself for the evening. Papa Toure sat up in his bed and said, "Thank you, Brother Gabriel. Sleep well."

"We have work to do in the morning," the old man said. Then he bowed and backed out of the doorway.

When Papa was sure he was alone, he reached into his rucksack, pulled out a thin titanium laptop, and fired it up. He logged in, placing the four fingers of his right hand on the computer screen. Once the machine recognized the user, Papa was connected to a secure satellite for his video call.

As he waited for the encryption software to load, Papa examined his temporary home. Bare whitewashed walls, a concrete floor with a reed mat, a slim mattress sagging on a rusty metal frame, a cinder-block table with a cup of tea and a kerosene lamp. *It was perfect.*

Papa's satisfaction was interrupted by the laptop announcing that the video call was connecting and, ominously, that any unauthorized use was punishable by a large fine and a lengthy sentence in a U.S. federal prison. He rubbed his scalp with his palms and sat up straight. The screen suddenly came alive with the face of Jessica Ryker.

"Ahhh, hello," said Papa, unable to contain the smile on his face.

"Bonsoir," she replied wearily. Papa noticed her eyelids were heavy and tired. She forced a smile.

"So, is it true?" he asked excitedly. "I'm sorry to ask so rudely, but I have to know. Is it true?"

"Yes," she said, dropping her smile.

"Let me hear it from you."

"It is done."

"You did it? Tell me."

"Solomon Zagwe is dead."

"How exactly did it happen?" he asked.

"I'm sure they're reporting this news in Ethiopia, Papa. It's just like they're saying in the press. An explosion at his house last night. A few minutes before midnight local time."

"An explosion? Really?" Papa checked the screen to confirm their call was encrypted. "That's not your style."

"I didn't choose the weapon. If it was up to me, I would have hung Zagwe by his toes, cut off his balls, and watched him bleed to death."

"That's not your style, either, Jessica."

"I know," she conceded, slightly embarrassed. "But it would have felt good to do it with my own hands. To see his face, to let him know it was me who killed him. For him to know why."

"That's not the Jessica I have known for so many years."

"That bastard got off easy, dying in a flash of heat and light. Never knowing who was pulling the trigger. Or why."

"Contain your emotions. That's one of your great strengths. The professor always said that about you."

"I know. I know. This one is . . . different."

"Tell me, Jessica. Really. How did you do it?"

"Misinformation."

"Enlighten me."

"I convinced one of Zagwe's business partners that he was stealing their money. I knew they'd do the rest."

"Chimurenga?"

"Yes. Chimurenga didn't even hesitate. Zagwe was dead within a few hours of our planting the idea. I knew Simba wouldn't mess around. I didn't know it would be that quick."

"See? That was better. No need to bloody your own pretty hands."

"What I didn't expect was Simba to go one more step and take out his other partner."

"Tinotenda?"

Jessica nodded. "We didn't have anything to do with that one. Simba must have gotten paranoid. But just in case, we're covering our tracks. Even if we can't prove Chimurenga killed Tinotenda, he is going down for the Motowetsurohuro massacre. We finally got evidence to pin that on him."

"UMBRELLA ROSE! Of course!"

She nodded again. "Chimurenga is already in custody. He was apprehended just after the embassy released the picture of the mass grave and announced the FBI was cooperating. The authorities are holding the general until the new government is in place and they can begin prosecution."

"Brilliant."

"We couldn't have done it without you, Papa. Your discovery of the Zagwe link to

Thailand led us to the banking records for Royal Deepwater Venture Capital and then to Max O'Malley, which then pointed us back to Chimurenga and the wire transfers. Without that, I'm not sure how we would have put it all together."

"Max O'Malley? I haven't heard that name for years."

"He came back to Zimbabwe. Instead of uranium, this time it was diamonds."

"Oh, my!" Papa tsked loudly and shook his head. "You've shaken the hornet's nest on this one, Jessica."

"That's why we're going to leave this one alone," she said with a sigh. "Better not to know all the dark secrets. We need to live to fight another day."

"You've brought down two mass murderers in one operation and your fingerprints are clean. That's a success! I don't see why you're harboring regrets."

"Langley."

"Figured it out, did they?"

"The deputy director was at my house just a few hours ago reading me the riot act."

"Merde," he cursed under his breath. "Charges?"

"No. But he's shutting down Purple Cell."

"It won't last. Once the deputy director blows off steam, he'll come back to you and reactivate. He'll need you soon enough."

"I hope you're right."

"Ahhhh, I've seen it all before."

"I know. That's not what has me worried."

"What is it? What have you not told me? Have you not covered your tracks?"

"It was *how* I tricked Chimurenga into killing Zagwe. *How* I planted the misinformation."

"Yes?" His eyebrow rose in anticipation.

"Judd," she said flatly, averting her eyes.

"Our Judd?"

"I lied to him."

"There is nothing new there."

"Yes, but this is different. My cover is one thing. This time I deliberately used my own husband as an unwitting participant in an unauthorized assassination. It violates just about every rule we have."

"Judd is a big boy. What does he know?"

"That's the thing. Even if I can live with the lie, I have a feeling it's only a matter time before he figures out something."

"Then it's time to run and be free. You have shed yourself of Zagwe. Now is the time to tell Judd the truth. Before he knows too much. Or suspects something that's not true. His imagination could be worse than the truth."

"You're right, Papa. I know you're right."

"And if Purple Cell is shut down, then it doesn't matter if he knows."

"You're right, Papa. I wish van Hollen was still here. BJ would know what to do. He'd know how to play all of this."

"We all miss the professor. But he is gone. Now you are the one. You have to take the mission forward."

"I don't know, Papa."

"When does Judd return home?"

"Tomorrow. He's already on the plane back to Washington."

"Good. You tell him tomorrow. Whatever happens, you'll deal with it. You still love him, yes?"

"Yes. Of course."

"*Inshallah.* That's all that matters, yes?"

"What are you going to do, Papa?"

"Ahhhh, an excellent question. I'm going to stay in Lalibela for a while, I think. Brother Gabriel, the monk who tends the Church of Saint George, has invited me to stay."

"Perfect," she said. "A Muslim from Mali staying in an Orthodox Christian church in Ethiopia."

"*Inshallah!*" he replied with a laugh. "The monk runs an orphanage here. They are doing God's work. I don't know which God, but they could use my help. I'm going to stay and set up a clean water system. Maybe find something else useful to do."

"You are a good man, Papa."

"I am old. It's the least I can do."

"And then what?"

"Who knows what comes next, Jessica? Who knows?"

"I guess we'll both find out."

"Good-bye, Jessica. Go easy on our Judd. You two are still young. You still have many things to accomplish. Consider it a new beginning."

"*Au revoir,* Papa."

"Run and be free," he said, a split second before the screen went blank.

Papa slapped the laptop closed and sat back thinking about Jessica, Judd, and their history together. He looked around his sparse room, absorbing his new home and pondering what he was about to do.

Papa lifted the mug of tea, blew gently, and took a sip. "Ahhhh," he exhaled. *Yes, perfect.*

■ ■ ■ ■

EPILOGUE: MONDAY

■ ■ ■ ■

70.

". . . I, Gugulethu Nehanda Mutonga, solemnly swear to uphold the constitution of the Republic of Zimbabwe."

"GU-GUUUUUUUUU!" shouted the crowd, which packed the national stadium to capacity. In the center of the stage stood Gugu Mutonga in a bright red business suit, one hand held up, the other on the Bible. A judge in full robes and a horsehair wig was reading the proceedings.

Standing immediately behind Gugu was an inner circle of her closest friends and supporters, including the beaming face of Lucky Magombe. The rest of the stage was crammed with chairs holding the nation's top judges, business leaders, and senior members of the Democracy Union of Zimbabwe. Hidden among this crowd, at the back, almost but not quite entirely out of view, sat Mariana Leibowitz.

Gugu finished the oath of office and solemnly accepted a sash across her chest, the conclusion to her inauguration as president. She turned to face the throngs of supporters, who raised their arms and screamed again. "GU-GUUUUUUUUU! GU-GUUUUUUUUU!"

A drummer on the stage began a celebratory beat. Gugu rocked her hips to the rhythm in a victory dance, igniting more cheering from the masses in front of her.

Among those closest to the stage were the faces of Tsitsi and Tinashe. The two young Zimbabweans held hands tightly and screamed until their voices were hoarse. As they danced, drunk with the dreamy jubilation of triumph and hope, Tsitsi could feel a growing queasiness in her belly, a sensation she knew was the first wave of morning sickness.

Once the drumming was finished, Gugu Mutonga raised both her hands, palms to the sky. This set off another frenzy. "GU-GUUUUUUUUU! GU-GUUUUU-UUUU!"

She then took the microphone and the stadium fell silent. She lifted it to her lips and paused. The crowd held their breath, waiting for the first words of their new president.

Then she asked, "Who is ready for a new Zimbabwe?"

71.

Bangkok, Thailand
Monday, 8:33 p.m. Indochina Time

Harriet Tinotenda pressed button 81 and felt the thrust in her thighs as the high-speed elevator rocketed toward the sky. The Baiyoke Tower, one of Bangkok's most exclusive addresses, was a suitable place to live, she thought. At least until she could find her own place.

The elevator's floor panel display flashed the passing floors: *19 . . . 20 . . . 21 . . .*

Once Harriet got upstairs and claimed her insurance policy, she knew she would have to start over. She had done it before. She could do it again.

Now she had nothing. Her husband was dead. Her lover was in custody and probably would be jailed for life. But she was still young. She had a life to live. Simba may have made mistakes, but she had to move on.

Worst of all, her country was in the hands of the traitors and sellouts. The most galling affront, she decided, was the uppity little woman claiming she had won the presidency. That cockroach actually believed she had won over the people! *Over my Baba! Outrageous!* "Tsaaah!" she tsked to herself.

And the Americans, she thought. They did this. The arrogant Americans and the wicked British. It was an insult. An affront! One day she would make them pay, she decided. Yaah, one day they would pay.

44 . . . 45 . . . 46. . . .

But today she had to focus on her immediate task, the first step in her new life. She had to claim the money her lion had stashed away for her. Simba promised she would be safe, that she would be kept in the style to which she had become accustomed. That, no matter what happened, she could still have it all.

Simba had called, just before he was arrested, to reveal his partner in Thailand was the gatekeeper. All she had to do was go to the office of Max O'Malley, 81F of the Baiyoke Tower in central Bangkok, and give the password. Simba told her all about the luxurious office, the photos of the rich and famous, the impressive view of the city, the soothing charm of his partner, who would welcome her with open arms and provide her with everything she needed. Max O'Malley would give her the code to the secret bank account. Max O'Malley held the key to all she had been promised, just in case anything went wrong.

Now everything had gone wrong, she lamented. She didn't even have her luggage.

Yaah, once she extracted the bank code from O'Malley, she would make a healthy withdrawal first thing tomorrow morning and go shopping at the Emporium. Or maybe at the Gaysorn Mall. That would make her feel better, she knew. Should she withdraw twenty thousand dollars? It was the beginning of her new life. She should start with a splash. At least fifty thousand dollars. Yaah. Just to start. The idea of a shopping trip already made her relax.

62 . . . 63 . . . 64. . . .

The rumble of the elevator racing upward toward the penthouse was an apt metaphor for her life, she thought. She'd begun as nothing, a poor girl from nowhere with little more than her wits and a pretty face. Saint Catherine's Mission School for Girls, Kwekwe Secretarial Academy, Ministry of Public Works, Office of the President, First Lady of the Republic of Zimbabwe. The events of the past few days were just a temporary setback, she told herself.

Harriet had parlayed her modest beginnings to become the wealthiest and most powerful woman in the country. She would just have to do it all over again. Regroup, rebuild, counterattack. Return to Zimbabwe to reclaim her glory. Maybe even as president herself?

But the first step on that road to redemption was to find this Max O'Malley. *Perhaps he is not only rich and powerful. Perhaps he is even handsome?*

79 . . . 80 . . . 81. Ding!

The elevator doors slid open. She stepped into the hallway, pausing to peer out a glass window at the bustling urban streets far below. From up here, from high in the sky, she looked down on all the little lights, all the little scurrying people. She suddenly felt on top of the world again. She was already nearly back on top.

Harriet extracted a bright pink tube from her pocket, one of the few items she'd managed to salvage when she fled to the private airport and began the hasty journey to Thailand. She applied the lipstick, smacked her lips, and blew the city of Bangkok a kiss. She then found door 81F and, just as Simba had instructed, knocked three times. Harriet called out, "The lioness is here."

No reply.

She knocked again and repeated, this time more loudly, "The lioness is here!"

Still nothing.

Harriet gripped the handle and, to her surprise, the door gave way. She cracked it open an inch and called out. "Hellooooo? Mr. O'Malley? You should be expecting me. The lioness is here."

When she again received no reply, she swung open the door.

"Tsaaah!" she screamed, eyes wide, in shock and horror.

In front of her was a room, entirely empty.

72.

Georgetown, Washington, D.C.
Monday, 9:25 p.m. Eastern Standard Time
When Judd opened their front door, Jessica was sitting on the living room sofa, ready. He set down his carry-on bag, walked over, leaned in, and kissed her. Jessica's lips tasted of red wine and she smelled of vanilla and honey.

"Welcome home, sweetheart," she said, and started to pour him a glass of pinot noir. "Sit. We need to talk."

"What is it?" he asked, still standing. "Can I take a shower first?"

"No. I need to tell you something important."

"Okay," he said and disappeared into the kitchen. Judd returned with a bottle of beer and sat down next to her on the couch. Judd took a deep breath and then a long swig of his drink.

"I haven't told you everything about my

life, about where I come from," she began.

"You told me you were adopted. You were an army brat."

"True. I was adopted. And my parents were both in the military and we moved around a lot. And yes, they both died before I met you. That's all true."

"Okay."

"What I didn't tell you is that I was born . . . in Ethiopia."

"Ethiopia?"

"I don't know much more. I really don't remember much more."

"You don't remember?"

"It's all a blur."

"You're Ethiopian and you never thought to tell your husband?"

"No. I'm American now. It was never relevant," she said.

Judd took another gulp of beer.

"Until now," Jessica said.

"Okay . . . I'm listening."

"Did BJ ever push you to go into public service?"

"BJ van Hollen? What does the professor have to do with any of this?"

"He introduced us."

"Of course I know that, Jess. I was there too. In Kidal twelve years ago when we met."

"Don't get mad, Judd. I'm trying to explain. Did BJ ever try to . . . *recruit* you?"

"Sure. He pressured me. He wanted me to work for the government. He hated after all his mentoring that I chose to teach. His disappointment was one of the reasons I jumped at the chance to create the Crisis Reaction Unit. BJ van Hollen was a big reason I took the risk and left Amherst to come to the State Department. But you know all this."

"Well, BJ recruited me, too. Only he *succeeded.*"

"Succeeded? Succeeded how?"

"I think you can guess."

Judd didn't say anything. Instead, he leaned over and took her hand. "I already did."

"You — you knew?" Jessica asked. "For how long?"

"I think I finally put it together when Noah told me on the phone about birds and purple umbrellas. Once I figured out you weren't telling me everything, all the other little clues started to fit together. All the advice arriving at just the right time, the insights, the observations, the *coincidences.* Even though it took a while for me to admit it, even to myself."

"So . . . are we good?" She squeezed his

hand and gave him a puppy-dog look.

"I'll need time to get used to this, Jess. You know everything about me and I'm still finding out everything about you. About your secret second life."

"I don't have a second life, Judd. It's just professional cover."

"So, who are you?"

"I'm me. I'm the same person. I'm Jessica Ryker. I'm your wife and mother to your children. We're a real family. None of that's changed."

"Are you an agronomist?"

"Yes."

"What else don't I know about you?"

"With time . . . I'll tell you everything with time, Judd. But just know our marriage is real, our love is real. That's what matters most."

"Is your water project in Ethiopia real?"

"No. That's a cover."

"Is Papa in the CIA, too?"

"I can't say."

"You can't say or you don't know?"

"Does it matter?"

"I don't know what matters anymore, Jess."

"Well, I do, Judd. I'll tell you what matters. You just helped catch two mass murderers and depose a dictator. You, Judd Ryker, just helped bring justice to thousands, maybe millions, of people. Why aren't we celebrating that?"

"Were you secretly helping me in Mali three months ago?"

"Yes."

"And now you were helping me in Zimbabwe, too?"

"Yes."

"Okay, okay . . ." he said, his mind still spinning. "Jess, I still don't understand."

"Understand what?"

"A lot. Why were you pushing me to get involved in Zimbabwe's election? Why were you strategizing for regime change? What was . . . your agenda?"

"Redemption," she said.

"Redemption for what?"

"And revenge."

"Revenge?"

"Solomon Zagwe," Jessica whispered.

"Ethiopia . . . the Red Fear . . . thirty years ago . . . I should have known," Judd said aloud, talking to himself. "But you never mentioned Ethiopia to me before."

"No, I didn't. I didn't need to."

"You didn't even ask me about Zimbabwe until" — Judd rubbed his forehead — "until last week, when that tourist jumped off the bridge at Victoria Falls . . . Wait, was that tourist one of yours?"

"Sort of."

"What does that mean?"

"The tourist was a private investigator. I contracted him to help build an evidence base against Zagwe. I couldn't discount the chance Zagwe might be arrested and I'd have to get him in court. But Zagwe must have caught him."

"What about the Justice Department? They were tracking him, too."

"I couldn't count on that. Their special investigator, your friend Isabella Espinosa, she's good, but she kept hitting brick walls. I just couldn't take the chance Zagwe might escape. Or be captured and then somehow find a way to get off."

"So the CIA hired a private contractor to collect evidence against a war criminal?"

"Not the Agency. Me."

"I don't understand, Jess."

"Hunting Solomon Zagwe wasn't an official operation."

"So you went rogue to help me?"

Jessica nodded. "Or . . . you could think about it the other way around. More like *you* went rogue to help *me.* Even if you didn't realize it."

"So you're the reason I was sent to Zimbabwe?"

"Indirectly."

Judd was hearing this new information faster than his brain could process it. Then he froze. "Are you behind the firebomb that killed —" Judd stopped and held up a palm. "Scratch that. Actually, Jess, don't say a thing. Don't say another word. I don't want to know."

"If you're asking whether I killed Zagwe, the answer is no. Chimurenga did. Did I have a hand in bringing about circumstances that led Chimurenga to believe he needed to kill his business partner? Well, there I think we both played a role."

"Both of us?"

She locked eyes with Judd and nodded.

"So . . . the whole thing was never about democracy in Zimbabwe? Concern over the election was just another cover?"

"In the beginning, yes."

"The supergrade uranium hunt was a ploy?"

"Sorry, yes. That too."

"UMBRELLA ROSE was just a cover for your rogue operation?"

Jess nodded.

"How did you pull that off?"

"I had to get S/CRU involved in Zimbabwe and find a reason for you to fly there immediately, before the election window closed. That was the only way. I figured I could get you to help me to get Zagwe and at the same time you'd get the big success you needed to save S/CRU."

"Helping me was a coincidence, then?"

"I think of it as collateral benefit," she said. Then, realizing how cold that sounded, she softened her voice. "I'm sorry I had to lie to you. I'm sorry about everything. But it couldn't be avoided. I just couldn't miss what might be my only shot at Solomon Zagwe. I had to do it."

"But why did you need me?"

"S/CRU was perfect. I had to force Zagwe out in the open. I needed to shake things up in Zimbabwe. I needed Tino to lose. And I needed *you* to make all that happen. We both needed the same thing to win."

"How exactly did I do that?"

"Another time, sweetheart, another time. But just know we had to create a window of chaos. It was the heart of the plan."

"Minute Zero," Judd said.

"Exactly. Your idea was essential to our success. Creating Minute Zero *was the strategy.*"

"It worked." Judd allowed himself to smile. "Minute Zero . . . *worked.*"

"Once we figured out what really happened at Kanyemba — that we could get two mass murderers instead of just one — we had to go for it. Seemed like the right thing to do."

" 'We'?" Judd's smile disappeared. "Who exactly is 'we'?"

"Please don't ask."

"Who else is working for you? Bull Durham? Brock Branson? Sunday? Jessica, does Sunday really work for you?"

"Who do *you* really work for, Judd?"

He thought about that as he drank the rest of his beer. *The Secretary of State? The President? Landon Parker? Some hidden puppet master?*

He set down his bottle. "I guess I don't really know."

"Right. What matters now is that we all played our part. And we prevailed. Zagwe is gone, Chimurenga's in prison, and Gugu Mutonga is president."

"And S/CRU will get credit," Judd realized.

"It all worked out."

"We make a pretty good team," Judd conceded.

"A powerful team."

"So I guess you were part of my Justice League all along?"

"In a way, yes," Jessica said. "If it helps you to accept all of this by thinking of it that way, Judd, then yes. Minute Zero was a success and the Justice League triumphed."

"So . . . if I'm Superman and this is my team, then . . . who exactly are you?"

"Oh, you're not Superman, Judd."

"I'm not? Who is Superman, then?"

Jessica lifted her wineglass and blew her husband a soft kiss.

"Me."

ACKNOWLEDGMENTS

Minute Zero would never have been written without the many people who helped me to fall in love with the beautiful nation of Zimbabwe. Mazvita Baba, Amai, Takudzwa, Tinashe, Blessing, and Biggie for your warmth and lifelong friendship. (Amai, you are greatly missed!) Andrew Meldrum and David Devlin-Foltz were influential early guides and still good friends. I'm grateful to Bobby Pittman, Bill Trombley, Charles Kenny, Markus Goldstein, and Kenneth Christian, who read early drafts and helped to make the story more readable and more realistic. Thanks to superagent Josh Getzler and Danielle Burby at HSG Agency. I'm tremendously grateful to my wise and cool-headed editor, Neil Nyren, and the amazing Putnam team, including Ashley Hewlett, Kate Stark, Elena Hershey, Alexis Welby, Anna Romig, Lydia Hirt, and Sara Minnich.

Most of all, boundless appreciation and love to Donna for your editorial clarity and eternal encouragement. *Ndinokuda!*

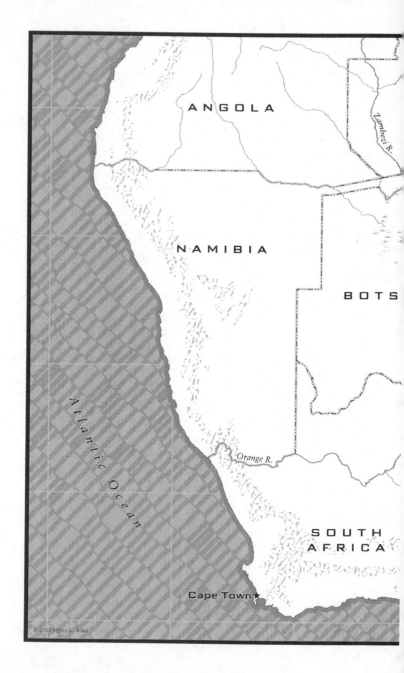

ANGOLA

Zambezi R.

NAMIBIA

BOTS

Atlantic Ocean

Orange R.

SOUTH
AFRICA

Cape Town ★

© 2013 Jeffrey L. Ward

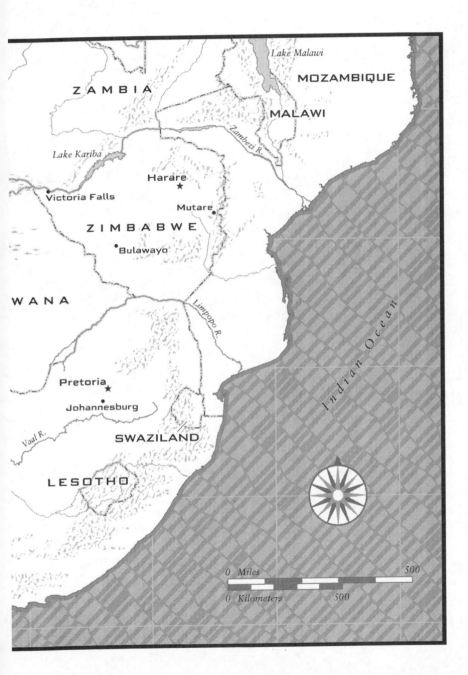

ABOUT THE AUTHOR

Todd Moss is vice president and senior fellow at the Washington think tank, the Center for Global Development and an adjunct professor at Georgetown University. In 2007-2008, he served as deputy assistant secretary of state in the Bureau of African Affairs, where he was responsible for diplomatic relations with sixteen West African countries. He lives in Maryland.

The employees of Thorndike Press hope you have enjoyed this Large Print book. All our Thorndike, Wheeler, and Kennebec Large Print titles are designed for easy reading, and all our books are made to last. Other Thorndike Press Large Print books are available at your library, through selected bookstores, or directly from us.

For information about titles, please call:
(800) 223-1244

or visit our Web site at:
http://gale.cengage.com/thorndike

To share your comments, please write:
Publisher
Thorndike Press
10 Water St., Suite 310
Waterville, ME 04901